EXPLOSIVE DISCOVERY

Inside the cardboard box were cardboard walls, to stop the olive oil bottles rattling. An empty cigarette packet lay on top. Chas threw it over his shoulder. Beneath, better things lay nestled in the cardboard compartments.

A gold pocket watch like Dad's. Stopped at twenty to eight because some idiot had opened the glass and tied little yellow wires round both the hands, so they'd jammed together as they passed each other. It made Chas mad, the way kids messed up decent things.

The yellow wires led to a battery, and a gray cylinder the size of a can of peas. . . .

"Run, it's a time bomb!" screeched Cem.

FATHOM FIVE

ROBERT WESTALL

BORZOI SPRINTERS   •   ALFRED A. KNOPF

New York

A BORZOI SPRINTER PUBLISHED BY ALFRED A. KNOPF, INC.
Copyright © 1979 by Robert Westall
Cover art copyright © 1990 by Darryl Zudeck

Library of Congress Catalog Card Number: 80-11223
ISBN: 0-679-80131-6
RL: 4.8
First Borzoi Sprinter edition: December 1990

Manufactured in the United States of America
10 9 8 7 6 5 4 3 2 1

*To Marni and Di
for all their patience*

1 Chas wakened in darkness, wanting the lav.

Out in the living room, the clock above the dying fire said midnight. Every night he wanted the lav, always midnight. Had he some strange disease?

No one to ask. The spaniel on the sofa thumped its tail without opening its eyes. Table laid for Dad's early breakfast.

After the lav, he always felt burningly thirsty. He drank two beakers of water from the kitchen sink. Tasted the best ever, even if Mam did use that beaker for soapflakes.

In the mirror above the sink, shadows made his face look mysterious. He moved his head to and fro, but couldn't get a new angle, even stretching up. His pajamas lost their grip on his hips. He grabbed, and tied the pajama cord more firmly. But the trousers immediately returned to their precarious balance on his hips.

He sighed. If his face was mysterious, his body was ridiculous. Six feet tall, and his feet got farther away every day. Every new pair of trousers they bought him climbed inexorably up his bony white shins. Lads would shout, "Who's died?" and when he shouted back, "What do you mean, who's died?" they'd shout, "Your flags are at half-mast." But trousers meant ration coupons, and clothing coupons were short. Even if, every year, fat boys and tall thin boys were lined up in the school hall, and weighed and measured by the school nurse. If you weighed and measured enough, you got extra coupons. But the queue for weighing was called the Freak Show, and other lads stood round asking where the Bearded Lady was . . . .

And still there were never enough coupons. Last winter, he'd split his trousers on the barbed wire round the Fish Quay, and Mam had refused to patch them; patches meant poverty, and they hadn't come to that yet. Instead, Chas got new trousers, and Dad had to do without a new winter coat, and Mam never let Chas forget it.

But in spite of his tallness, his stomach still stuck out like a kid's. He pulled up his pajama jacket to look; sucked his stomach in. His pajama trousers fell down again.

Retrieving them, he rolled up a sleeve and flexed his bicep. It looked like thin white rope. Disgusting!

In his American cop comics was a guy called Charles Atlas; his *grin* had muscles; even his Brylcreemed hair had muscles. He sold a sure-fire way of making muscles. But you had to send fifty cents to America. Even if you *had* the money, some rotten U-boat would just sink your letter. . . .

He suddenly remembered Mam said it was bad luck to stare in a mirror after midnight. You might see the devil standing behind you. He made himself look, and only saw two tea towels hanging on the pantry doors. Devils was daft; Mam was daft. Still, he got out of the kitchen quick. Somehow, the world worked by different rules after midnight.

He fled back to the spaniel; poked it till it gave him a sleepy lick. It smelled warm; dusty fur and waxy ears. Good cure for devils.

Then he heard an explosion. His stomach tightened from old practice. But it wasn't an antiaircraft gun; they echoed round the whole sky. Nor a bomb, because the ground didn't tremble.

A small explosion, far away. He remembered it from before the war: the maroon which called out the Garmouth lifeboat. When Mam was young, the maroon was always going. The women of Garmouth would fling their shawls over their heads and run to Collingwood's Monument. Watch aghast as schooners went onto the rocks, and poor sailor lads drowned in sight of their own front doors.

Chas imagined the lifeboatmen running, pulling on black oilskins. Then that wizard splash as the lifeboat hit the water. He wished he could see it. It would impress the girls at school tomorrow. Make a marvelous article for the school magazine.

But his parents would stop him going. Not for any real reason. Just 'cause of what the neighbors would think. Mam's whole life was ruled by what the rotten neighbors would think.

But were his parents awake? He tiptoed to their bedroom door. Damn; they were mumbling in a blankety way.

"What's the matter, hinny?"

"Aah thought Aah heard a gun."

"It was the maroon."

"Ye sure?"

"Sure Aah'm sure. It's wild night for sailors."

Bedsprings creaked as Dad turned over. Snores resumed. But he'd have to watch it. Mam, once wakened, never really went back to sleep and she had ears like radar.

Taking trousers and sweater from the neat pile Mam always made when she came to say good night, he tiptoed to the back door, avoiding creaky floorboards. Got his bike from the coalshed, holding the back wheel off the ground so the freewheel wouldn't click. He felt guilty about leaving the back door unbolted, but burglars only existed in Mam's mind. After four years of war, the McGills had nowt worth pinching but the dog and the butter ration, and this week the dog had eaten the butter ration.

Pedaling drove icy wind up his sweater. It used to be a racing bike, but he'd turned the handlebars upside down like cowhorns, tied an old car number plate to the saddle, and a stick that rattled against the back spokes making a motorbike noise. Such things made girls look at you, but they didn't help fast pedaling.

Still, the Coast Road sloped down all the way to the sea and was empty as the sea, in spite of the explosion. Garmouth folk were more tired and less nervous than in 1940. And the wind was at his back, driving thin clouds across the moon toward Germany.

He swept down the Monument approach at thirty miles an hour, the wind so cold and hard it felt like swimming. He gulped in lungfuls, like drinking water. He shot across the narrow plank bridge with a great *Whee-hee* and didn't have to pedal again till the great statue on the Monument looked over him.

Collingwood's Monument, raised to honor the great Northumbrian Admiral. Thirty years after he was dead and pushing up daisies. Huge sandstone base, short column, then the statue. The statue's head was far too big, making it look like one of the Seven Dwarfs; but no one noticed till it was up. Still, it made a good aircraft carrier for seagulls; the Admiral always had plenty of white hair.

But the best thing about the Monument was four real cannons from Collingwood's ship. Their barrels were blocked up, to stop kids stuffing down fireworks on Guy Fawkes' Day. The sandstone base of the Monument was hollow, and much used by drunken sailors caught short going back to their ships. It had a curious Egyptian-pyramid smell that varied with the weather. Whenever the *Garmouth Evening News* ran short of war disasters, it ran an article headed: *Is Collingwood's Monument Falling Down?*

Chas chained his bike carefully, and climbed the steep steps. He paused. There were people on top of the Monument. Slum roughs? Courting couple? Couples were worst. They glared at you, making you feel guilty even if you weren't.

A man's voice said authoritatively. "There she goes now!"

Chas tried not to feel glad there was a sensible adult there.

The group on top opened to enclose him. The man said again, "There she goes now," specially for Chas's benefit. The man was wearing a tin hat, naval duffle coat and a huge pair of binoculars. He looked at least a lieutenant-commander. Mam said Chas had lieutenant-commanders on the brain; but he'd never actually *seen* one. He peered at the man, trying to make out details of his uniform. His stare embarrassed the man, who repeated for a third time, "There she goes now!"

Chas looked left, toward the river mouth. Under the patchy moonlight, the water was broken and restless. Out beyond the piers, the small black blob of the lifeboat was tossing about as helplessly as a milk crate. It was a poor reward for pedaling two miles in the middle of the night.

"Seen anything else?"

Old Binoculars looked offended. "No, but I was up here two minutes after the maroon went."

"Aye, less than two minutes," said a woman, tucking her hair into her headscarf. "He'd just Come Off, you see. I was getting his supper; it's getting cold on the table." She hugged herself against the wind, shivering so violently that the whole group began shivering in sympathy. "I've only got me nightie on under me coat," she confided, pulling the coat tighter round her.

Chas felt suddenly depressed. Old Binoculars couldn't possibly be a lieutenant-commander. Lieutenant-commanders' wives didn't walk round the streets in only their nighties. Perhaps these people were from the Low Street. . . . Chas moved away a slight distance. Mam had a way of saying "The Low Street."

He felt freezing and ridiculous. Why hadn't he put more clothes on? Why had he come at all? Nothing was going to happen. *And* he would have a hard pedal home against the wind. And a geography exam tomorrow. He tried to take his mind off it by enjoying the view. It was a super view.

Garmouth Cliffs didn't stop at the coast; they swung inland, up-river. This northern cliff was called Bank Top. All the interesting things in the town lay at the base of Bank Top. On his left, stretching out to sea, was the North Pier. Waves broke right over it when the sea was rough. It was a great game, walking along it in a storm with a bunch of lads, trying to dodge the waves, seeing who was last to get soaked.

Below, awash with foam tonight, were the rocks called the Black Middens. Sometimes ships got wrecked there, in spite of the piers.

Next thing up-river was a little crescent of beach called Fish Quay Sands. You could always find something smelly and interesting washed up on the Sands. Next came the Lifeboat Station, stuck out over the river on stilts. Then came the Fish Quay itself, also stuck out over the river on stilts.

Fish Quay was the best place he knew. Dead herring flung all over the place; waiting underfoot to send you arse-over-tip like a banana skin. Herring squashed to a pink pulp by the wheels of lorries and carts. Some old gaffers kept alive by picking them up and cooking them. Chas tried bringing some home once, but Mam said the herring weren't nice, you didn't know where they'd been, and threw them in the bin.

There were herring gulls on the Quay, big as geese. Walking round your legs bold as brass. You left them alone; one snap of their beaks could take your hand off.

Trawlermen were great. Swearing nonstop. Mad generous. There was a spaniel dog sat outside the Fish Quay Tavern. Trawlermen reckoned it was lucky; patted it on the head before they sailed, and when they came back safe they gave the dog things. Once it had a pound block of chocolate in its mouth. It got fatter every day.

Trawlermen could sleep any time. Dad said they could sleep stretched along a clothesline. Trawling all night, they took their sleep when they could.

The ways they talked, life was one big laugh. Trawling up German mines in their nets and firing rifles at them. Fighting off German bombers that tried to machine-gun them; calling them names like Horace the Heinkel.

A great place, the Quay; but the next place up-river was scary. It was really Old Garmouth, but everyone called it the Low Street. Because the land at the bottom of Bank Top was so narrow, it was only one street wide. People had to build their backyards, even their houses, out on stilts over the river. Every backyard had steps leading down into the water. People kept a rowboat moored like posh folk kept a car.

Years ago, everyone in Garmouth lived down Low Street. Then the toffs moved up Bank Top, into Albion Road and Northumberland Square. But even that didn't content them. They kept on moving outward. Now they were three miles up the coast at Whitley Bay, with their rockeries and crazy-paving paths; well clear of the smell of the fish they still made their money from.

After they went, anybody who was *anybody* moved up Bank Top. Only the riffraff were left, the feckless rubbish who hadn't two pennies to rub together. Sailors tired of the sea moved in, and married the pale lank-haired daughters of the riffraff.

They were harmless enough—except the Maltese. The Maltese kept cafés; and Women. The Women lured drunken sailors into the cafés, where the Maltese knifed them and lifted their bulging wallets. Then the dead sailors were dropped through the trapdoors in the floor, straight into the river. On an outgoing tide, the bodies were carried out to sea, and No Questions Asked. Or so people said.

Actually, it must be true, because once it went wrong, and a woman's body was washed up on Fish Quay Sands. The fish had been busy, and her only distinguishing mark was that the big toe on her left foot was much smaller than the second toe. The papers said the police were making inquiries. Everybody else said ha-ha. Because the Low Street lot stuck together and wouldn't even tell a policeman what time it was. The police were so scared they went down the Low Street in pairs. Anyway, people said, women like that deserved all they got. It was a nine days' wonder—till the curate ran off with the church-warden's wife. . . .

But it was OK, because the Maltese, like all riffraff, knew their place. They didn't mess about in the Upper Town, where decent folk lived. And it was great, going down Low Street in daylight, because most Maltese would be sleeping off last night's booze, and the others just looked at you and you stared back, daring them to try anything because you came from a decent home. Nothing ever happened, but it made you feel tingly. And when you got through the Low Street, to the safety of the Fish Quay, you felt like Dick Tracy or something. But you never told Mam. . . .

"What's that?" yelped Old Binoculars, lifting his glasses so sharply they rapped against his helmet.

"Where?" Everybody shoved their heads close to him.

"Just beyond the South Pier."

Chas moved even farther off, so he could use Mam's old opera glasses. He was ashamed of them; they were coated with pink mother-of-pearl and obviously

Women's Things. He trained them out to sea, but all he got was bigger and fuzzier moonlit waves.

"*Thought* I saw something," said Binoculars miserably.

"They work him *that* hard at the naval base," apologized Binoculars' wife. "That admiral's onto him day and night."

Somebody passed round fags, and hesitated at Chas.

"I *am* sixteen," said Chas defensively. But he had to fumble with the packet a long time before he got one out. Thank God it was dark.

Someone was clever with cupped hands and lighter.

"Mind that light!" shrieked the woman, and laughed like a cock crowing. They *must* be Low Street types.

Chas didn't inhale; it made you sick. He held the smoke in his mouth and blew it out again. But the little fire under his nose made him feel warmer; orange against the dark-blue night. "Cup your hand over that fag, lad," said someone sharply. "They show up three miles away at sea."

Chas nearly said "So what?" but it was the bloke who'd given him the fag. . . . Instead, he began revising facts for his geography exam . . . products of Czechoslovakia: Pilsner beer at Pilsen, Bren guns at Brno—except the Nazis put a stop to that . . . it was stupid, revising lessons that went out of date in 1938.

"There it is again," said Binoculars. "A light at sea— no, it's a ship on fire."

Chas focused and refocused desperately. Opera glasses were useless. Then he saw it. A ship's bridge, one tall funnel, a lick of flame for'ard.

"God help him if there's a U-boat!"

"There's a tug."

"That'll be Dick Burley in the *Hendon*. He's on harbor-watch tonight. Moored just inside the piers last thing."

"Dick'll see him right. Dick knaas the sea."

Somebody asked to borrow the opera glasses, because Old Binoculars wasn't sharing. The glasses were passed from hand to hand.

"Want a look, son?" asked someone reluctantly at last.

"Thanks *very* much!" said Chas.

"Watch your lip, lad. Eeh, bairns have no manners these days."

"Take the world off you as soon as look at you."

Chas struggled to focus again. Some fool had put fingerprints all over the lenses. He hadn't got a hanky, so he surreptitiously pulled out his pajama tail and wiped the lenses with that. It spread the fingerprints around without making things clearer.

Then, far left, came a small blinding flash. A bang rolled across the sea, echoed round the cliffs and faded up the Gar. The woman screamed. A white column climbed out of the sea near the burning ship.

"It's—it's a bliddy U-boat on the surface . . . the cheeky sod. Look . . . LOOK!"

Lost behind fingerprints, Chas couldn't see a thing. Again a flash and bang. He abandoned the glasses as another white column grew between ship and shore.

"The bliddy nerve. . . ."

"You wait—the Castle guns'll have him. They've been waiting for a chance like this."

As if in answer, the Castle searchlights came on, waving wildly overhead.

"Geddown, lads—it's not a bliddy air raid!"

The searchlights descended with agonizing slowness, and weaved across the waves.

Flash and bang from the U-boat.

"They've hit the bugger!" screamed the woman.

"They've not fired yet," said Chas.

"Less lip, you!" said Binoculars.

Then the first Castle gun fired. A white rose of piercing intensity lit the sky.

"Ooh, they've missed by *miles*," said the woman.

"They're firing star shell, hinny, to light him up."

And, far out, there was a tiny black square against the sea.

"U-23—coastal type," said Binoculars. Who was he kidding? The thing looked no bigger than a floating oil drum.

Then all four Castle guns fired together, red trumpets of flame whose noise filled the world. The U-boat vanished in a snarl of foam. Everybody cheered. But when the foam subsided, the U-boat was still there, moving right.

"He's getting behind the ship, so the guns can't shoot."

Again the U-boat vanished in foam, only to reappear. The star shell went out, leaving darkness and the burning ship.

"Oh, those poor sailor lads," wailed the woman.

When the next star shell came, the U-boat had vanished behind the freighter. The guns were silent.

"Why don't the armed trawlers go out?"

Chas glanced down at the Fish Quay. Smoke poured from several funnels of the armed-trawler fleet; but none moved.

"They're trying to get steam up," said Binoculars. "They'll never do it in time. . . ."

"She's going to make it!" shouted somebody. And indeed, guided by the *Hendon*, the burning ship was turning in toward the piers. Pink-lit smoke poured from her for'ard hold, obscuring the lighthouse at the pier's end.

"Thank God." Everybody sighed.

Then a U-boat shell hit the freighter's bridge. It must have crippled her steering gear, for she began heading straight for the granite pier. The *Hendon* yipped indignantly, like a zoo keeper trying to cope with a very large elephant. The tug's propellers churned the water white, but to no avail. The freighter's bows kept straight for the granite wall. And still the U-boat fired.

"Why don't our guns fire back?"

"U-boat's too close. Can't lower their gun barrels enough."

Chas could have wept. Sodding U-boat, so close to the lighthouse that the lighthouse-keepers could have thrown stones at it. And no one doing *anything*.

Then the *Hendon*, despairing of saving the freighter, slipped her towing cable and, turning like a Dodgem car, headed straight out toward the U-boat. Clear across the water came a faint *tacca-tacca-tacca*.

"What's that?"

"Dick Burley. He's got Lewis guns on his bridge. He's going to ram Jerry!"

"The mad sod!"

Chas watched aghast. The tugboat was tiny. The U-boat would eat it. . . . But on the tug went, a tremendous wave surging from its bow. The U-boat fired again; Chas closed his eyes.

When he opened them again, the shell had flown wide and burst in the middle of the harbor. And the U-boat was making off, picking up speed.

"Go on, Dick. Go on, lad, run the bugger down!" It was like the home-team center-forward getting the ball and heading for goal. The tug seemed about to burst with speed, steam and indignation.

Tacca-tacca-tacca went the Lewis guns.

Wheep-wheep went the tug's siren. It was gaining on the sub.

Then the sub's conning tower vanished beneath the waves.

"*Ooooooh,*" groaned the crowd. "Too late."

Too late for the freighter too. Her bow hit the pier with a rumbling crunch. Steel sparked against granite as she ran alongside and stopped. Pink smoke wreathed the pier. Little figures of men leaping to safety. Then with a long hissing the ship sank, till only masts and funnel showed. The flames went out. It was suddenly very dark.

"She's gone." Everybody sighed together. Chas unclenched fists that had pins and needles.

"By—Dick Burley deserves a medal."

"Did ye see him? Straight at it."

"Fancy a U-boat running away from a bit of a tug."

"Mevve he thought Dick was a battleship!"

Chas slipped away to his bike. On the way home he met ambulances heading for the pier.

There was a light in the kitchen. Mam in curlers and dressing gown, Dad in his warden's uniform; drinking tea.

"Where the hell you been?" asked Dad.

"You've had me worried sick," said Mam. "Tuck your pajamas in. I don't know *what* you think you look like. Anybody see you looking like that?"

"It was *dark,*" said Chas wearily.

"Don't cheek your mam. Where you been?"

"You never used to be like this," continued Mam,

as if Dad hadn't spoken. "You were a different lad before you went into that sixth form. That sixth form's turned your brain. I don't know what the Head would say if he saw you in pajamas like that. . . ."

"Where you been?" repeated Dad. But Mam was still in full cry.

"I don't know where you get your ideas from. What your Aunt Aggie would say. . . ."

"I'm *trying* to answer my father's question," snapped Chas. "*If* you don't mind. . . ."

Dad's fist thumped the table. "Don't come that grammar-school talk wi' us."

From the glint in Dad's eye, Chas knew it was time to change tack. "There was a U-boat off the piers—Dick Burley tried to ram it."

"You coulda bin *killed*," wailed Mam. "I knew I was right to worry. I told your dad so."

But Dad was no longer listening. There was a different, small-boy glint in his eye. "Dick Burley, eh? How'd he get on?"

Mam went on huffing and puffing about pajamas; but she might as well have gone to bed. When Chas had told everything, Dad looked at his pocket watch and got to his feet.

"Sunk against the North Pier, eh? I'll just have a quick look before work."

"But you haven't had your breakfast. That U-boat might come back—"

"Hush up, hinny," said Dad, and was gone.

"Now you'll make your dad late for work. You're both as bad as each other. I suppose you want some breakfast."

"Please."

"Then go and clean your filthy face—put those pajamas for washing . . . did you feed your rabbits last night?"

Chas slammed the bathroom door. But Mam nagged straight through it, as if it didn't exist.

2 Audrey Parton leaned on her typewriter and thought of headlines she might have written. *Garmouth Hero Tackles Killer U-boat*.

Waste of time. The censor wouldn't even let the *Garmouth News* tell its readers they *had* been shelled from the sea. But that didn't stop the rumors. People ringing up from Hartlepool asking about the German pocket battleship. . . .

Then there were readers' letters. *Mother of Five, Chirton* demanding the whole British Navy be called in to defend the Gar. *Borough Road*, a Communist gentleman, saying such things wouldn't be allowed to happen off Murmansk.

The censor would drop those in the wastebasket too.

The *News* had tried doing a profile of Dick Burley. Their photographer tried opening up Dick with whisky. He might as well have poured his whiskies into a bottomless pit. Dick had called Audrey "ma bonny lass," sung doubtful songs, and blown cigar smoke to spoil the photographer's pictures.

It was *useless* being a reporter in wartime. You couldn't tell people a *thing*. The port commander had declared the *Corwen Star*'s cargo "Top Secret," and posted sentries on the pier to stop sightseers. Immediately, the fish queues became convinced the *Star* was full of poison gas that leaked nightly after dark and had already killed thousands of seagulls.

But after the first low tide, men in pea jackets who were "something on the Fish Quay" began passing American gunsights from hand to hand. Audrey bought one for five bob. Beautifully made by "Fine Instrument Co. of Detroit," wrapped in yards of greased paper—and totally ruined. You could see through it, but darkly, through a rainbow mist. The moving parts grated with rust.

Then there were the ghouls who flocked to the Monument every fine evening. Contemplating the blackened wreck as the tide washed in and out of its shell holes, their enjoyment enhanced by the fact some of the crew were Still Missing; and by the licking of horrible yellow ice cream sold by a Maltese off a homemade barrow.

Funny. People glared at that Maltese; said he made his ice cream from Black Market stuff. But they still bought the ice cream. . . .

But none of it was News. Tonight's big headline was:

Ex-Mayor Bought Stolen Butter.

Audrey lit another coffin-nail Woodbine, and tucked her knees under her desk because the chief reporter was leering at them again. She returned to her half-finished article, *Tasty Rissoles from Whalemeat.* Leaving school hadn't been anything like she thought. She missed Chas McGill's gang. 'Course, Chas seemed just a kid now; a nutty kid. But a nice nutty kid. Better than married reporters who asked you out for a drink. . . .

*

The *Corwen Star* was to be raised the first Saturday of the Easter holidays. Mam packed a picnic basket, and they caught the eight o'clock bus to the Monument to beat the crowds. The Monument was already lively. Kids pushing each other off the cannons and parents saying endlessly they had a lovely day for it.

The *Star*, too, was a hive of activity. The pier's crane, usually used for lifting granite blocks, was swung out to the sound of cheers. The *Star's* hull was lined with long shapes, low in the water.

"What's them flat things?" asked Mam suspiciously.

"Pontoons, to lift her with the tide."

"Pontoon's a gambling game!" Mam dreaded gambling. One of her brothers had Ruined Himself at Cards and Died Young.

Dad raised his eyes to heaven and said, "Let's have a sandwich!"

"You've just had your breakfasts!"

They munched steadily all morning. And rearranged tartan rugs, complaining how hard the steps were and how cold the wind, even for April.

"I don't know why they want to move the nasty thing," said Mam. "It's best left where it is. It's not in anybody's way."

"It's a danger to navigation," said Dad, brooking no argument.

"But what do they want to lift the ship onto the pier *for*? Nobody'll be able to get past to the lighthouse. And it'll make the place look so *untidy*. . . ."

"*Hinny*." Dad groaned, putting his face in his hands. "Hinny, they're not lifting it onto the pier. They're lifting it into deep water to blow it up."

Chas kept his face straight with an effort. Cem, his friend, collapsed helpless over a cannon.

"But it's full of water," said Mam.

"They're pumping it dry."

"But more water will run in through them holes."

"They have blocked off the holes wi' cofferdams."

"Aye, they'll need coffins, for them poor sailors still aboard."

"God give me strength," said Dad. Chas kicked Cem to stop him laughing.

Slowly, as the tide came in, the *Star* lifted for her last voyage. Every time the crane clanked, Mam worried in case it would topple over into the water.

"They knaa what they're doing," said Dad. "What's them gray boxes they're putting aboard?"

"That'll be the coffins," said Mam darkly. "Want another sandwich, our Chas?"

"Here comes the towline." And there was Dick Burley, maneuvering the *Hendon* as easily as if she were a rowboat. Everyone cheered and shouted advice. Dick stuck up two fingers in what might have been a victory sign. Then the crane clanked rapidly, and the *Star* wallowed sideways, a hundred yards clear of the pier.

Men leaped from her decks onto the pontoons, the pontoons pulled clear, and the *Star* sank with a great glugging and bubbling, like the toy submarine Chas used to play with in the bath when he was a kid.

"What they done that for?" demanded Mam. "They can't blow it up now—the gunpowder will get all wet."

Before Dad could think of anything to say, the *Star* blew up like a thousand depth charges. A bit of her funnel shot high in the air like a merry crazy bird, then fell back into the water. Everyone gave a satisfied sigh and began rolling up rugs and finishing sandwiches, agreeing through mouthfuls it had been better than the pictures.

"I'll bet that bang smashed a few windows," said Mam. "Hope ours are all right."

"Hinny, our house is two miles away!"

"Blast plays funny tricks," said Mam.

"Well, let's get cracking," said Dad. "Standing here won't buy the bairn a new shirt."

But Mam didn't seem to hear. She was staring fixedly out to sea. Chas scanned the horizon; it was totally empty. Chas wondered for a moment whether Mam was seeing things; then he realized she was deliberately *not* seeing things. Or rather, not seeing somebody. Somebody undesirable was approaching. He looked round. Audrey Parton was coming down the broad steps.

Chas could never make out why Mam had taken against Audrey since she left school. Admittedly she was a *bit* different. She wore a dirty white raincoat all the time, and her hair pulled back in an elastic band. And her face was often shiny, like she'd just got out of bed. But what difference did that make?

"Hello, Audrey," said Chas loudly.

"Hi, Audrey," said Cem even louder; he had an incredible nose for seeing something was up.

"Hello, Audrey," mumbled Dad in a half-hearted way. A bit miserable.

Audrey paused, one foot poised above the steps. She'd have liked to stop. Then she saw Mam's ramrod back turned on her. So she just said, "Hi!" dispiritedly, and walked on.

"Hey!" said Chas loudly, at Mam's back. "That was Audrey Parton."

"I know it was Audrey Parton," said Mam, unrolling the tartan rug and rerolling it tighter.

"What you got against her?"

"That'll do, Chas," said Dad.

"She drinks," said Mam through tight lips.

" 'Course she drinks. We all drink. We've got to eat and drink to live."

"You know what I mean," said Mam. "She's been seen drinking with *men*, in the Rex Hotel at Whitley Bay."

"What's wrong with the Rex Hotel? Me Aunt Aggie had her Silver Wedding there. . . ."

"That's different."

"How is it different?"

"That'll do, Chas!" said Dad. People were starting to stare, but Chas didn't care.

"I was at school with her. She was all right *then*."

"It's what she learned since she left school that worries me."

"Like what?"

Dad picked up the picnic basket. "I'm off. If you lot miss the five o'clock bus, you can walk."

But there was a devil in Chas. Which made him say:

"Me and Cem'll walk home by the Fish Quay Sands. We'll take the short cut through the Low Street. It'll save the bus fare."

Mam's pale face flushed. "You'll do no such thing. Over my dead body you will. You won't go near *that place*."

Dad glanced round the intrigued bystanders. "Shove off then—an' make sure you don't drown yourself."

Chas looked back once; his parents were walking up the hill to the bus stop. Yards apart, like they never did normally. Must be a hell of a row going on; once Mam started on about the Low Street she never stopped. Chas was sorry for Dad; but he'd paid Mam back for Audrey. . . .

They cut across the cliffs to the Fish Quay.

"It's funny," said Cem.

"I can't hear anybody laughing. That noise you hear is seagulls, friend."

"Oh, ha ha," said Cem wearily. "I mean it's funny about Jerry sinking the *Corwen Star*. Hasn't been a ship sunk round here since 1940, and that was only a collier."

"Pinpointing strategic targets," said Chas, grandly.

"Ye what?"

"Hitting one's enemy smack in the breadbasket. Like when our bombers hit that German ball-bearing factory. No ball-bearings means no planes, no tanks, no nothing. Well . . . same here. If that U-boat had sunk a collier it wouldn't have mattered. We got plenty more coal. But I bet those gunsights cost five hundred quid each. Now they'll have to fetch more from America. It might hold up the Second Front. . . ."

"Yeah," leered Cem triumphantly. "But how did Jerry know what the *Corwen Star* was *carrying*?"

There was a long awful silence before Chas said, "Lucky fluke!"

"Lucky fluke nothing. Jerry wouldn't have taken those sort of risks for a rotten collier. Right under the Castle guns? Like my Aunt Fanny. Jerry *knew*."

"I suppose he knew the armed trawlers wouldn't have steam up, either?"

"Yeah."

"Talk sense. You'll be saying next he knew what the crews had for supper."

"Maybe he did." Cem was grinning in a way Chas

didn't like. Gloating 'cause he knew something no-body else did. Or pretending he did. You could never tell with Cem.

"How *could* Jerry know?"

"A spy . . . ?" said Cem slyly.

"Don't talk wet. A spy wouldn't last five minutes in Garmouth. Everybody knows everybody."

"Do *you* know everybody?"

"No, but my gran does. She's always working it out with Mam. Which street they were born in. Who they married. They spend hours at it."

"She doesn't know everybody."

"Like who, clever-dick?"

"Foreign sailors."

"What, the Free Dutch, the Free Danes? They're on *our* side."

"What about the Swedes? They're neutral."

Chas was silent.

"Why couldn't it be a British sailor?" Cem's gloaty tone got louder.

"Stands to reason. . . ."

"Lord Haw-Haw's a traitor, and he's British." Cem did his awful impersonation. "Jairmany calling, Jair-many calling. Here is a message for the people of Gar-mouth. Look your last on beautiful Garmouth Priory, for tonight it will be destroyed by the bombers of the victorious Luftwaffe."

The Germans had raided that night. Demolished a public lavatory in Wellington Street. It had been a good joke—two years ago.

"Haw-Haw's really American," said Chas trium-phantly.

"I've got a newspaper cutting," said Cem, reaching inside his jacket pocket. "Want to see it?"

Chas hesitated. Cem's cuttings were always exciting; but afterward you wished you hadn't read them. They were about things like a girl's headless body being found in a suitcase. Or some American army doctor amputating his own leg in the jungles of Guadalcanal.

Cem dangled the tatty, much-folded cutting under Chas's nose. "No guts!"

Chas snatched it, nearly tearing it in half.

"Watch out, you oaf!" yelped Cem. "It's *precious*."

"Huh!" Chas read it. It was from the *Daily Express* of November 4, 1942.

THIS WAS THE PRICE OF A TRAITOR

Eighteen pounds was the price for which Duncan Scott-Ford, British merchant seaman, betrayed his country.

The enemy agent who handed it to him in Lisbon promised more, for more convoy secrets. But he never got any more.

And early yesterday morning, they took him out at Wandsworth Jail and hanged him. Duncan Alexander Croall Scott-Ford, a 21-year-old Plymouth man, was sentenced to death for treachery at the Central Criminal Court on October 16 after a secret trial before Mr. Justice Birkett.

He was a pub-crawler who drank with fellow seamen for the information he could get and pass on to the enemy agent—a nightclub hostess—who employed him.

But when he arrived in Lisbon with more information, the agent refused to pay, and threatened to expose him unless he continued to work for her.

For his £18, Scott-Ford gave information about his own ship, imperiling his shipmates' lives.

He paid with his own.

Chas felt sick.

Cem snatched back the cutting triumphantly. "Toldja!"

Chas exploded. "He was a *nutter*, giving away his own ship!"

"There's plenty of nutters," said Cem. "There's probably another nutter down there now." He nodded gloomily at the ships in the river.

"He was a toff!" roared Chas. "All toffs have a black sheep in the family."

"How do you know he was a toff?"

"With a name like Scott-Ford?"

"He wasn't doing a toff's job—he was only a seaman."

"That *proves* he was the black sheep of the family. And he was south country—from Plymouth."

"What difference does that make?"

"A Garsider wouldn't be a traitor—sell his country for eighteen measly quid."

"I'm a Garsider. I'd do it. Not for eighteen quid—but for eighteen million. Think of all the racing bikes you could buy—one for every day of the year."

"You'd do anything. You stink. You'd join the Waffen SS and bayonet babies and roast them over a fire and eat them."

Cem laughed in pure maniac joy.

"And never, never, never show me your rotten cuttings again! You've got a mind like a *sewer*."

Cem went on laughing. "Well, if you're going to be childish, I'm off."

"Let's see that cutting again," said Chas suddenly.

"But you just said. . . ."

"Show me or I'll smash your stupid face in!" Chas's fists were clenched.

Cem sighed with elaborate tolerance; handed back the cutting.

Chas stared and stared at it, trying to find some kind of comfort. Stared at the blurred photo of the dead spy; a pale, cocky young face with Brylcreemed hair and turned-up greatcoat collar. He didn't *look* wicked or a traitor. That was the terrible thing. He looked like somebody out of the *Garmouth Evening News* who had won a prize for ballroom dancing or got married, or been killed doing his duty against Rommel. Like somebody down your street. . . .

Chas gazed miserably at the Castle guns, the barbed wire on the clifftop, gray lines of ships and swinging cranes. Britain's War Effort. Everyone doing their bit, just like 1940. . . .

Like hell. It was 1943. War going on too long; people turning funny. Miners striking, when the country was desperate for coal; helping Hitler. Shipyard workers pinching iron rations from ship's lifeboats, so torpedoed sailors died. Sailors in port, drinking themselves stupid, peeing up side alleys where ladies could see—three up in court last week. No Allied landing in Europe; no Second Front. Everyone too busy boozing and going with prostitutes. Britain going rotten inside. Hitler winning from sheer boredom.

Chas glared down at the Low Street. That's where Scott-Fords got their info. And passed it on. Nightclub hostess? Just a posh word for prostitute.

It all became very clear.

Who ran the brothels? Maltese. And who was boss-Maltese?

"Cripes," said Chas. "Nico Mintoff!"

Mintoff was never up in the police court. Dad said he was too clever by half. But when something nasty happened, people nudged each other and said "Nico." Chas had never seen him. But years ago, they'd played a game called "Knocking up Nico." You slithered down Bank Top, holding on to tufts of grass, getting nearer and nearer the Blue Café where Nico lived. There was always a guard in the doorway, sitting in a tipped-up chair, hat over his eyes, pretending to be asleep. You never saw his flick-knife—but you knew it was there in his pocket.

At the bottom you started shouting.

"How many sailors you knifed, mister?"

"Hey, tell Nico we want to see him!"

The guard pretended not to hear. But when you shouted, "Nico's a dope!" he'd leap off his chair and make a blind run at you. Then you climbed like hell, panting and slithering till you reached the safety of the top. Then the Maltese would shout:

"Nico see you one dark night, Johnnie, yes-no?"

As far as they knew, Nico had never seen any kid one dark night.

But there was always a first time.

Then *you'd* be floating down the ebb tide, with the blackjacks nibbling at your big toe. . . .

"What you mean?" asked Cem. "Nico Mintoff?"

"He's the spy."

"What spy?" Cem sounded incredibly innocent; even concerned.

"The spy you were bloody talking about. . . ."

"Oh, Chas, Chas, Chas," crooned Cem soothingly. "I was only pulling your leg, little Chas."

Chas tried to kick him, but missed.

"There, *there*," soothed Cem. "Why don't you lie down, Chassy-Chassy? You'll soon feel better. . . ."

"Why shouldn't there be a spy?" yelled Chas. "Why shouldn't it be Mintoff?"

"That rubbish about Nico was years ago. Kids' stuff."

"That dead woman in the river wasn't kids' stuff— it was in the paper. The *Corwen Star* wasn't kids' stuff."

"Oh, hell," said Cem. "It was just meant for a laugh. . . ."

"Everything's a laugh to you. If Hitler won, *you*'d start laughing."

"Let's go down Fish Quay Sands. It'll take your mind off it."

Fish Quay Sands faced up-river. Anything thrown off the ships ended up there. Mainly waste from fish-gutting. It was like a stricken battlefield in some War between Fishes. Bodyless codfish gaped at all angles, displaying sharp teeth in snarls of mummified viciousness. Other fish were only head and tail, whole flanks carved away by gigantic swordstrokes. Families of flies rose buzzing. Herring gulls only gave up their prey with a savage slash of yellow bill when the boys were about to tread on them. One was fighting a noisy duel with a black tomcat. They were well matched.

Among so much death, the inanimate debris of the river assumed living shapes. Old boots displayed their nails like sharks. A pair of sodden trousers looked foully murdered.

It would have smelled horrific, but for the salty breeze. With the breeze, it just smelled interesting. On holiday, the smell of rotting fish always made Chas homesick.

The river was as littered as the beach. You could hardly see the water. Some stretches were covered with sawdust from a sawmill a mile up-river; others with the iridescent green and purple of oil. Out of this soup protruded sticks, bottles and broken fish-boxes, bobbing together in rhythm with the shallow waves.

"What's *that*?" said Cem.

There was an interesting object on the far edge of the soup. About a foot long, fatly curved and browny-yellow. Could be one of those musical instruments that guys played, in movies about schooners sailing into tropical islands at sunset. Where mysterious dark women waited with a glass of wine in their hands— or danced on tables, stamping their feet and swirling up their skirts and. . . .

"Stop daydreaming, you dozy bugger," said Cem. "Let's get it ashore, whatever it is."

They started a long-practiced routine: lobbing half-bricks to splash beyond the object, so the splashes would drive it in to the shore. You had to be careful, though; one ill-placed brick falling short could undo half an hour's work. When they had it moving nicely, Chas said, "Suppose there was a spy. . . ."

"Suppose your granny played fullback for Arsenal. . . ."

"No, seriously—how would a spy get his messages to the U-boat? Radio?"

"Oh, God," said Cem despairingly. "He's off again. You been watching too many movies, mate. Look." He pointed to the bristling radio masts above the naval base and the Castle. "The Navy's listening in, night and day. They've got a secret device. If a spy transmitted for two minutes, they'd be able to work out exactly where he was transmitting from. Then—good night." Cem drew his hand across his throat and made glugging noises.

"All right then. He could write to a neutral country—like that woman German agent in Lisbon."

"And the ship he was writing about would be a thousand miles away by the time the letter got there. Give over, Chas. You're a bore."

Cem made a brilliant shot that drove the object in the water a whole foot nearer, and looked unbearably superior.

But an hour later, the object was still six oily yards from shore. It was nearly dark; teatime. Cem, getting impatient, picked up four bricks cemented together. He got very near the water's edge, thrust his foot forward onto a patch of sawdust, and threw.

Unfortunately, the sawdust was sawdust-on-water. Cem's foot vanished up to the knee. The bricks fell with an enormous splash on the near side of the object, driving it out again three whole yards.

"Clumsy great sod!"

"I'm bloody soaked. Me best shoes."

"Now I'll have to come back for it *tomorrow*."

"If some other kid doesn't get it first," said Cem spitefully, wringing out an evil-smelling sock.

3 It was a lovely morning, sun streaming through the kitchen window. Mam would have said it was showing up all the dust, but she wasn't up yet. Only Dad, frying his breakfast, wearing his grease-black cap and whistling a tuneless song that he reckoned was called "The Whistler and His Dog."

"Want fried bread? There's a thrush on the back

lawn; she's caught three worms since I've been watching."

Chas said "Yes" to both remarks, twisted back the lace curtains and watched the thrush. He liked being with Dad before Mam was up. It was more relaxed, with an open milk bottle on the table that Mam would never have allowed. Dad never talked about Life and its Meanings; only fried bread and thrushes.

"What's got you up so early?"

Chas told him about the thing in the water.

"It'll be a mandolin, floated off a sunken ship mevve. Your Aunt Mary-Ann used to play one; very sweet. Won a competition once, at Cullercoats Methodist Church."

They pedaled down the road together. As Dad turned off for the gas works, he said, "Don't get drowned at the Quay. Aah nearly drowned there as a lad. And your granda. Never was a McGill didn't." But Chas thought there was a wistful look in his eye.

The Low Street looked washed, empty, innocent. To his left, Bank Top was a-twitter with birds. To his right, the houses towered up to the sky, leaning together, brickwork patched like an old coat. Every window seemed different, some gabled, some boarded up, some broken and fluttering dark-gray curtains like filthy petticoats. Not a sly face visible. The lower windows had shutters across, held by iron bars and padlocks. The Low Street lot mustn't even trust each other.

Sunlight glistened on dew-wet cobbles and broken beer bottles in the gutter. A bowler hat floated shallowly on a stream of brown frothy liquid wending its way to the river. Chas wouldn't have known the liquid was beer, except a white cat was lapping it warily.

A brand-new woman's shoe, black patent-leather, lay alone in the middle of the road.

The height of the houses oppressed him, but every so often it was broken by an alley winding down to the river, giving a glimpse of blue sky and the yellow funnels of moored tugs.

The Blue Café windows were shuttered too. Nico sleeping off the booze. Emboldened, Chas dismounted, leaned his bike against the café wall, and went to look at the Wooden Dolly.

The Dolly stood in an alley of her own, leading to Wooden Dolly Quay. Once she'd been a life-sized woodcarving; a Garmouth fishwife, creel of herring on her back. Done by a Victorian lady called Miss Spence.

But for a hundred years, seamen had thought the Dolly lucky, as trawlermen thought the spaniel lucky. They carved their names on the Dolly; hacked off bits to take back to sea. Now she stood, terrible, face a noseless, eyeless skull. Handless, armless, greasy-shining with the touch of seamen's fingers. The more they hacked off, the more terrible she became. Must be splinters of her all over the world. Oil-soaked splinters floating the North Atlantic, from ships that burned all night like a torch on the ocean and ships that groaned once and went down like a stone. Against the U-boats and Fokke-Wulf Condors, even the Dolly couldn't always be lucky. . . .

Suppose all the splinters of her were brought together again; and drowned men brought them. . . .

A door opened behind Chas, making him jump. It was a thin little woman, clutching a washed-out dressing gown to her skinny chest and putting out a milk bottle. So the Low Street lot got milk delivered just like decent people. . . .

She stared at Chas, with the same blank hostile stare as the white cat.

He fled back to his bike.

The mandolin was still there. He picked up the first half-brick of the day, and paused. Such a *great* morning. The piers blue in the distance and the tiniest ripples whispering up the Sands. The world was super—when there weren't stupid people around to spoil it.

He made the bricks land just where he wanted; knew they were right before they landed. Like when your first serve went in at tennis. Why was life composed of days like this, and other days when you kept on double-faulting? Specially when you were playing some sneery bugger?

There was a girl walking along the gangway to the Lifeboat Station. Wearing slacks. All Mam's friends wore slacks, but they bulged embarrassingly. This girl didn't. She had a dog on a lead, and was holding back her long hair with her other hand like something out of a magazine.

He watched her all along the gangway. When she turned, he started throwing stones again.

She waved. Chas looked round to see who she was waving at. But the beach was empty.

She waved again. He waved back timidly, then blushed to the roots of his hair.

It was Sheila Smythson.

He'd watched her profile every day for three years, choosing his seat in the classroom so he could slump against the wall and watch her without being noticed. He knew that straight nose, infrequent smile and lock of hair that curled round her ear better than he knew the back of his hand. But he'd never spoken to her.

Once she had spoken to him. He'd fled and buried his head in his desk. Later, they told him she'd only asked to borrow a pencil sharpener.

'Course, it was different in daydreams; after he'd saved her from being raped by a platoon of sex-crazed Japs. Killing them single-handed. Then he and Sheila walked off arm in arm into the sunset. That walk often went on for hours, without anything much happening. Sometimes he asked her to marry him and she always said yes. But then the daydream always ground to a halt like the Saturday matinee movie when all the kids jeered and whistled.

He had different daydreams, about girls who let you do things. But Sheila wasn't that sort. Her father'd been lord mayor of Newcastle and they lived in the biggest house in Whitley Bay. Anyway, sixteen-year-old girls only went out with grown men. She probably had a fighter-pilot boyfriend with an MG sportscar.

He returned to lobbing bricks; at least she must find his accuracy impressive. When she came off the gangway she would turn away toward Whitley Bay and he could have a last long look at the fascinating way her bottom moved inside her slacks. And he could feel comfortably sad all morning about missing a chance to speak to her.

She passed along the gangway and out of the corner of his eye. He counted to ten and turned for a good eyeful.

She was walking along the beach straight toward him. He turned back quickly and flung a brick that missed the mandolin by an inch. He'd better throw well clear till she'd gone.

Her footsteps crunched nearer. Stopped right behind him. He was throwing stones so fast now that the sea was boiling like Dunkirk.

"What *are* you doing?"

"I'm getting that mandolin thing—or whatever it is—in to the shore." He punctuated the sentence with savagely flung stones.

"Why?"

"Because I—want it."

"Whatever for?" *Very* snooty.

"To make—a wooden leg—for my grandfather." Oh, she must be loving this—a smelly little tick throwing stones in the river like a *kid*. *Big* laugh when she told the fighter-pilot boyfriend. . . .

"Don't you want to talk?" Her voice was so rueful, he whirled in amazement. She was sitting on a cleaner patch of beach, arms around knees and chin on hands. Her dog was running loose, miles away.

He'd never really studied her so close before. She had a white scar on her chin, and her wrists were thin.

Goddesses don't have scars. So he sat beside her and said, too loudly, "What are *you* doing here?"

"Taking the dog for a walk. I do it every morning. I'd go nuts but for him. I talk to him. All the time."

"Why don't you talk to people?"

"Mummy's in the hospital for her nerves and Daddy's so busy and the housekeeper treats me like a statue, and there's nobody else much. It's worst in the holidays. I walk for *hours.*"

"What about boyfriends?"

"D'you have girlfriends?"

Chas laughed; goodbye fighter-pilot.

Then, horribly, they could find nothing to say. Sat side by side, staring at a cod's head as if willing it to speak. It was a siren from the river that saved them; a line of gray warships issuing out of the Gar.

"That's my cousin Robert," said Chas.

"What is?"

"That is. That's his escort group. He's on East Coast Convoys."

"His what?"

"*Escort* group. The destroyer *Virago*—1500 tons—four 4.7-inch guns, eight torpedo tubs, four depth-charge throwers, four depth-charge racks, speed of twenty-nine knots, launched 1922. The corvette *Acanthus*. . . ." Chas rattled on till he reached the armed trawler *Lord Coyne*—two hundred tons, one twelve-pounder gun.

"Don't you talk a lot?" said Sheila. "And you still haven't told me who Cousin Robert *is*."

"He's in *command*. Commander Robert McGill, DSO, DSC and two bars. He's sunk three U-boats."

"I know him. Mummy and Daddy had him round for cocktails. He didn't mention *you*."

"He wouldn't. Never met him. They're the posh side of the family. Live in Whitley among the *toffs*. Oh—"

"Don't mind me—I didn't choose where to get born."

Chas struggled on. "Got a scrapbook of cuttings about him—picture of him getting his medal at Buckingham Palace. Keep an eye on him—whenever he's in port. After Arctic convoys he's in a terrible state—lifeboats smashed, handrails all twisted up the air . . . he had his funnel shot off at Dunkirk—hey, what you laughing at?"

"Him getting his funnel shot off—sounds painful."

In the face of Chas's ominous silence she struggled to stop laughing, turning bright red and giving occasional snorts. "Oh, I'm sorry—don't be so *huffy*."

"Would you like a piece of chocolate?" said Chas calmly, thinking he was being pretty decent under the circumstances. Pity that when the chocolate emerged, it was covered with fluff. He tried to wipe the fluff off, only to find that his hanky was green with yesterday's river slime.

"That happens in my handbag too," said Sheila hastily. And ate the chocolate.

After a companionable munch, Chas asked, "Your father was lord mayor, wasn't he?"

She pulled a face.

"Not you too! It's all people talk about. Makes me feel like a Martian. It was *years* ago. We're quite an ordinary family really. What does your father do?"

"Gas works."

"Is he the manager?"

Chas wanted to say yes. So when he finally said no, just the foreman-fitter, it came out a bit savagely.

"You mean he mends machines? With his own hands?"

"Yeah. Well, it's honest. Not like bosses and lord mayors always eating banquets. I'm a *socialist* and when the war's over, Attlee will get power and then *we*'ll say what goes. Everyone will have to work and get their soft white hands dirty, just like my dad."

"My father works as hard as yours. Brains are just as important as hands. Look how brainy you are at school."

Chas's voice rose to a squeak. "My dad's *cleverer* than me. He can mend anything. I'm hopeless at mending things."

They glared. Then Sheila put out her hand help-lessly.

"Sorry. I didn't mean to be rude about your father. I just keep saying stupid things. That's probably why I've got no friends. Everyone's got it in for us, just 'cause Daddy was mayor. People are so *catty*."

Chas found such stark honesty unbearable. Staring out at the river he said, "I haven't got any real friends either. I go about with people, but you can't trust them—they're nice one day and bloody horrible the next." Then, to cover his confusion, he turned on to explain the Gar's boom defense system, and threw in a character sketch of Dick Burley for good measure.

"Why *do* you talk so much?"

He bridled. But she started laughing, so he had to laugh too.

"To impress girls," he said.

She went all solemn again. "Shall I tell you some-thing? Girls would much rather be liked than im-pressed. Men are always trying to impress me. Or stare up my skirt in buses. That's why I wear slacks. And that's why I like you. You don't *stare* at me."

Chas blushed; and stared at the mandolin instead. "It's drifting away. Better get to work."

Sheila was helpful. Didn't try throwing bricks; just fetched them. They nearly had the mandolin when a shout echoed down the beach.

Cem. In his idiot mood, from the way he was drag-ging his feet through the sand in huge strides, imper-sonating Frankenstein. He ignored Sheila completely, banged Chas on the back with agonizing bonhomie, and picked up the biggest boulder in sight.

"Never fear—Cemmy's here. Cemetery Jones in

person, at great expense, by popular request. Great strength rings the bell."

"Careful!" screamed Chas. Too late. The boulder sailed through the air and landed smack on the mandolin. In an instant, the water was covered with splintered wood.

"Oh, you SOD! That was *deliberate*."

Cem was laughing like a drain, fending off Chas's fists. Chas flung a cod's head at point-blank range. It hit Cem in the face and *that* stopped him laughing.

"Oh, c'mon, Chas. It would have fallen apart anyway, as soon as you took it out of the water."

"It WOULDN'T. It even had two of its strings left. I spent hours getting it in, and all you can do. . . ."

"Hours getting it in? What were you talking to that *thing* Sheila Smythson for, then?"

Chas glanced round, startled. Sheila and her dog were already distant silhouettes on the cliff top; going home.

"You spoiled that on purpose, too. She's a *friend* of mine."

"Since when?"

"Since this morning. Till you bloody came. Oh, you SOD!" And the fight was on in earnest. At first Cem still couldn't believe it was happening; sixth-formers never fought seriously. He kept fending Chas off, asking if he'd gone mad. Till Chas really hurt him with a plank of wood.

Ten minutes later they stopped, out of breath, Chas sucking a cut lip and Cem with a trickle of blood down his face. Feeling childish and more full of hate than ever, Chas stormed off along the beach, pretending to look at things in the water and seeing nothing. Cem sat on a post, dabbing his forehead accusingly with a filthy handkerchief. After a bit the bleeding must have stopped, because he began throwing stupid stones in the water again. Chas thought what a useless sort of person Cem was; why had he put up with his stupidities all these years?

It was then Chas noticed the big enamel bowl, floating in the whorls of scum. The sort whole families got washed in; the sort women bathed their babies in. Chipped round the edges and stained with rust. Oddly, it contained a cardboard box, marked *Queen of Sheba Olive Oil. Produce of Cyprus. One gross of bottles.* It looked oddly like a model boat; the kind of thing kids put in the river to throw stones at.

He drew it ashore. Immediately Cem came bounding along the beach.

"Get away!" yelled Chas. "You're not spoiling this as well."

"Spoil what? It's only rubbish. Even *you* can't want that."

Inside the cardboard box were cardboard walls, to stop the olive oil bottles rattling. An empty fag packet lay on top: Gold Flake. Chas threw it over his shoulder. Beneath, better things nestled in the cardboard compartments.

A gold pocket watch like Dad's. Stopped at twenty to eight because some idiot had opened the glass and tied little yellow wires round both the hands, so they'd jammed together as they passed each other. It made Chas mad, the way kids messed up decent things.

The yellow wires led to a battery, and a gray cylinder the size of a tin of peas. . . .

"Run, it's a time bomb!" screeched Cem, heading up the beach so fast, sand spurted from his heels. Chas was only a yard behind. Twenty yards away, they circled round the bowl like wary bullfighters.

"You're kidding."

"I'm bloody not. Didn't you see that film about General Mihailovic and the Yugoslav freedom fighters? They used a bomb just like that with wires and a watch to blow up a bridge." Then Cem laughed. He *was* kidding. On the other hand, he always laughed just before the headmaster caned him. With Cem you never could tell. . . .

"Stands to reason it can't be a bomb. Not big enough to blow up a fly. And what could they blow up down here—the town sewer outlet?"

"Would ruin the war effort—universal constipation." Cem was really enjoying himself—you could tell.

"Anyway, it should have gone off when the watch hands touched. It's a dud."

"Famous last words."

"So what would *you* do? Tell the cops? Get laughed at when it turns out to be kids messing about?"

"Don't ask me. You're the boss. . . ."

Stuff him! Rage drove Chas back toward the bowl, stiff-legged, quivering all over. He circled it again. Cem stayed at a safe distance, shouting Chas was a nut case. But there was worry in his voice that was not unpleasing. Chas picked up a stick and poked at the bowl. He knew it was crazy; a bomb could kill you at two yards as easy as if you were holding it. But he'd wiped the sneer off Cem's face.

He poked a bit too hard. The cylinder moved. Toppled over. Chas was ten yards away before he could stop himself. Then he turned back confidently. The way the cylinder had moved, the noise it made, told him it was very light, nearly empty.

He picked up the whole contraption and undid the yellow wires. The gray cylinder felt like aluminum. When he shook it, it rattled like an electric light bulb. He tossed it up and down like a feather, enjoying Cem's face.

With the wires removed, the watch started going. Perfectly good watch; worth pounds. He put it ostentatiously in his pocket. Finders keepers; losers weepers.

"Rubbish, eh?" he said, as Cem came up.

"What else you got?" asked Cem, reaching.

"Gerroff." He was feeling more tolerant now. But not *that* tolerant.

The battery was the sort radio sets worked off. Big, heavy, because when you broke it open you'd find dozens of little lead cells like miniature depth charges. Only you had to be careful, because sticky stuff oozed out that burned your hand. Chas licked the battery's terminals, but his tongue didn't prickle. The battery was dead. But interesting because it was marked *U.S. Navy.* Anything American was worth keeping.

Cem looked wistful.

"OK—you can have the battery," said Chas.

"Ta," said Cem humbly.

Chas turned back to the cardboard box. It was glued so tight to the bottom of the bowl he couldn't budge it. And the cardboard was thick with—he smelled it— lard. Somebody had smeared the box with lard to waterproof it. Because while there was quite a bit of water slopping round in the bowl itself, the inside of the box was bone dry.

"Funny!"

"Kids messing. There's nowt else worth having. Chuck it back in the river an' we can bombard it."

"That's just like you—brainless. If you can't understand something, smash it. This lot is *for* something. Too carefully made for kids. I want to work out what it's *for*. Give us that battery back."

"Mingy swine. You can't carry all that lot home."

"Can."

"What about your bike?"

"I'll wheel it."

"You'll look a right twerp walking through town with that bloody great bowl."

"So what? Give us a hand."

"If you give me back the battery. . . ."

"Get lost."

They wheeled their bikes huffily on opposite sides of the road. Cem alternately scrounged and sneered all along Low Street. Chas found bike and bowl nearly impossible. He dropped the bowl in the middle of Low Street with a clang that turned every head. A bunch of Maltese on the corner said something in Maltese and sniggered. Cem went walking on ahead as if he was a complete stranger.

"Fine mate you are!"

"Mates give each other things."

"Aw, wrap up."

It got worse. Low Street turned away from the river and became Tanner's Bank, steep as Mount Everest. Tanner's Bank had copped it in 1940, when the Germans tried for the docks. All that was left was five-story walls and waist-high grass between, full of rusty prams. But Tanner's Bank had been derelict before the Germans came: a rotting gap between Low Street and decent folk, that the Germans had just made a bit wider.

Nearly at the top of Tanner's, the bowl escaped.

Chas propped his bike carefully against the wall before pursuing it.

It rolled right to the bottom.

"Ancient British Customs number five," announced Cem in his film commentator's voice. "Tanner's Bank Bowl-Rolling. Here we see a typical Ancient Briton. . . ."

They finally climbed into Northumberland Square, where decent folk were coming out of Chapel and catching doubledecker buses. At least the women were. The men were off to the pub for a quick one, before going home to carve a Sunday roast as big as an Oxo cube.

Chas dropped the bowl a third time. The decent folk make remarks about Low Street hooligans and put their noses in the air and said it shouldn't be allowed. . . . Making Chas feel as if he was in church with his trousers undone. He collapsed onto a bench.

Cem made a last peace move. "Wanna fag?"

"You barmy? Half these nosy old bags know my mam. I'd never hear the end of it. Yak, yak, yak. Smoking'll stunt your growth. Break your wind. You'll lose your place on the school rugby team. . . ."

"Suit yourself." Cem put on his cycle clips. "Seeyaround."

Chas stuck up two fingers at his retreating back.

"Chas McGill! What would your mother say? I'm sure that's not what they teach you at the grammar school." It was Mrs. Spalding, the next-door neighbor, in full cry. With her son Colin, wearing his Sunday-best expression. Behind which he was killing himself laughing.

Chas eyed the passing buses in stark despair. Why had he ever thought this a smashing day?

4 Sunday continued ghastly.

He tried getting the bowl down the greenhouse unobserved, but Mam followed him. Did her nut about the amount of rubbish down there. Which wasn't on. The greenhouse was male territory. Chas told her so, reasonably and logically.

Mam called it cheek. She would tell Dad when he got home for dinner. Then Mrs. Spalding came across and put her two-penn'orth in. Chas was reasonable and logical again. Mrs. Spalding departed in hysterics. What *was* the point of being taught to argue logically at school if, the moment you tried it at home, they just called it cheek?

But dinnertime wasn't too bad. Mam made the mistake of opening the battle by telling Dad what Mrs. Spalding had said. Dad was no fan of Mrs. Spalding's; he expressed wonder that Tom Spalding had kept his hands off her for twenty years, because a workingman was entitled to a bit of peace when he got home after a hard shift.

Mam asked if she was meant to take that remark *personally*?

Dad said she could take it any way she liked.

A frost descended over the eternal Sunday rice pudding, and Chas was able to slink back to the greenhouse unobserved. If he sat on the floor, below window level, he couldn't be seen from the house. They'd think he'd gone out.

But what was there to do, now he'd lost Sheila and quarreled with Cem?

Blacky and Whitey bounced wildly round their

hutches till he fed them. Then they sat up on their hind legs and pulled down their ears to wash.

Big thrill! They were the sole survivors of the twenty-six rabbits he'd had during the 1940 rabbit-keeping craze. The rest had gone for rabbit pie. He was glad Blacky and Whitey were too old and stringy to eat; sometimes they seemed the only true friends he had in the world. If he died, they could be buried with him, as ancient chieftains used to be buried with their faithful followers. . . .

Suppose that bowl had been a bomb? And he'd been blown up this morning? His rotten parents would be weeping now, instead of snoozing under the *News of the World*. But the pathetic graveyard scenes soon palled. He tried rescuing Sheila from a Jap armored brigade, but in the face of a gray English Sunday, the Japs were reluctant to fight. Besides, memories of the real Sheila kept breaking through. . . . Bugger the Japs.

He poked the gray cylinder irritably. Couldn't be a bomb, *could* it? Far too light. He turned it over, looking for a way to open it. But there were no screws to undo or anything. Give it a bash with the hammer? But by the time he'd hammered it open, the inside would be mashed to a pulp and he'd never find out *anything*.

If only the battery hadn't been dead, he could have wired the whole thing up again, reset the hands of the watch, and waited for whatever was going to happen. . . .

Then he remembered the old radio set. The one they'd used before Dad bought the plug-in one. Dad hadn't thrown it away; he'd stored it under the stairs, just in case. . . . That had a battery.

But he mustn't be seen nicking it. He did a leopard

crawl up the garden path, dodging behind the sprouting chrysanthemums like the Yanks at Iwo Jima. Got halfway before he realized Mr. Spalding from next door had stopped his hoeing and was watching him closely.

They eyed each other a long moment. Then Chas said softly:

"Advanced biology. Beetles."

Mr. Spalding nodded knowingly. "Sixth-form work."

Chas leopard-crawled on, under Mam and Dad's window. Eased the back door open without its usual creak, and the cupboard under the stairs. Next door the radio was playing; Mam and Dad talking, off and on. Mam was still trying to get Dad to take Chas in hand. Dad was saying yes in a way that meant he was reading the paper. Chas was tempted; it was deliciously terrifying to hear what people really thought of you, as opposed to what they said to your face. But he had the battery in his hands now, and a wild excitement was crawling up his thighs into his stomach.

On the way back, the battery really got Mr. Spalding going. His eyebrows were all over his face.

"Beetles," said Chas. "Electrocute them. New technique."

"Sixth-form work," repeated Mr. Spalding as if to preserve his sanity. Chas reached the greenhouse and locked the door.

He wired up the whole gadget. Battery to watch; watch to cylinder; cylinder to battery. Then he wound up the watch, set the hands five minutes apart, and waited, cross-legged, with his fingers in his ears. Any minute now he, Blacky and Whitey might be little bits of red meat all over the landscape. And old Spalding wouldn't be much of a loss. All he ever did was hoe his cabbages.

The hands of the watch touched. The watch stopped ticking. Nothing happened. The world returned to a dull gray. Why? Because he hadn't been blown to bits? Did he *want* to be blown to bits?

He reached out a hand to rip the whole stupid contraption apart. Now he *would* take a hammer to it. But when his hand touched the gray cylinder, he paused.

The cylinder was gently vibrating. He held it to his ear. It was buzzing softly, like the Morse code tapper they had in Scouts. He removed the bare ends of the wires from the hands of the watch, and pressed them together. The cylinder buzzed again, just like a primitive Morse code tapper.

Pressing the wires together, he softly tapped out, "S—O—D—O—F—F." He did it several times to get it right. Then the game palled. He looked up to the house hopefully, wondering if it was time for a cup of tea.

The living room light was on, against the gray of the afternoon. It was like looking into the lighted stage of some play. Dad was on his feet, doing his nut; pointing at the radio. Hey, this looked interesting. He shoved the gray cylinder in his pocket and ran up to the house.

Dad was threatening to go to the police. "Cheeky swine!" he shouted at the radio. "Morse-coding 'sod off' like that. Ought to be locked up."

"Are you sure it wasn't just interference?" asked Mam. "The atmospherics was terrible last night. I couldn't hear the Saturday Night Play. Neither could Mrs. Spalding. An' such a lovely love story. . . ."

"Woman, Aah know Morse code when Aah hear it.

'Sod off,' it was, plain as the nose on your face. Some radio ham messing, mevve.''

"Could it be a spy?" asked Mam nervously.

Dad laughed harshly. "The way the war's going, I wouldn't blame a German spy for telling Hitler to sod off. But he wouldn't risk his neck to do it."

"Are you sure it isn't a spy? I couldn't rest safe in my bed. . . ."

"No. Rest yourself, hinny. Mevve it's just some Navy lad on radio duty and bored on a Sunday afternoon."

Chas fingered the gray cylinder in his pocket. So that's what it did. It didn't blow up at a set time. It sent out a buzzing radio signal instead. And it had started at twenty to eight last night, in time to spoil the Saturday Night Play. And everyone thinking it was just atmospherics. . . . Wonderingly, he turned the cylinder over and over in his pocket.

"What are you doing, Chas?" asked Mam.

"Scratching."

"Don't scratch *there*, dear. It's rude."

"Well what do you do, if you *itch* there?"

"You'll be a grown man soon. Ladies don't like seeing a grown man scratching there."

"He's not scratching," said Dad. "He's playing wi' something. C'mon, let's see it."

Chas passed it over, reluctantly.

Dad held it to his ear and shook it. "Radio valve."

"Found it down the Quay. Can't get it open."

"Easy," said Dad, taking a pocket knife out of his waistcoat and selecting one narrow blade from about fifty. He pressed the blade into the base of the cylinder, and the whole thing fell apart, black glass gleaming and a gold top to it.

"Oscillating valve," said Dad, "Oscillator."

"What does it do?"

Dad frowned. "I'm not much of a dab-hand at radio. But they do use oscillators in the RAF, your cousin Gordon tells me—for Air-Sea Rescue. When one of our bombers comes down in the drink—in the North Sea after a raid on Germany—the bomber lads get into the inflatable dinghy. The dinghy's got a black box wi' a handle to turn and an oscillator sends out a continuous radio signal. Then those high-speed launches the Air-Sea Rescue has—wi' radio direction finders—can home-in on the signal an' rescue the bomber lads. Six hundred megacycles is the wavelength the RAF use."

"Do the Germans have radio direction finders and all that?"

"Reckon so. 'Cause sometimes our lads get rescued by the Germans instead; then it's prison camp for them, 'stead of Blighty. Anyway," Mr. McGill tossed back the cylinder, "that's not an RAF oscillator—that's some foreign rubbish."

Chas huddled in the corner of the sofa, while Mam got the tea on a tray, before Mantovani and his orchestra came on the radio to play her favorite, "Roses of Picardy." Chas had a lot to think about.

Last night the oscillator had been floating in the river, broadcasting its buzz, ruining the Saturday play. Somebody had gone to a lot of trouble and expense to play a pointless joke.

Or had the RAF been practicing Air-Sea Rescue in the dark? No, the whole contraption was too crude and homemade for the RAF—they'd have had the proper thing.

So, who . . . ?

And then everything became clear in a flash. Some Maltese down the Low Street, getting news of a ship from a drunken sailor. Putting together bowl and box and oscillator. Only he'd have them all ready beforehand. Putting a message into the bowl; slipping it into the river through a trapdoor in a café floor. Then the outgoing tide (the tide *had* been going out last night) would carry the bowl out to sea, with all the other garbage that came down the Gar. Past the unsuspecting boom-defense vessel. Carrying the bowl miles out to sea. (The Amazon carried mud fifty miles out into the South Atlantic, the geography teacher said.)

Once out at sea, in the dark, at twenty to eight precisely, the gold watch had switched the oscillator on. And a German Air-Sea Rescue launch—no, the U-boat, stupid, the one that sank the *Corwen Star*, would pick it up easily, using a radio direction finder. Diabolical!

And pick up a message! Maybe there was a ship in danger now! Chas gave a convulsive leap that made Dad cock an eyebrow up from the *News of the World* and say:

"You sickening for St. Vitus's Dance or something?"

No. It was OK this time. Because this particular bowl had never got out between the piers. It had gone ashore on Fish Quay Sands, and Chas had found it instead.

So . . . the message to the U-boat must be still in the bowl. Sitting down in the greenhouse at this very moment.

"Jesus!" said Chas.

"I *beg* your pardon," said Mam ominously, as she came in with the tea tray.

"Sorry. I was remembering our homework for the

Easter holidays. Scripture homework; three Miracles of Jesus."

"Why don't you write down what you're set for homework, so you don't forget it? You'd forget your head if it was loose. You'll be out in the world in two years' time—in the Army mevve. *They* won't let you forget things. In one ear and out the other . . . you don't know you're born yet—hey, where d'you think you're going?"

"Just down the greenhouse for a minute."

"Oh no you're not. You're going to sit down and eat your tea like a civilized human being. *Then* you're going to help me wash up. Then you're going to have your bath. And then you're going to do that homework on the Miracles of Jesus."

"Aw, Mam!"

"Do as your mother says," said Dad, reaching up for a hot scone.

5 Chas lay in bed and *seethed*. Five putrid pages on those rotten Miracles and they still hadn't let him go down the greenhouse. In case he got dirty after his bath; because it was dark; because of any other stinking reason Mam could think of for not disturbing the way things were *always* done.

He'd tried reading *Jane's Fighting Ships* under the bedclothes with a torch, but even *Jane's* was meaningless tonight. He'd tried summoning up the whole Jap army but they'd surrendered unconditionally. He'd wriggled so much, the sheets had come unstuck at the bottom of the bed.

Out in the living room, Mam and Dad had yakked till ten past eleven. Now they were in bed, yakking still. What did they find to talk *about*, after twenty years of marriage?

He returned to *Jane's Fighting Ships*.

Wakened at midnight, wanting the lav. The torch was still shining right into his left eyeball. The battery was nearly used up. But silence had fallen at last. He got into his dressing gown and tiptoed across the living room.

"Chas?" came Mam's faint beddy call.

"Just going to the lav." He nearly said "bog" to nark her, but that would really wake her up.

"You've got weak kidneys, just like me," came the faint declining murmur. Now she had something to worry about, Mam might really go to sleep.

He squeezed out through the lav window and crept down to the greenhouse, shading the torch. People said Tom Spalding sometimes hoed his lettuces by moonlight, just to escape the sound of his wife's voice. People said she talked to him even when he was fifty yards away down the garden. . . .

Besides, there were still policemen and air-raid wardens, officious buggers, who loved to jump out at you shouting, "Put that light out!" even though there hadn't been a serious raid for a year. Just to prove how important they were.

The bowl leered at him mysteriously. He pulled the cardboard walls out of the box and separated them. Nothing. He tried prising the layers of cardboard apart, but it just tore off in little strips. He couldn't imagine a U-boat commander taking that much bother.

The box itself revealed only a few grains of mouse dirt. Perhaps the message was concealed between bowl and box? But that glue was set like concrete. And the bowl itself revealed nothing but chips and rust spots, and a small hole mended with nut and bolt and a pair of shiny washers.

He sat back on his heels, shivering. There must be something he'd missed.

Then he remembered. The first thing he'd found in the bowl had been an empty Gold Flake fag packet. Or rather, a nearly empty packet. Something had rattled insides as he threw it carelessly over his shoulder. He punched his forehead with his fist; rocked backward and forward in agony. What a fool. . . .

He considered cycling straight to the Fish Quay in his dressing gown. But hunting for a fag packet on a moonless beach with a dying torch. . . .

The sun would be up in five hours.

He wakened weary as a dog.

"Look what the cat dragged in," said Dad. "Fried bread? Still after that mandolin?"

Chas told him about Cem.

"That lad gets dafter. He even makes you look sensible. So what you after now?"

"Something peculiar, floating . . . can't quite make out what it is."

"You'll find something down there you wish you hadn't, one of these fine days. That woman they found—"

"I *know*. Her big toe—"

"Watch your lip." Dad flipped a piece of fried bread onto Chas's plate, in a shower of yellow grease. "Get that down. It'll put hairs on your chest."

"Da-ad?"

"Ye-es?"

"What are German spies *like*?"

Mr. McGill eyed him warily. "Why?"

"Just settling an argument with Cem," said Chas, with careful casualness.

Mr. McGill considered. "Strikes me the spies the Germans are sending over are rubbish, mainly. Last one they caught landed from a sub, walked into the nearest railway station soaked to the waist on a lovely sunny morning and asked for a single to Edinburgh."

"What's wrong with that?"

"Station had been closed to passengers for ten years. . . . They weren't much better in the last war either. They had one called Mata Hari—dancing girl she was. Aah used to have a postcard of her, lying on a couch in a grass skirt. They caught her and shot her. She was a bit too conspicuous for her own good. Best spies are people nobody would expect, like the insurance man."

"Tubby Tolliver?" Chas laughed. Tubby was a plump bachelor of fifty, with a lisp. Kids ran after him shouting, "I thaw thithter Thusie thitting on a thee-thaw."

"Yeah, Tubby. Because no matter what Tubby got up to, the police would just laugh like you did, and say, 'What? Old *Tubby*?' "

Chas was so impressed, he nearly told Dad everything, there and then. Even broadcasting "sod off" on the radio. . . . But Dad would just tell Mam, and Mam would just go on and on.

Still, they cycled down the road together.

Chas searched Fish Quay Sands for an hour. It was quite handy for searching, because each tide left a separate band of rubbish, and he could work along between the bands. He found a Capstan packet, complete with whelk shells. A full packet of Woodbines that collapsed wetly in his hand. Four Player's Navy Cut. But no Gold Flake.

The tide had been in and out since yesterday.

No fag packet, no spy. Just Monday washday, cold-meat fritters and Cem's jokes. Unbearable. He smashed three fishboxes, but it didn't make him feel any better. Then he ran along the Lifeboat gangway, frightening the gulls off their posts. All but one Greater Blackback which held its ground with open beak. Chas considered going back for a brick to heave at it, but it wasn't worth it. So he leaned on the rail, contemplating the gulls seeking their breakfast in the river. So graceful, till you realized they were feeding at the town's sewer outlet. How like life—apparently beautiful; suddenly disgusting.

"Hello. Don't you look *cross*?" Sheila's voice made him jump.

"That's *my* business."

"No wonder you haven't got any friends."

"Who says I haven't got any friends?"

"You did, yesterday."

"I said I hadn't got *many* friends. It was you said you hadn't got any friends. I've got Cem."

"So I noticed. If that's friendship, give me enemies."

"We're friends *really*. Everybody falls out sometimes."

"He doesn't like *me*."

"He doesn't go with girls."

"He was jealous. That's why he smashed that thing. Anyway, I don't care about his dirty little habits. Do *you* go with girls, Chas McGill?"

She leaned nearer. A faint nice smell came through the pong of rotting fish.

"Sometimes. When I feel like it."

She kept giving him sideways looks under long lashes. He felt torn in half. His mind was angry; his mind *wanted* to be angry. But his body was starting to feel all relaxed and cheerful.

"Where's your dog?"

"Didn't fetch him. Came to see you."

"How'd you know I'd be here?"

"Oh, girls know these things."

"I didn't come to see *you*. Came to find a fag packet."

"Do you smoke? Thought you were on the rugby team?"

"No, I don't smoke. But Cem does, and he's on the team and he can run faster than anybody. So don't say it breaks your wind. . . ."

The breeze blew her hair across her face. Her eyes peered through the newly washed strands, large and blue. She opened her mouth slightly.

Then the thought hit him: Cem smoked; Cem had offered him a fag yesterday, while they were quarreling in Northumberland Square. A fag from a Gold Flake packet. . . .

"Must go! Seeya!" Sheila or no Sheila, he pelted for his bike.

Cem lived at the cemetery, which was why he was called Cemetery. His father was the Cemetery Superintendent. They lived in a large dark house that looked like a cathedral with smoking chimneys. It was called *Cemetery Lodge*, which was not cheerful, even carved in gold letters over the front door. So Mr. Jones, in a fit of grave humor, had renamed the house *Dun-roamin*.

Only fools went to the front door. It had a bell handle which you had to pull like hell, and then about two minutes later a bell rang, that sounded like the one Quasimodo swung on in *The Hunchback of Notre Dame*. Sometimes the bell pull came off in your hand, and you had to give it to the person who finally answered the door. The Jones family all thought that a real scream.

Sensible people went to the back door, which was quite normal except it afforded spacious views of about ten thousand tombstones.

Cem's mam came to the back door, up to her elbows in washday suds.

"He's not Up," she announced. "He's been down for his breakfast, but he's not Up."

" 'S important."

"Nowt's important to that one in the holidays. You'll not see him before lunch. He's playing that Arctic convoys again. I've told him to stop it twice, but he won't. He'll cop it when his dad finds out. His dad only wallpapered that room last month; posh paper an' all." She paused. "I suppose you'd better go up, if you can get."

It wasn't hard to find Cem's bedroom. A trail led to it: schoolbooks open on the stairs, a half-built Meccano crane on the landing, a crushed box of birds' eggs by the bedroom door, punctuated by sharp cracks.

Cem's bedroom looked as if a clothes shop had received a direct hit from a fifteen-inch shell. Heaps of togs lay everywhere, about two feet apart. Here, his rugger kit, still plastered with mud. There, tennis whites, no longer white. There, mucking-about gear, thoroughly mucked-about. In the corner, his posh chatting-up-the-tarts gear, hardly used.

Through this sartorial sea sailed the German navy. U-boats lurked behind socks; a destroyer sailed the strait between a pair of rugby boots. In the lead, the *Bismarck* thrust through the waves of a gaberdine raincoat.

Cem's bed showed signs of long siege. It was strewn with copies of *The Beano*. (How even a member of the *Science* sixth could still bear to read *The Beano*. . . .) Between comics were plates of dried-up porridge and coffee mugs. In the center of operations crouched Cem in striped pajamas.

"Siddown. Mind your bonce."

Something banged against Chas's skull. He looked up. A super wooden model of a Stuka bomber hung by a string from the lampshade. It even had a tiny pilot, complete with goggles. Cem was a fantastic model-maker.

Chas sat down, avoiding a slice of buttered toast. Just in time.

"*Whoop, whoop, whoop,*" wailed Cem, like a destroyer's klaxon. "Action stations. Dive-bombing attack on the port bow. *Gnaaaaaaaaaah!*" He flung himself full-length on the bed, aiming at the Stuka with an ancient Webley air pistol.

"*Bang!*"

It was a good shot. The cockpit canopy of the Stuka shattered, sprinkling Chas with celluloid. The tiny figure of the pilot leaped toward the ceiling. The air-pistol pellet whanged off to bury itself in the posh wallpaper.

"*Gnaaaaaaaaaaaaaaaah!*" wailed Cem, on a despairing note. "*Splosh!*"

Chas presumed the Stuka had hit the sea. "Can I have a word with you," he said, "if Convoy PQ 17 is safe for the moment?"

Cem brushed some wet cornflakes from his pajama elbow onto his pajama trousers and said, "What's up?"

Chas explained his theory about the spy.

"Yeah," said Cem. "It'd make a good program for Children's Hour. 'Cept not even four-year-olds would believe it."

"I'm serious."

"You're more than serious. You're *fatal*."

"The fag packet would prove it."

"Yeah, yeah," said Cem. "Well, we mustn't mock the afflicted. I did take your Gold Flake packet. It had two fags left in it."

"Where's it now?"

"Shoved it down the bottom of the dust bin, where Mam can't find it."

Cem got dressed in thirty seconds. "We must get Mam out of the way. She doesn't like me grubbing in the dust bin." He said this apologetically, as if his mother had some peculiar habit. "Look, you go downstairs and say goodbye to her, like you're leaving. Then nip round and ring the front-door bell. She'll be five minutes undoing the front-door bolts. Then nip back and meet me by the bin."

"Thanks! The neighbors will think I'm a lunatic."

"They know that already. Anyway, it's you wants the fag packet."

Chas did as he was bid, and was back at the dust bin in a flash. Cem pulled the lid off. The bin was empty, except for one pink paper flower, stuck to the bottom.

"Hell," said Cem. "The bin men came this morning. I've just remembered."

Chas's heart sank. Then Cem's mam came back and gave him a funny look, and muttered that she had more to do on washing day than play Some People's silly games. . . .

They jumped on their bikes and scarpered.

"Let's chase the dust cart. They mightn't have emptied yet," yelled Cem. "Leave this to me. My dad knows the bin gaffer, Mr. Ernest. He calls him Deadly Ernest."

They ran Deadly Ernest to earth five streets away. He was carrying a shiny new bin from a posh house. For a gaffer, he was carrying it clumsily. The lid fell off, and tin cans scattered across the neat crazy-paved path. Deadly Ernest glanced back at the house windows, then helped a few more tins out with a mittened hand. Then he banged the new bin so hard on the edge of the dust cart that a great dent appeared.

"That house won't give the bin men a Christmas box," muttered Cem. "Ernest's a great man for bearing grudges. But he's OK if you handle him right. Good *morning*, Mr. Ernest!"

"It's fricking Jones's fricking lad. Wot *you* want?"

"Me mam put one of my Dinky toys in the bin by mistake, and you emptied it this morning."

"Wot a *shame*." Deadly Ernest put down his bin and stared into the distance, eyes glazed.

"Got any money?" whispered Cem. Chas reached reluctantly for the two shillings he'd been saving toward a new tennis racket. Cem slipped the coins into Ernest's top pocket. Ernest's eyes came back into focus.

"You're too late," he said with satisfaction. "We emptied at the Tip half an hour ago." His eyes returned to the horizon.

"We got no more money," said Cem firmly.

No response.

"We both saw you mess up that bin. My mam knows the woman who lives in that house."

"Bleeding little blackmailer," said Ernest. "Is that what they teach you at the grammar school?" But doubt had appeared on his face. "You can go to the Tip and tell old Tin-tash to let you in. Tell him you only gave me a shilling. . . ."

At the Tip, Tin-tash said, straight off:

"How much you give 'im?"

"Five bob," said Cem, with a dead-straight face.

"I'll have half of that," said Tin-tash, "or I'll report him to the sanitary inspector."

"You do that," said Cem warmly. "Where'd they tip?"

"By the incinerator. Live at the cemetery, don't you?"

"Yeah."

"Look for the dead flowers. Mostly daffs, this time o' year. And watch where you put your hands. Found a lovely parcel this morning—all done up in red-and-gold Christmas paper. What do you think was in it? Dog dirt! That's your haristocrats for you—always doing down the workers. Hitler had the right idea— shot all the haristocrats when he came to power."

"You don't support Hitler, do you?"

"There's a lot of good in Hitler. I has a chance to think about things, working the incinerator. You know what Hitler really wants? Strength through Joy!" Tin-tash took a false-tooth-powder tin from his pocket, and opened it to reveal a dozen fag ends. Some were stained bright yellow from the Tip. He lit one, drew on it, and doubled up coughing. "Strength through Joy—remember that! And look for the dead daffs."

They delved through the daffs.

"We're near," said Cem, unearthing a tin of tomatoes. "That was yesterday's breakfast. *And* that catapult I thought I'd lost. I'll kill my mam."

They heaved up the wired carcasses of two wreaths. One was labeled *Dear Father. Gone but not forgotten.*

"He's forgotten now," said Cem. Chas thought it must make you very heartless, having a cemetery superintendent for a father. . . .

But there was the Gold Flake packet, no longer forgotten. Just tea-stained.

Chas opened it. Empty. He pulled it apart. Nothing.

"Maybe it's the wrong one," he said hopefully.

"No chance," said Cem gleefully. "Look at those holes. I put two slugs through it, doing target practice."

Chas played miserably with the silver paper, teasing the tissue off the back.

"Look!" screamed Cem. "Writing. Numbers!"

But already the inky writing was spreading and blurring across the damp surface of the silver paper.

6 Chas stared bleakly. The silver paper was now pale blue all over, with dark-blue creases. The writing had dissolved.

"D'you think it was *designed* to do that?"

"More likely me mam's tea leaves. They were all

over the packet. Dad says Mam's tea's so strong it takes the coats off your stomach."

"Well . . . that's that, then."

"No it isn't," said Cem. "I copied it down."

"You *couldn't*. It went too fast. Pull the other leg— it's got bells on it."

"I did, honest. I've got a photographic *mind*."

Chas glared. "That's the first I've heard of it."

Cem laughed, meaning nothing. "Don't you want to see it then?"

"As an example of your stupid practical joking; yes."

Cem handed him a mucky card. It read *Dear Father. Gone but not forgotten.* Chas turned it over, and read: "*240074 ESPERANZA KUGELLAGEN.*"

"Look at that continental seven," said Cem coaxingly. "Foreign. That's not kids messing about. What kids know about continental sevens?"

"Every kid who does French at our school," said Chas wearily. "They use it all first year, till they get sick of it. And *Esperanza* sounds Spanish, not *German*."

"Yeah—but *kugellagen*. . . ."

"Look—I don't *mind* you trying to make a fool of me all the time . . . but you might do better than that. That wouldn't fool a *baby*."

If only Cem would own up, they could both forget it. But Cem began getting very het up, like he was really serious.

"But I can see what it *means*. 2400—2400—midnight. It's the twenty-four-hour clock, like the Home Guard use."

"*And* what about 74?"

"Seventh day of the fourth month—which was last Saturday night when your bowl is supposed to have broadcast. I can see the whole message—it means a ship called the *Esperanza* was due at midnight last Saturday with a cargo of *'kugellagen.'* If only we can find out what *that* means in German. . . ."

"It just so happens," said Chas, "that I know."

"WHAT?"

"Chimpanzees."

Cem nearly went mad. He went bright red and grabbed Chas by the shoulders, and shouted in his face, covering him with spit. "Will you stop fooling about? This is *serious*."

"You'll burst a blood vessel," said Chas condescendingly. But he was impressed. If Cem was acting, it was acting of a very high order. "Tell you what. Let's find out what *'kugellagen'* really means. Then if there really is a ship in the river called *Esperanza*, and if she did come in at midnight, and she really has a cargo of *'kugellagen'*, I'll give you my Meccano electric motor. And if there's not a ship, you give me your air pistol. How's that?"

Cem took a deep breath, and his eyes went blank. The air pistol was his most precious possession. Then he made up his mind and nodded.

"Done."

God knew what Cem was up to, but an air pistol was an air pistol. . . .

"Who would know what *'kugellagen'* means?"

"The girls at our school in the commercial set. They do shorthand, typing, French and German."

"Those silly tarts. . . ." Cem was suddenly reluctant.

"Audrey Parton took that course."

"She's *left*," said Cem mutinously.

"I still see her occasionally."

"*Do* you? Sheila Smythson, Audrey Parton? You running a harem or something?"

"Shut up! And . . . being on the *Evening News* Audrey might be able to find out about the *Esperanza* too."

Chas felt great. He could almost feel the air pistol in his hand already.

They rang Audrey from the phone box in Northumberland Square. Cem moaned about coughing up twopence, till Chas pointed out that *he'd* coughed up two shillings for Deadly Ernest. Chas popped the twopence in, and asked the operator for the *Evening News*.

"Hold the line, please."

It was then that Cem discovered the phone box had a pleasing echo, like singing in the bath. He began impersonating Bing Crosby.

If he thought that was going to save his air pistol, he was very much mistaken.

"*Garmouth Evening News,*" said a gruff busy male voice. Chas was so flustered he pressed Button B and got his money back. The gruff voice cut off with a click.

"Fancy pressing Button B," jeered Cem. "Try pressing your belly button next time."

Chas tried again. Cem began practicing Tarzan calls.

"Are you fooling about?" asked the operator, very narked. "That's a crime, you know. You'll end up in the police court."

Chas managed to land a kick on Cem's knee. The Tarzan yells descended to a yelp.

"What's that noise?" demanded the operator.

"There's a dog going mad outside the phone box. That's what I'm phoning the *News* about."

"You need the *police*," said the operator threateningly.

"No—the police are already here. They've caught the dog."

"Hold the line."

"Garmouth Evening News."

Chas managed to gasp out, "Can I speak to Audrey Parton, please?"

The gruff male voice gave a yell that nearly shattered Chas's eardrum.

"Hey, Audrey, another one of your fellers for you. Are you in?"

"Ask who it is." Audrey's voice came faintly through the clack of typewriters.

"My name is Charles McGill," said Chas, with all the dignity he could muster.

"He says he's Charles McGill," mocked the male voice. "Sounds about twelve years old. Cradle-snatching again, Audrey?"

A lot of other male voices chimed in, making crude remarks and laughing in the background. Chas's face burned.

"He is not twelve, and he's a lot nicer than you, Bill Shanks," said Audrey's voice, coming nearer. Chas could tell she was narked, from the way she was banging her heels down.

"Hi, Chas. What's up?"

"We've got a smashing story for you, Audrey."

Audrey groaned. "Not *again*. I haven't forgotten those Siamese twins you invented, down Cullercoats."

"No, this is serious."

"So was the Siamese twins. I nearly lost my job—oh, all right, I'll come. I'm only writing up a wedding."

She took them to the British Restaurant in the Square. It was an old Methodist church, armed with sixteen-inch tea urns. The walls were dark brown except where plaster had fallen off, and noisy with lettering.

God is Love.

Try our delicious Woolton Pie.

There were great fat smirking posters of Lord Woolton. Bet he didn't eat Woolton Pie, which was mainly composed of boiled potato peelings on which the dead body of a rabbit had been allowed to lie in state. . . .

Audrey bought them weak cups of tea. Chas apologized for not buying her one. She smiled, in that tolerant way he could hardly bear.

"It's OK, Chas. I'm a working girl now. I can charge this to expenses. Schoolboys are always hard up."

"Won't be hard up, once I've been to University."

"No, Charley. But I can't wait five years for a cup of tea." She crossed her pleasantly plump knees in a sophisticated way. She always wore nylons these days. Only American soldiers gave girls nylons, and everyone knew what for.

She took out a cigarette case and lighter combined. Had her initials on.

"You two don't smoke, do you?" she said carelessly, as an afterthought.

"Yeah," said Cem shamelessly, and took one.

"No," said Chas, sulking. Who had given her that posh cigarette case? What for? Why *was* she so different these days? A year ago, she'd been one of his gang.

Hanging on his every word. She'd only been left school six months. Now she was light-years away. . . .

"Cheer up, Chassy-Chassy. Why worry—it may never happen." She ruffled his hair affectionately, as a pretty young aunt might.

"Will you come to the flicks tomorrow night?" he said desperately. "It's a good flick, about the ghost of a bomber pilot. Starring Spencer Tracy and Irene Dunne. . . ."

"Seen it. Bill Shanks took me."

Chas took a private vow to smash Bill Shanks's face in; after he'd been to University, of course.

"C'mon, Chas, I'm a busy girl. You didn't bring me all this way to ask me to the flicks, I hope. . . . Tell Momma *everything*."

Chas ran his hands through his hair with exasperation. Why could girls never understand anything about physics?

"Look," he said. He drew a triangle in the dirty tablecloth with a teaspoon. "There's a triangle of wire. Here, on the right-hand corner, is an oscillator. It's a kind of little radio station. When it's working, it sends out a buzz you can hear on your own radio set. Right?"

"Check," said Audrey. Chas flinched; only girls who'd been out with Yanks said check.

"And here on the left-hand corner is a battery, which makes the oscillator work. Right?"

"Check."

"But the thing *can't* work, because up here in the top corner of the triangle, the wire is broken. So the current from the battery can't flow round the triangle, or circuit. Right?"

"Check."

"But if you attach the two broken ends of wire to the hands of a watch, when the watch hands pass each other, the wires are pressed together, the circuit is completed, the current flows from the battery, and the oscillator sends out its buzz. Right?"

"Check."

"Now, both the Germans and British have ships with radio direction finders, which can trace an oscillator buzz like a bloodhound tracks down a criminal. Right?"

"Check."

"So, this bloody spy fits up the apparatus and puts it into an enamel bowl, disguised as any old rubbish. And he puts a written message in the bowl as well. Then he slips the bowl into the river when the tide is going out. The river carries the bowl out to sea, past the defense boom and guardship, past the piers. When the bowl is well out to sea, the watch hands come together, the oscillator buzzes and, under cover of dark, the U-boat surfaces and tracks it down, and gets the message. The message will tell the U-boat when an important target ship is arriving off the Gar. So the U-boat torpedoes it. Q.E.D."

He looked up. "You do get it now, Audrey, don't you?"

Audrey nodded cheerfully.

"Then what do you think?" asked Chas.

"Oh, Chas, you're *such* a baby. Spies, secret radios. It's Herman the German, straight out of *The Beano*. On the whole, I thought the Siamese twins the funnier. . . ." She snapped her handbag shut and rose to go.

"OK," said Chas miserably. "But at least translate us the German in the message. We promise not to bother you again."

Audrey gave him a sharp look and held out her hand. She frowned. "Your German spy can't even spell—it should be *kugellager, not kugellagen.*"

"I had to copy it down dead quick," said Cem. "The message was smudging with the wet."

Chas shot him a look of pure hate. "What does *kugellager* mean, Audrey?"

"Ball-bearings."

"Strategic target," said Cem, and whistled.

Audrey collapsed back in her seat, and lit another fag. "It's daft. It's crazy. You two must be infectious. You're making me as daft as you are . . . but it's *spooky*. No, I'm not going to tell you—it would just encourage your stupidness. . . ."

"WHAT?"

Audrey laughed weakly. "Talk about coincidence. The *Esperanza* is in the river—tied up way beyond Newcastle. And she did arrive about midnight on Saturday. When you two were tucked up safe in bed, and it was too dark to see her name from the shore anyway. I know, because I've just been covering the captain's daughter's wedding. He was frightened he wouldn't get home in time. How would you two know all that?"

Chas glared at Cem. "He's got an auntie lived in Newcastle, down by the river. Did you go there for your Sunday tea, Cem?"

"No, no. Honestly. No." But he was laughing again. It was hopeless once he started laughing. If the Gestapo ever caught Cem, he'd just start that laughing and drive them nuts. He could spill the whole beans and they wouldn't know if he was kidding or not. "Anyway, how could me auntie know about the ball-bearings?"

"That's *it*," said Audrey, closing her handbag with a decisive snap. "If the ship is carrying ball-bearings, that would be top secret. And if it's not, that settles this whole *stupid* business. I'll know where I am—back in Siamese-twin land. I shall go back and see that captain again, and I shall make it my business to find out. Seeya!"

Cem shouted after her, "Ve haf our spies everyvere," in his best Peter Lorre accent.

"But if the ship is carrying ball-bearings . . . ?" said Chas.

"You owe me one Meccano electric motor."

7 Chas stayed excited until lunchtime, then it wore off and he was bored again. Cem was weeding the graveyard for money, and refusing to share the loot. Blacky and Whitey dozed in the greenhouse heat and refused to respond either to fresh dandelion or to pokes with a stick. Funny, you looked forward to the holidays all term, yet when they came they were a drag.

Sheila. He felt rotten running out on her like that. Suppose he went to see her at her house?

The thought turned his throat dry. Suppose the lord mayor was there? But he'd be at work. And Mrs. Smythson was in the hospital. And the housekeeper would only be some ordinary old granny. Anyway, they couldn't hang you for it.

He changed into his best shoes and trousers, and RAF sheepskin flying jacket. He knew the jacket would be too hot, but it was the most impressive garment he owned.

He knew the Smythsons' address because they were always in the papers: 17, Brinchdene Avenue.

He was sweating freely by the time he reached Whitley Bay, and sweating always made him feel panicky. The houses got bigger and bigger; the gardens posher and posher. Brinchdene Avenue was poshest of the lot; a cul-de-sac, so you couldn't cycle down it pretending to be going somewhere else. Brinchdene was the kind of road you didn't enter *at all*, unless you had definite business. People in Brinchdene didn't like kids and rang the police if you hung around, and the police always took their side.

Inevitably, number 17 was at the very far end.

There was one fat old guy cutting his hedge, and another mowing his lawn. They looked up and stared as Chas passed. When they saw him stop at number 17, they crossed the road to talk to each other. Chas propped his bike against the gatepost, and it immediately fell over.

The lawn was big as a prairie. The front door was varnished oak, with black studs, a big black knocker and a porch lamp with knobbly colored glass. When Chas used the knocker, it sounded as though he was knocking the door down. Too late he noticed the little bell-button.

Silence, except someone was playing the piano. Romantic. Tchaikovsky? If it wasn't Tchaikovsky, Chas didn't know what it was. Tchaikovsky was the only composer he knew, except the guy who wrote the *Warsaw Concerto*. He got terrible marks for music at school. Only sissies got good marks for music. But it was nice to imagine Sheila playing by a French window, breeze blowing through her long hair. Perhaps he could turn the pages for her. . . .

The door had opened. A personage stood there: black dress and black-rimmed spectacles and black tight-permed hair; white pinny and white collar and a mouth like the whole Gestapo.

"Yes?" she said, in a voice that meant No. Beady eyes took him in, from flying jacket to well-polished shoes. The mouth tightened even further.

"I've come to see Sheila."

Old Gestapo said, "Wait," and closed the door to within half an inch, very pointedly. But Chas could still hear her saying:

"There's a *boy* at the door, asking for Miss Smythson. No, he's not from round here, madam. Yes, madam."

The front door reopened.

"Come this way."

The hall was paneled and dim; yellow tulips on a table. A pong of polish so strong you couldn't tell what they'd had for dinner. Chas's best shoes slid nastily on the gleaming floor as he turned at right angles through a door.

It might have been Sheila sitting at the piano; same straight nose and long dark hair. But it wasn't Sheila, unless someone had taken a pencil and drawn cruel lines deep into the forehead, and between nose and mouth.

"Sit down, please." It was the way the headmaster said it, when there was trouble. Chas blundered to the edge of a chintz settee.

"*Why* do you want to see my daughter?"

"Met her at the Quay this morning. We were having a crack—a chat, when I suddenly remembered I had something to do. I dashed off sudden—suddenly—and I thought after—afterward I'd been a bit thick—unmannerly . . . so I came to apologize." He knew he was talking much too loud. Almost shouting.

"The Quay? That's not a place Sheila *goes*. She walks her dog on the promenade. You must have met her *there*."

"Erm . . . yes."

"Have you spoken to my daughter before?"

"She's in my class at school."

"Oooh . . . you to go the *High* School." Some of the icicles in the voice melted, but not many. "What's your name?"

"Charles McGill."

"Oh, yes. I've heard you *mentioned*. You're rather clever. Eight distinctions in school certificate and you won the Blower Memorial Prize."

"Yes." The hated blush came and went on Chas's face. But the woman's voice was now perceptibly warmer.

"What are you going to read at University?"

Chas felt like saying "Books," but something warned him to say "English."

"Who's your favorite poet?"

"T. S. Eliot." Chas breathed easier. This was ground he knew. He tried a little joke the English master had liked. "I'm measuring out my life in coffee spoons."

"Ah—*The Love Song of J. Alfred Prufrock.* Dear, *dear* Prufrock. But that's not Eliot's best work; not his deepest. Have you read *The Waste Land*?"

"No." (Dad said when you were dealing with bosses and other crafty buggers you should never pretend to know more than you did.)

"Pity," said Mrs. Smythson. "I think you'd rather

enjoy it. Like to borrow it?" She walked over to the biggest bookcase Chas had ever seen. It covered a whole wall; with lattice windows and more books than the school library. Mrs. Smythson took a book down, and paused.

"McGill? Can't say I've heard the name except from Sheila, of course. What does your father do?"

A yawning gap seemed to open at Chas's feet. He wanted to get it over with; leap into the yawning gap shouting, "He's a foreman-fitter, you snobbish cow!" But he liked the books too much, and the grand piano, and adults you could discuss T. S. Eliot with. So he merely said, "Engineer."

"Which firm is he with?"

"Gas works."

"Is he the manager?"

"No. Foreman-fitter."

"Oooooooh." It had a descending note, like Cem's Stuka falling into the sea. The hand holding the book wavered, then vaguely put the book down on the arm of a chair. The voice changed to brisk dismissal.

"Well, Charles, I'll tell Sheila you called. She's rather busy at the moment—she has her own friends at the tennis club. But I expect you'll see her at school."

At that very moment, Sheila walked in.

"*Hello!*" she said, amazed but pleased.

"Charles was just going," said her mother, leading the way into the hall.

"Can't I give him a glass of lemonade?"

"Not now, dear. Daddy will be home soon."

"He won't be home for *hours* yet."

"And it's time for your piano practice. . . ."

Sheila looked as if she was going to make a row. Chas shook his head slightly.

"Seeyaround, Sheila." He winked.

"Seeyaround, Chas."

Gestapo, as if she was telepathic, had appeared at the end of the hall, and was holding the front door open, just as wide as it would go. As Chas stepped through it, he heard Mrs. Smythson say:

"Seeyaround? I wish you wouldn't use such expressions, Sheila. That's why I object to you going to that school. *I* wanted you to go *away* to school. But you're so stubborn; you can twist Daddy round your little finger."

Gestapo closed the door.

8

"If that ship *was* carrying ball-bearings . . ." said Chas.

"Oh, my God, he's off again," said Cem.

"We'll have to plan what to do next."

"Simple. You hand over your Meccano electric motor."

"But after *that*?"

"Why do anything?"

"But if there's a spy. . . ."

Cem gave a long and earth-shaking yawn, nearly as long as the first verse of "God Save the King."

Chas said, "Well . . . ?"

"Simple. You go to the chief constable and say, 'I've got a spy, like I once found a machine gun.' He'll *love* that."

"Talk sense."

"You tell *me* to talk sense? What sense is all this spy rubbish?"

"But you believed it yesterday."

"That was yesterday. Today it's too hot." Cem rolled over, stretching slowly, exposing his thin freckly back to the sun. All the knobs showed on his spine. Not a pretty sight. . . . They had cleared a stretch of Fish Quay Sands and were sunbathing.

"I thought—"

"That's a lie for a start."

"I thought we could build a raft, like we used to, and go and look for the trapdoor under the Low Street where the spy put the bowl in the water. . . ."

"Chas, for hell's sake! Rafts are kids' stuff. Really, I sometimes worry about you."

"C'mon, you're not *doing* anything."

"I'm waiting for the tide to come in."

"What'll you do then?"

"Watch it go out again."

"C'mon."

"Give over, Chas. It's too hot. Mind you, I'll build a raft on one condition. . . ."

"What's that?"

"If you give me that pocket watch."

"I can't—it's part of the evidence. Tell you what— after it's all over, I'll give you the battery and the oscillator."

"Get lost. Watch or nothing."

Chas swore under his breath. First the Meccano motor and now the watch. This spy was expensive. But only Cem was good enough to build a raft.

"OK. After we've caught the spy."

"Or by the end of the Easter holidays, whichever comes soonest."

"Done."

Cem sat up briskly. "Right. Get searching. You know what we need. Driftwood and oil drums."

Sheila showed up mid-afternoon.

"Keep an eye on those oil drums," said Cem crossly. "I'm going to look for more." He put on his shirt in a hurry and stalked down the beach, tucking it into his trousers.

"Huffy, isn't he?" asked Sheila.

"He doesn't go with girls."

"Thanks for coming yesterday. I'm sorry Mummy chewed you up. Should have warned you."

"Thought she was in the hospital."

"She's in and out all the time. It's a nursing home where they pamper her. But she soon gets bored."

"I'm not coming again. Apparently you have friends of your own; at the tennis club."

"Have I, hell! She chews up everybody I bring home. Nobody's good enough for her. Not even Daddy. She chews him up most of all. You'd like *him*."

"He has my sympathy. Why does she go on like that?"

"Daddy says she's highly strung."

"*Painful!* How'd you get out of the house? I'd have thought she'd keep you chained up from now on. In case I was lurking in the front garden, waiting to rape you."

Sheila giggled, not displeased. "Oh, she *tried*. But I mooned about, playing my records too loud till she got one of her headaches. Then she couldn't get rid of me quickly enough. So I came to be *raped*!"

"No raping today—against union rules."

"I sometimes think she's not my *real* mother. I

sometimes think she's my stepmother and Daddy's never had the heart to tell me."

Chas looked sadly at her straight nose and long black hair and said, "Yeah. Expect she is your stepmother. Maybe you'll find out when you're twenty-one."

"What're you doing with all the oil drums?"

"Building a raft tomorrow."

"At *your* age? Why?"

He took a deep breath and told her. She sat there, head on one side, smooth brow all wrinkled. She had no more grasp of physics and logic than Audrey. At the end, she just said, "Mmmm."

"You don't believe me, do you? You think it's all comic-book stuff."

"I'd like to help. It's better than sitting at home."

"Better than the tennis club?"

"Better than the tennis club."

"We'll have to paddle right up-river, past the Lifeboat Station, through the Fish Quay, and then under all those piles that hold up the back of the Low street. Just before the tide starts going out."

"Why then?"

"Because that's when the spy put *his* bowl in the water. We've got five old bowls, and we'll paint big numbers on them. Then we'll drop them off the raft into the river, one by one. Watch where they drift to—learn the river currents. That way, we might be able to work out which trapdoor the spy used. . . . Do you still think it's all daft?"

"I don't mind. It's nice being part of a gang. I was never in a gang before."

Just then Cem came striding back, with two oil

drums under each arm. They were still dripping from the river, and not doing his clothes any good.

"Hey," he said to Chas, "there's a good plank floating in the Gut. Stop standing about. D'you want me to build this raft or not?"

"Sheila's staying to help," said Chas. "We could do with another pair of hands."

"Hmmph," snorted Cem; a thousand words couldn't have said more.

They worked till teatime, fishing planks and beams from the oily bosom of the all-providing Gar, and piling everything in a disused fishyard, ready for the morning. They covered everything with old fishnets, and made out a notice saying *Property of B. Hastie, Fishmerchant*, to keep thieving kids out. Sheila departed soaked to the skin, saying she'd have to tell her mother she'd fallen on the rocks.

"Well," said Cem. "She got her hands dirty, anyway."

Mam looked up from her teatime kipper. "A letter came for you. From a *lady* by the smell of it." She sniffed archly at the pink envelope.

The envelope just said *C. McGill*. Chas's stomach went tight. Was Mrs. Smythson making trouble already? He jammed his thumb under the flap and gouged it open, nearly tearing the envelope in half.

"How often have I told you," said Mam, "to use the paper knife? We could've reused that envelope with an economy label."

"Uhuh," said Chas, through an inert mouthful of bread-and-marge. He stared at the pink notepaper in panic; but it only said:

Dear Chas,

You were right. The cargo was ball-bearings. I went back to the captain's house, to ask for more details about the bridesmaids' dresses. When I asked him if he'd got all his ball-bearings ashore, he nearly went crazy. Who had told me?

I had to make out it was gossip I'd heard round our office. I swear if I hadn't been a girl and so young, he'd have called the police in. But I sweetied him up, and he only went on and on, for about an hour, about how careless talk by dock workers cost seamen's lives. I gather it's serious, and some dock workers might get into trouble. Hope it's been worth it.

It doesn't sound like one of Cem's inimitable jokes, does it?

What do we do next?

Audrey

Chas folded up the letter and stuffed it in his pocket.

"Aren't you going to show us?" asked Mam, coyly.

"No!"

"Oho!" Mam's eyes narrowed. "Something you're *ashamed* to show us?"

"No. Just *private*."

"We don't have secrets in *this* house. . . ." Mam raised her voice in the way that always got Dad's attention.

"Show your mother," said Dad, without raising his eyes from the *Daily Express*.

"I'm entitled to *some* privacy."

"Show your mother," said Dad, louder. He'd take his head out of the paper next.

"Just a sec," said Chas. "The fire's going out." He

got up and poked the fire into a blaze, then dropped the letter on top. It began curling up round the edges.

"Look what he's doing!" wailed Mam.

Dad leaped from the table, pushed Chas aside with a large hand, and grabbed the letter off the fire.

At that very moment it burst into flames. Dad waved it frantically, like a child waving a flag as Mr. Churchill went past. The flames went out, in a trail of blue smoke. Dad licked the tips of his fingers, and said something unprintable.

"Now you've burned your dad's fingers," said Mam.

"That's just like you!" stormed Chas. "Always setting me and Dad against each other. He wasn't even *interested* till you started."

"What's in that letter, Jack?" asked Mam.

Dad looked embarrassed and handed it over. "Can't make no sense of it. It's not much." He went back to his newspaper.

"It's signed *Audrey*," said Mam. "That'll be that Audrey Parton. So you're mixed up wi' *that* one?"

"So what?"

"So them reporters drinks themselves to death. She's *fast*, that one, *fast*."

"Like a Spitfire?" asked Chas.

"Jack, do you hear the cheek he's giving me? You might listen. After all he is *your* son. . . ."

"Don't cheek your mam," said Dad automatically.

"Is that all you've got to say, Jack? Are you listening? I think your only interest in him is teaching him bad language. Do you realize what word you used in front of him just now? I won't have such language in this house."

Dad put down the *Express* and got up heavily. "I am going," he announced, "to water my tomatoes.

And when I come back, I want to hear no more." He departed.

"Now you've put your dad in a bad temper." She switched her attack. "It's not that we don't want you to lead a *normal* life, you know. Bring some nice girl home—one of our own sort. But if you get that Audrey into trouble, that's goodbye to college. You'll have to support her—it'll be clerking at Smith's Dock for you. Not that you could get that Audrey into trouble. She knaas too much, that one."

Chas wondered if Sheila's father qualified as "one of our own sort."

"You can wipe that grin off your face an' help with the washing up. Here's your dad back from the greenhouse."

9 For the third morning running, Chas got out of the house before Mam was up. He even had time to make dripping sandwiches, because he wouldn't be home till dark. His alibi was a picnic in Holywell Dene with Cem.

"What's so great about Holywell Dene all of a sudden?" asked Dad.

"Nature study."

"You won't get far wi' a lass, feeding her dripping sandwiches." Dad liked his joke, but he left it there; that was the great thing about Dad.

Chas reached Fish Quay Sands long before anybody else. He spent the first half hour in frantic activity, carrying the oil drums down to the highwater mark, and arranging them in five rows of three. Then he put two in front, and one in front of that, to make a sharp-end for the raft. "Bow" was too grand a name for a raft. He was careful to put the battered oil drums in the middle, and save the smooth ones for the outside, so the raft would float smoothly through the water. He tied them all together through their handles, with Mam's second-best clothesline. That clothesline would take some explaining, but he had all day to think up a good lie.

Then all he could do was wait; Cem was the wood-worker. But it was toward the coast he kept looking, the way Sheila would come. He'd never had a girl-friend before, and he wasn't sure he wanted one now. Girlfriends had drawbacks. Lack of money. Lads making sneery remarks when she wasn't there. Like, "What d'you want to go round wi' *that* thing for?" or, "Does she *let* you?" Or saying that she had tits like gooseberries or a face like Frankenstein. You could thump *one* guy, but they always did it in crowds.

And now he sort of *owned* Sheila, he wasn't so im-pressed with her. That scar on her chin. . . . On the other hand, lots of lads said she was a bit of all right.

Just then she appeared on the cliffs by the Monu-ment. Chas gave a guilty start, and made up for dis-loyal thoughts with frantic waving. She was carrying something heavy, which turned out, on closer inspec-tion, to be a hold-all.

"What you got there?"

"Coffee, among other things." They drank it on the beach, after Chas had cleaned a space. Sitting side by side was OK because you didn't have to look at each other.

"Mummy's gone back into the hospital—for tests."

"Oh, good. I mean. . . ."

"You mean 'oh, good,' " she said, and laughed. Her hand was lying carelessly on the sand beside him. Did she want him to hold it? Or would she wriggle and sigh and pull it away?

The problem was solved by a noise like a blacksmith's shop on the move. Cem rode his bike down onto the beach, tried to pedal through the sand, and predictably fell off with maximum drama.

"Oh, *you're* here!" he said to Sheila. Well, at least he was speaking to her.

"Audrey's coming this afternoon," said Chas. "I rang her. And that ship *was* carrying ball-bearings."

"All the more reason for not lounging about," said Cem. "Don't *I* get coffee?"

"Those who ask, don't get," said Sheila. "One strychnine, or two?"

Cem drank with maximum slurping, and then announced he didn't like coffee. After which he proceeded to empty hammers, saws and tins of nails from his saddlebag. Chas hoped Cem's dad wasn't doing any emergency coffin-shortening that day.

Cem was good at making things, but he was a right prima donna. Fetch this, fetch that, until Chas and Sheila were panting. Any bit of wood he didn't like he smashed to smithereens. Six-inch nails were hammered in, like stakes in Dracula's heart, to the accompaniment of screams so piercing that once they fetched the Fish Quay policeman running. Maybe it was because all the time Chas and Sheila were handing things to each other their hands kept touching. Sheila's fingers were warm and smooth against the rough wet wood.

But in the end, the great framework was finished,

and lowered over the oil drums. Then it was only a matter of nailing on a deck of fishboxes, and waiting for the tide to come in and lift the raft. Gray whorls of scum came swirling in, glugging between the oil drums, while Cem nailed waste wood together to make paddles. Audrey arrived, wearing trousers and looking more like the old Audrey. Especially after Cem smeared green slime on her cheek.

"That inimitable caveman charm," said Audrey, kicking him on the shin. "Had any lunch, you lot?"

"Chip-butties," said Cem, pulling a curiously banana-shaped package from his hip pocket. The sandwiches were two inches thick, and the chips had turned slate-gray.

"Scientists have discovered," said Audrey darkly, "that *rats* fed on a diet of pure starch go *mad*."

Cem offered Sheila a chip-buttie.

"Slap his face, dear," advised Audrey. "A chip-buttie is attempted rape."

"I've . . . brought some lunch," said Sheila. "Enough for everyone, I think." She began unpacking all manner of delights: cold chicken and apple tart.

" 'S all black market," said Cem, but he was so far impressed as to wipe his hands surreptitiously on his trousers. "Wot? No caviare?"

"There's some in the fridge at home," said Sheila. "Off a Russian tanker. But I didn't think you'd like it."

"Ker-*runch*," said Audrey. "Put the boot in! I warm to you, Sheila."

They ate, till the raft gave a convulsive heave, and began to swing to and fro on its mooring rope.

"Time to go," said Cem.

Audrey pushed down on the raft with her foot. Water smacked up through the deck at one corner. "Sure it'll float?"

" 'Course it'll bloody float!" roared Cem. "If you don't mess wi' it. I spend a whole morning giving meself blisters, and all you can do is criticize."

"I'm too young to die," said Audrey.

"Anyway," said Cem, "*you* aren't going on the raft. You're staying here to guard our bikes, and track the enamel bowls as they float down-river."

"Drop dead," said Audrey. "I've not taken a half day off just to stand here and freeze."

"I'll stay," said Sheila. "What do I do?"

"You're *soft*," said Audrey. "Why should girls do all the dirty work?"

"Thanks, Sheila," said Chas. "Will you be warm enough, just standing?" He took off his check scarf and draped it round her ears. "Take my gloves as well—they'll only get wet on the raft."

"What do I *do*?" asked Sheila.

"Stand on the Lifeboat gangway and watch for the bowls floating out to sea. Try to get the exact time they go between the lighthouses. Here." He hung the pink opera glasses around her neck. "Let's synchronize our watches. I have ten past two."

"If you've finished, Errol Flynn," said Cem, "would you mind fetching the enamel bowls?"

Chas fetched the bowls from their hiding place in the fishyard. Cem and Audrey were already on the raft; Cem standing up, pretending to fall into the water and making the raft rock wildly, Audrey pouring out the old acid nonstop; but Cem was guaranteed acid-proof.

"Cheeroh," said Chas.

"Take care," said Sheila. "Come back safe."

"For God's sake," said Cem. "We're going to the Low Street—not Berlin."

They pushed off, and it wasn't like a movie anymore. Too damn real. The raft proved a real bitch, even for a raft. She'd a nasty tendency to turn left. Chas, who was on that side, had to paddle twice as hard or they simply went round in circles. The low waves of the river came at them *thump, thump, thump,* with the monotonous regularity of a clock. After each wave the raft sagged downward sickeningly. Everyone had grown a lot bigger and heavier since they were last on a raft.

The oil drums below knocked together in a funny jiggling rhythm, sounding as if they were going to break loose at any moment. If the waves had been any higher, they'd have been in real trouble. As it was, it was just exhausting and humiliating. Everything seemed a hundred miles away, or a hundred feet high. They felt like drowning flies, making feeble motions and getting nowhere.

They struggled round the end of the Lifeboat house, and turned up-river toward the Fish Quay.

"My bottom's getting wet," said Audrey. "The waves are splashing up."

"That's your explanation," said Cem. "You should have excused yourself before you came."

"You're the vulgarest little tyke I know."

"I try. Nice to be appreciated." Cem fished a rough map of the Fish Quay and Low Street out of his jacket, and passed it to her.

"Shove that up your sweater. The bowls too, if you like."

"What's it for?"

"Marking where we drop the bowls in the river; and where the trapdoors are."

"Hope the Maltese don't notice," said Chas.

"Or we'll end up," mocked Cem, "floating down the river with the big toe. . . ."

"Grow up," said Audrey. "Just because the Maltese keep brothels, it doesn't make them the Waffen SS."

"What you come for then, if you don't believe they're up to something?"

"I'm after a headline for the paper."

"Like what?"

"Two Boys Drown in River? Two Boys Saved by Intrepid Girl Reporter? Someone's got to look after you."

That silenced even Cem. Moving the raft was a terrible slog, even at slack tide. And the time for the tide to turn was getting very near. The homemade paddle began to chafe Chas's raft-building blisters; he wished he hadn't been so gallant with his gloves.

But eventually they reached the Quay. People stared down at them; old men with check caps and mongrels. Kids holding lines baited with mangled herring.

"Hope those kids watch it," said Cem. "Don't want a fishhook in my ear."

"Duck!" said Chas. "There's a dog just cocked its leg."

Cem ducked. Chas and Audrey fell about.

"Drop the first bowl," said Chas.

"Those little swine fishing will just sink it," said Cem.

They edged between the towering rusty riveted hulls of the *Henry and Agnes* of Grimsby, and the *Jolly Nights* of Aberdeen. Caught by an extra large wave, the tall hulls moved menacingly toward each other.

"Paddle, *quick!*" yelped Cem. "I'm too young to be a trawler sandwich."

As they rounded the stern of *Jolly Nights*, a bucket of potato peelings showered all over them.

"Watchit, you stupid gyet!" bawled Cem.

A red face peered down at them in wonder. "Wadinfockineel yese stupid lummmocks daeing there?"

"Diving for sunken treasure," yelled Cem. "Sporrans captured after Bannockburn."

"Dump that bowl quick," said Chas. "Before he's back with something worse than potato peelings."

The something missed them by inches. Cem told the Aberdonian where he might stuff his haggis.

"Hasn't been a war with Scotland since 1601," said Chas. "But any moment now."

"I'm not coming out with you two again," said Audrey. "I could have done something worthwhile, like washing my hair or changing my library book."

They pressed on. Dead fish and bits of planking began moving past them down-river.

"Tide's turning."

But they were past the last of the rusty trawlers; nearing the beginning of Low Street.

It looked for all the world as if someone had started to build a rickety wooden bridge across the river. Then stopped after forty feet, and built a house on top instead. Behind that failed bridge pressed another, and another. Failed bridges with houses on top stretched along the river for a quarter of a mile: an inextricable tangle of gable ends, bay windows, corrugated-iron fences with rusty teeth on top, laced with barbed wire. Wooden staircases descended to the river and continued down under the dirty water. Pipes dribbled nameless liquids. Ropes trailed, rotten and forgotten. Rowboats bobbed at their moorings, some sunk to their gunwales. On every rail, wireless aerial and post sat a gull. Windowsills were thick with their nests; every wall smeared white with their droppings. It looked the last place God made, the backside of the Low Street.

And beneath the failed bridges, dark caverns stretched, full of the sound of wave-slap. That was where the trapdoors would be.

"We're not going under that?" said Audrey.

"We sure are, sister."

"I'm getting off!"

"It's a wet walk home," said Cem.

With a couple of bumps and a bit of fending off, they passed inside. It was black as night till their eyes adjusted. Then they could see where the sunlight, bouncing off the river, made rippling patterns of light on the jumbled planks overhead. They forged ahead slowly. The great wooden piles that held up the Low Street were about ten feet apart, like tree trunks in a forest. The raft was just able to squeeze between, except when something sunk underwater blocked the way.

"Eeurk, what a pong!" said Audrey.

"The Maltese have no sewers," intoned Cem, who had discovered an echo. "The tide carries all away."

"I wish it would hurry up, then."

"Shurrup and drop Number Two bowl." Number Two floated away gently, pinging against the piles. Then a gorgeous floral smell assailed their nostrils.

"Nelly Stagg's had a bath," said Chas.

"Who's Nelly Stagg?" asked Audrey, innocently.

The boys hooted. "She's on the *Evening News* and she doesn't know who Nelly Stagg is!"

"Nelly's Queen of the Low Street!"

"Nelly's done you-know-what with every sailor in the Navy!"

"Nelly slips the chief constable ten quid a week to look the other way!"

"Even *Nico*'s scared of Nelly!"

"You wouldn't," said Audrey, "be referring to Eleanor Mary Stagg, who was fined fifty pounds last week for keeping a disorderly house? Who was fined similar sums on the 20th of March and the 20th of February for similar offenses? I've seen her in court—a very *ordinary* little woman. . . . I don't just cover weddings, you know."

"Drop in Number Three bowl," said Chas.

Their progress became even slower. The outgoing tide was making gurgling ripples round the base of every pile, and a six-inch band of dripping seaweed was showing everywhere.

"Look!" yelled Cem. Chas waved his torch around vaguely. Two feet above their heads was a trapdoor, big enough to let through a body *or* enamel bowl.

"Been used recently," roared Cem. "Look at those scratches."

"Shurrup, or they'll hear."

Too late. The trapdoor moved; a light blinded them and a hoarse voice spoke.

"Hey, Johnnie, what you doing, yes-no?"

"Fishing for blackjack," said Chas in his best innocent first-form voice.

"Go catch blackjacks somewheres else. Nico not like you fishing here. You know Nico, yes-no?"

"Yeah." They paddled like mad, and made some progress. The sound of the tide running round the piles was like a waterfall now.

"Not that way, Johnnie. Nico not like that. Go back Fish Quay, yes-no?"

"Aah, get lost," shouted Cem in distant echoing defiance.

"Oh Gawd," groaned Chas. "Does this boy have to fight all the Free Nations of the World?"

Twenty yards farther on they dropped bowl Number Four. Chas was keen to be rid of them now.

"Johnnie? Why you drop tings in water?" The voice, so near, made them jump. The Maltese was standing at the bottom of a wooden staircase, dead ahead. He was wearing pajamas, and the oddest shoes Chas had ever seen: brown with white tops. He had obviously just got out of bed, for his hair stood up wildly all over his head. He'd have looked ridiculous, if you didn't know he had a knife in his pajama pocket.

"Hell," said Cem, steering away from the staircase so wildly he almost threw Audrey in the water. But the Maltese began to follow, walking delicately along the weed-covered beams that joined the piles. They paddled like maniacs, but the tide was now so strong he caught up with them.

He reached out and grabbed the back corner of the raft. Audrey slithered frantically away from him. The raft tilted; the Maltese overbalanced and fell between raft and beam with a tremendous splash.

They left him clinging to a beam like a drenched kitten. It was obvious he couldn't swim.

"Get back to the trees, monkey!" shouted Cem. "Get back in the circus!"

"I *remember* you, Johnnie. . . ."

"Let's get out of here," yelled Chas.

"One more basin to go," said Cem stubbornly. "Fifty yards more and we're clear of the piles and out at the ferry landing. Then we can drift back down to the Sands on the tide. No more paddling."

"Hey, there's a ship coming down-river."

Peering out through the piles, they saw a great bow sweeping past, very close. Then a gray wall of hull, with tiny jets of water spurting out.

"It's the *Ortabes*," said Chas. "Tanker—ten thousand tons—one of the regulars."

"But look at those waves!" cried Audrey. "Coming straight for us. . . ."

"It's only the tanker's bow wave."

"But it's *two feet high!*"

"Hang on. Keep your hands off the sides of the raft, or you'll get your fingers smashed." They clung, as the bow wave hit, picked up the raft, and threw it against a pile. There was a crash of splintered wood, and a *boing* of oil drums. Then they were lost in a maelstrom of water and piles that whirled them till they were dizzy, and beat at them like fists.

When it finally stopped, the raft was ominously low in the water; the last shallow bow waves slapped mercilessly in their crouching faces.

"We're sinking," said Audrey, rather unnecessarily.

"Lie flat or we *will*. Where's the paddles?"

The paddles were gone.

"I still have the last enamel bowl," said Audrey, maddeningly calm.

"Doesn't matter," said Chas. "The tide'll take us down to the Sands anyway. We may have to swim at the far end, that's all."

And indeed, the current was drawing them out from the piles. The tanker was halfway past now, but it still loomed as big as the Houses of Parliament.

The current grew stronger. But it wasn't just taking them down to the Sands; it was drawing them toward the back of the tanker, faster and faster.

"God," said Chas. "The propellers!"

They were being sucked in by the tanker's screws. The ship was unladen; high in the water. Her port propeller was half-exposed, so that its blades smashed down into the water like a never-ending succession of huge bronze axes. Chas felt like a condemned murderer being dragged face down to the guillotine. He squinted up the tanker's towering side, but there was no one in view. Audrey began screaming for help like a steam whistle, but her voice was lost in the throb of engines and the beat of the propeller.

Fifty yards away; forty, thirty, twenty.

"Shall we swim for it?" yelled Cem.

"The prop would pull you in just the same."

Audrey gave up yelling.

Ten yards. *Whump, whump, whump* went the prop blades, throwing dirty yellow foam in their faces. Ten more whumps, thought Chas, and I'm dead. It's not possible . . . not fair . . . University . . . I've hardly been *born* yet. . . .

Somewhere down-river, far away, a tugboat yipped commandingly. The tanker's deep siren responded; dignity answering impudence.

The great propeller stopped.

Had they been seen? But no. Chas remembered ships always stopped engines at this point, to give the tugs time to pull their bows round toward the open sea.

The raft bumped gently into the great bronze propeller blade. Another blade hung dripping overhead. Had they time to drift astern, to safety?

But some perverse force of the water kept the raft clinging there. And at any moment the propeller might start to turn again. Ships never stopped engines for long. Audrey shouted and shouted, but nobody noticed.

Then the forces in the water slowly relented. The raft grated along the side of the tanker's great rudder, and was left spinning on the smooth surface of the river.

Just in time. The tug hooted again, the tanker replied, the propeller turned.

They had left one of their oil drums behind. The propeller hit it. It vanished in a clang of tortured metal and didn't resurface. Chas dropped his head furtively to thank a God he hadn't believed in since he was ten.

But he gave thanks too soon. Another enormous blast echoed across the water. Chas screwed his neck round and peered up-river. A tall gray two-funneled shape was just clearing the river's bend.

"Hell, it's the *Huddersfield*. Must be a convoy coming out."

The cruiser hadn't bothered with a tug. She was slimmer than the *Ortabes* and, with four props, much more maneuverable. She was moving at speed, throwing up a big bow wave. Heading straight for them.

10 Blast after blast came from *Huddersfield*'s siren, but she didn't slacken speed. The siren was a general warning: Get out of my way! From her bridge, the sinking raft must look like the usual flotsam that littered the Gar. Her lookouts would be watching for bigger stuff, farther ahead.

Chas eyed the knife of her bow, willing it to turn left or right, but it didn't waver. What a din the cruiser was making! The skipper must be as mad as hell about *something*.

"She'll run us down for sure," whispered Cem. "I knew I shouldn't have built this raft with coffin nails."

Nobody laughed.

Then a strong wave came from behind, throwing them toward the cruiser. Chas turned his neck frantically. A second, blunt black bow hung right over them. Chas nearly died, till he realized it was hardly moving.

Large white letters spelled out *Hendon*. A grinning blond head peered down.

"I tink I go fishing, huh? And what jolly-odd fishes!"

A rope fell across the raft. Cem seized it, and with one convulsive leap, shinnied up the tug's side like a monkey. His take-off forced the whole raft under water.

Chas surfaced in a panic, with only one thought in his head. The cruiser was going to collide with *Hendon*, with himself as the filling in the sandwich. He forgot everything about swimming he'd ever known, flailed wildly, and went under again.

Then strong hands had hold of him; a blond head, sleeked with water like a seal's, was swearing at him in a foreign language. Then his own hands were on a rope ladder and he was on the tug's deck, and it was all right, only freezing cold.

"Audrey?"

She was there, lying on the deck, coughing up greasy water.

"Sorry," said Cem. "I didn't think."

"Do you ever?"

But further bickering was cut out by the arrival of the *Huddersfield*, screws thrashing the water in reverse. Neat blue sailors were lowering a collision mat, to stop her paintwork being scraped against the tug. And her siren called all heaven to witness the indignity to which she'd been subjected. An electronic voice boomed:

"Ahoy, *Hendon*. I shall report this to the harbor master."

In reply, a figure bearded like a prophet appeared on *Hendon*'s bridge, megaphone in hand. "Ahoy yerself, ye monkey-suited ponce. Caall yerself a sailor? Ye ought to get yer eyes chaarked. Nearly runnin' doon three bits o' bairns. Aah wouldn't gie ye charge of a model yacht!" The prophet foretold the captain's parentage and prospects, in language that brought color even to Audrey's frozen cheeks.

The sailors with the collision mat doubled up laughing. The electronic voice did not deign to reply. The cruiser crept past, then put on speed, white ensign fluttering with outraged dignity.

"Come and see Dick," said their blond-haired rescuer.

By the time they got up on the bridge, Dick Burley had returned to his rocking chair in the wheelhouse. Chas studied him, fascinated. He had eyebrows big as moustaches, and a beard that blanketed his chest.

Tiny purple veins covered his face from nose to ear-lobes. Naval cap, very greasy. Boots with thick white stockings rolled over the top. Old pin-stripe suit with waistcoat, watch and chain. The waistcoat descended over his belly in a series of greasy folds. He had a cigar in the corner of his mouth, and as he talked, rings of ash dropped into the waistcoat folds. When he stood up, ash fell to the deck like a miniature snow storm.

"What the whoremongering—ahah, ladies present. Sorry, madam, pardon ma French." He laughed, causing an ash avalanche. Then sat with furrowed brow, as if thinking of something fit for a lady's ears.

"What's yer name?" he asked at last.

"Chas McGill."

"Chas McGill?" There was another ash avalanche. "Well, it's as well Aah saved ye, Chas McGill, 'cause Aah nearly killed ye once!"

"Nearly killed me?"

"Aye, on accoont of some fish and chips, doon West Hartlepool."

"But I've never been to West Hartlepool in my life!"

"Aye you have—afore ye was born. Yer mam was seven month gone, an' yer da thought a touch of sea air would do her good. Aah was taking the *Hendon* doon Hartlepool to pick up a tow, so Aah give them a sail. At Hartlepool, yer mam took a fancy to some nice fish and chips—ye knaa how ladies are when they're seven months gone. Very headstrong. Wey, we had 'em and enjoyed 'em, but on the way back to the tug, the sky turned a nasty color. So Aah says to yer dad, why don't you tek her home by train, round by Newcastle? But yer mam would ha' none of it. She wanted to go to the pictures that night, to see Al Jolson in *The Jazz Singer*. And they couldn't afford railfare an' all.

"Anyways, we set off, and the weather was even rougher than Aah thowt. Yer mam threw up that fish and chips aal the way to the Gar. Aah thowt she was going to throw *ye* up at one point. She had to have a week in the infirmary, an' even then she almost lost ye—and she never saw *The Jazz Singer* from that day to this."

Chas gaped; somebody who'd known you before you were born was almost like God. Except God wouldn't say things that made Cem laugh like a rotten drain. . . .

Dick turned to the blond sailor. "Hey, Sven, nip doon the slop chest an' get some togs for these young 'uns, afore they catch their death. . . . The young lady can get changed in the chain locker, an' these lads'll have to get changed up here. Nobody'll see anything they haven't seen afore, eh, lads? And brew up, Sven—something ye can stand the spoon upright in."

The mugs of tea were thick and sweet as treacle. Dick added some dark liquid from a bottle in his pocket.

"That'll put hairs on yer chest—begging yer pardon, miss! Anyway, what were ye doing out on the river on that heap of floating junk?"

Chas thought hard, then decided to risk it. Somehow, he had a claim on Dick, and Dick knew it. And Dick knew the river. He'd never get another chance like this.

So he told him everything. It took time, because the *Hendon* was busy getting the convoy out; dazzle-painted Liberty ships, smart new tankers, old tramp steamers with funnels like factory chimneys. Ships with strange names like *Jan van Leyden* and *La Republique* and *Hiram S. Greenbaum*. Every so often, Dick would rush out onto the wing of the bridge to converse with their captains through the megaphone. Each time he returned, he apologized to Audrey anew.

"Foreigners, miss. Aal they understand is swearing. Universal language."

When Chas had finished his story, Dick tapped his empty mug against the binnacle thoughtfully. At last he said:

"Leave it alone, bonny lad."

"Don't you believe. . . ."

"Oh, Aah believe you about finding the basin, an' what was in it. The basin's an old trick. Sailors gettin' stuff ashore afore the Customs men search their ship. They tip the wink to a foyboatman, an' he picks it up in his foyboat. Nylons . . . watches—good Swiss watches bought up half-price in Portugal or Gib. . . ."

"But not a spy . . . ?"

"Not very likely. Aah've known this river forty years, an' those buggers ashore is capable of anything . . . but no, not likely."

"I do not agree," said Sven, stiffly. "We Norwegians thought German spies were just a joke, till it too late was. Then one morning the Nazis had landed, and the schoolmaster and the police sergeant are wearing swastika armbands and smiling and shaking hands."

Chas looked at Sven; his face was like stone, and his eyes looked tiny.

"Steady, Sven-lad," said Dick. "Ye're in England now. No need to look for Jerries under every bed."

Everybody laughed, except Sven. "We had Major Quisling under *our* bed." He walked off onto the wing of the bridge, and began to play with the canvas cover that kept the spray off the Lewis guns when they weren't in use.

"He cleans them guns like they were his bairns," whispered Dick. "He's had a bad time. The Jerries shot his da in Tromsö, after the British left. They sent Sven to the Lofoten Islands as slave labor. When our commandos raided Lofoten, they brought Sven back. Half-starved. Ye coulda played a tune on his ribs. Tried to join the Free Norwegian Navy, but he wasn't fit, so Aah took him on. Mention Jerries, he goes out of his mind. Ye remember the night we chased the U-boat? That was Sven's idea—had me potty as himself. If he hadn't had them guns, Aah swear he'd have gone after that U-boat wi' a knife between his teeth. Ah wish ye hadn't mentioned spies—he'll brood for a week now."

Dick stopped abruptly. Sven was coming back. He didn't look at Dick, he looked at Chas. Chas couldn't bear to look back at him. Sven gripped Chas's arm so hard it was all Chas could do not to flinch.

"You find spy—you tell me. Promise?"

"Yeah," said Chas, staring at the deck. Why did he feel *ashamed*, all of a sudden?

"Good. Now I your friend am. Anything you need—just ask and you get. Here. . . ." He handed Chas two keys.

"What . . . ?"

"Keys for my old boat—moored at Wooden Dolly Quay—better than raft. Keep as long as you need. . . ."

"Thanks."

But Sven had gone off the bridge, and was tidying up the foredeck with violent movements.

"If you *think* you've found out something else," said

Dick softly, "you come and tell *me*, not Sven. Aah don't want him going off half-cock an' murdering some poor bugger in a pub on *your* say-so. . . . Sven's a bit touched in the head."

Chas shifted his feet uncomfortably.

"See what Aah mean? Leave it *alone*, bonny lad. It's not a game."

"But if there *is* something going on?"

"Oh, there's always *something* going on. Tell ye what—Aah'll make a bargain wi' ye. Ye promise to leave it alone, an' Aah'll keep my eyes an' ears open—specially for that crackling on the radio. How's that? Aah feel responsible to your mám and da. . . ."

"You won't tell them?"

"Not this time. Aah've been young meself, though ye'd hardly think it to look at me now. Now, bugger-off before I set ye on chipping rust. Keep the togs—they're not worth fetching back. Sven'll row ye ashore."

Sven took them in the little rowboat that the tug trailed astern. "Now, no more building rafts, I think. I too busy am to keep on fishing you out of Gar!"

They laughed. He laughed. But his face was still white and bony, and his eyes still looked too small.

11 They walked up an alley onto Low Street.

"Seeya," said Audrey. She crossed the street and started up the stairway to Bank Top, wet bundle under one arm, and her bottom wiggling inside a pair of men's trousers big enough to fit Hermann Goering.

"OK for her," said Cem. "Hope our bikes are all right. Bet your woman's just pushed off and left them."

"Sheila's not like that. She'll wait."

"You must be kidding. D'you know how long we've been gone? Five hours!" He waggled his wristwatch in Chas's face.

They quickened their pace. But the bikes were OK, just where they'd left them. And a lonely figure was still standing at the end of the Lifeboat gangway.

"Never fear, Cemmy's here," shouted Cem.

The figure did not turn.

"Sheila—it's us."

Still the figure didn't stir. It was so hunched up, it could have been anybody.

"Are you sure it is her?" asked Chas uneasily.

"Can't you recognize your own stupid scarf?"

"Why doesn't she answer, then?"

"Your problem, mate." Cem swung one leg over his bike. "Seeya."

Chas started along the gangway, thumping down his feet heavily. But still Sheila didn't turn. Was she dead or something? Six feet away, he stopped; noticed her left hand on the wooden rail, clenched white round a very wet hanky. Suddenly, he felt scared.

"Sheila?" He touched her shoulder, timidly.

It was like touching a loaded mousetrap. She grabbed him so hard he could scarcely breathe, and clung on, burrowing her face into his shoulder. He looked round surreptitiously, to make sure no one was watching. The Sands were empty, thank God.

"What's the *matter*? "

She turned to him a face ugly with tears. It had that same bony look as Sven's. He'd never seen a face like it in his life. Much worse than Mam's when Granda died. Mam had just looked pale and ill, and bit her lip, and her eyes had glistened sometimes.

"WHAT'S THE MATTER?" Was everybody potty today?

"I thought you were *dead*. I waited and waited, and it was so *cold*. I only saw one bowl go out between the piers—Number Five. At half-past three. Then I saw a whole lot of oil drums come floating out. All tied together and mashed up, with bits of splintered wood. I knew it was the raft and some ship had smashed it, and if it looked like that—you. . . . Oooooooohhhhh!" She began sobbing like nobody had ever heard before, gasping as if she was choking.

"You shouldn't worry about me," said Chas, rigid with embarrassment. He patted her on the top of her head, as if she was a dog. "I always turn up, like a bad penny."

"Is—that—all you can say. Don't *worry*?" She continued sobbing. He went on mechanically patting her head, her shoulders, the small of her back. By now he was actually looking round in the hope of seeing somebody. If somebody came she'd *have* to stop going on like this.

"*Do* something. . . ."

"Like what?" asked Chas desperately. Was she going to faint? How was he going to get her home in this state? Everybody would stare. "Like *what*?"

"Kiss me, idiot!" Chas groped till he found her chin, and lifted it. Her eyes were shut, and all her eyelashes stuck together, and little pools of tears formed in the blue hollows under her eyes. He kissed her cheek experimentally. It was hot and sopping wet, and marked with red marks from being pressed against his sweater. God, she looked *ugly*. Why had he ever thought she was a smasher? It was dicey enough kissing a dry girl, let alone a sodden howling mess. He tried to back away, but she fell against him in a warm heap, and he had to hold her up.

"Kiss me again." But she did sound a bit better. He aimed for her cheek again, but she twisted round so he was kissing her mouth instead. She wouldn't let his mouth go. He breathed in hard through his nose, feeling he was drowning for the second time that afternoon. He felt she was sucking something out of him. What . . . life? . . . freedom? He felt he was going down into some prison. But a prison getting warmer and cozier by the minute.

Best of all, she'd stopped crying. She was just gasping now. She gave a wriggle against him, as if she was almost enjoying herself. Well . . . it wasn't bad. He maneuvered his nose into a position where he could breathe easily. After about five minutes, she looked away toward the river and said:

"Give me your hanky—I feel a *hag*."

"Haven't got a hanky—lost it in the river."

"You're *hopeless!*"

"Sorry."

"And stop saying you're sorry."

"Sorry."

She fussed in her shoulder bag and produced another hanky, and dried her face. He took his arms away, but she replaced them firmly round her waist. Then she put on some lipstick, pressing her lips together. He watched these female operations with lazy, sleepy interest. He'd never seen them close-to before, except with Mam.

But really, for someone who'd thought someone was dead, she was looking remarkably perky. Whereas *he* now felt like death-warmed-up. But humbly peaceful and grateful, because she'd stopped crying.

"Give me another kiss!" He realized he'd lost all power to refuse. But he didn't really mind. He was getting quite good at getting his nose in the right place.

"Walk me home." She held her body against his, making it quite inevitable that he put his arm round her waist as they walked. He had his other hand resting on his handlebars, and the pedal of his bike kept knocking against the back of his leg. He kept worrying he'd see some lads he knew.

But a gentle dusk was falling, and the riverbank was empty as far as the eye could see. And Sheila was talking more than she'd ever talked before.

"When I saw the raft, I didn't know *what* to do. I ran up and down the Low Street and the alleys looking for you. If that nice little policeman hadn't come along to help, I think I'd have gone mad."

"What policeman? Where?" asked Chas, with the nervousness of long experience.

"A little dark policeman in plain clothes. With ever such funny shoes."

"Funny? How—funny?"

"They had brown sides and white tops."

"God . . . that was the Maltese. . . ."

"He said he was a policeman. . . . I *thought* he was a bit small, but he knew all about you and Cem and the raft."

"You didn't tell him anything, did you?"

"Only your names and addresses. He said he would go and make inquiries. But he never came back. Did I do something wrong?"

"If you find me floating down the river one dark night. . . ."

"Don't talk like that. Or you'll start me crying again." Her face had a wide-eyed fanatical look, like a stormtrooper going into action for the Führer. It scared Chas even more than the Maltese.

"Where have *you* been?" said Mam. "D'you know what time of night it is? Where did you get those clothes—you look like a scarecrow. You'll have to take this lad in hand, Jack!"

The atmosphere was like an Arctic thundercloud. But for once, Chas knew he couldn't lose.

"I fell in the river, Dad. Nearly drowned. And you'll never guess who fished me out? Dick Burley. Took us for a ride in the *Hendon*. Told us about you and Mam at West Hartlepool."

"Aah knew Dick was clever wi' the *Hendon*," said Dad dryly, "but Aah never knew he sailed her up Holywell Dene. Did you give him a dripping sandwich?"

Chas had the grace to blush.

"What's all this about Holywell Dene?" said Mam, ready to make trouble out of anything.

But Dad just said, "Nowt, woman." He was content with his private joke.

"Dick Burley," said Mam, with a lightning change of attack that would have impressed Field Marshal Rommel. "Dick Burley. That man could have been captain of a *liner*, but for the drink. If only he'd stayed teetotal with the Methodists."

"Dick Burley a Methodist?" asked Chas innocently, looking at Dad. Dad laughed till the tears came.

"Aye, Dick was two years wi' the Methodists—till their vicar talked him into giving the Sunday School an outing on the *Hendon*. Aall went well, till they reached the Quay coming home. Then Dick, wi' the vicar next to him on the bridge, turns to the mate and says (everyday-like, and forgetting what company he's in), 'Shove her arse roond a bit more, Tommy,' meaning the ship. The whole congregation walked off the ship poker-faced, wi'out as much as a thank-you, and Dick never dared go back."

Dad passed from one Dick Burley story to another. As the family would've said, he was off. . . .

Mam walked stiff-backed into the kitchen, and closed the door so quietly it was worse than a slam.

Chas and Cem stood on Fish Quay Sands next morning, gloomily surveying enamel bowls Two, Three and Four bobbing among the flotsam.

"Better rescue Number Three," said Cem. "Me mam's looking for it everywhere."

"You'll not rescue Number One," said Chas. "It never left the Fish Quay. Those kids fishing have just sunk it."

"But your woman saw Number Five going out through the piers."

"She's not my woman—we're just friends."

"What's that lipstick on your face, then?"

Chas reached up a guilty hand.

"Ha-ha, *caught* you," said Cem. He did a kind of ballet dance in a circle on the Sands. "There wasn't any lipstick, but there *miiiiight* have been," he yodeled, to two completely innocent passers-by, who quickened their pace. Chas threw a dead crab to bring him back to order.

"Number Five *worked*. If it had been at night, a U-boat could have picked it up."

"Yeah, yeah," said Cem, grudgingly. "But where was Number Five bowl put into the water?"

"Audrey still had it when that tanker caught us."

"But after that? Nobody knows. Nobody knows. Nobody knooooows." He did his singing ballet dance round the Sands again. Then he came back and said, "The whole operation was a *cock-up*. The only time we get a bowl through the piers was the time we weren't trying."

"We have got some negative evidence," said Chas. "We know that any bowl launched under the Low Street just ends up *here*; and any bowl launched from the Quay doesn't go anywhere at all."

"Negative evidence," jeered Cem. "What a posh *phrase*. All you've done is prove it wasn't the Maltese with their famous trap doors. That baloney about the Maltese putting bodies in the river is all . . . BALONEY."

"Maybe the currents act differently on *bodies*—they're lower in the water. Anyway, a Maltese could've rowed out into the middle of the river and launched his bowl from there."

"What? At seven o'clock on a Saturday night, with half the population admiring the sunset over the Gar, before retiring to the pub? Not to mention the River Police launch? Suppose *they* asked him what he was doing? He could hardly say, 'I always play with boats in my bath, but now I'm getting more ambitious.' "

"There *must* be an answer."

"I've got news for you. You haven't got an answer, you haven't got a spy, and from the looks of it, you haven't got a woman, either. She's very late this morning."

"She's *not* my woman. And she's been and gone already."

"Is her passion for you on the wane?"

"No. She's gone to try and buy a bottle of olive oil."

"To anoint herself? Bring on the dancing girls!"

"Queen of Sheba Olive Oil, stupid. Same as the cardboard box in the enamel bowl. Maybe we can find out which shop sells it. That might give us a lead. It's not a common brand."

"You don't give up, do you? Anyway, here's your woman now."

"She's not. . . ." But Sheila immediately took Chas's hand in a tight warm grip.

"Excuse me," said Cem, and did an impersonation of playing a romantic tune on a violin.

"What's up with you?" said Sheila with unexpected spirit. "Jealous? Can't you get a woman of your own?"

Cem switched to a fine rendering of Stanley Matthews dribbling down the right wing of the beach, using a cod's head for a football. He reached the far end and began returning. Immediately, Sheila kissed Chas warmly. Then she looked at Cem, to make sure he'd noticed.

"Not in *public*," hissed Chas.

"*He's* not the public."

"He's OK, when you get to know him."

"I'd try to get him a girlfriend, only I don't know any female Frankensteins. Hello *again*, Cem." She kissed Chas warmly a second time.

"I'll go and weed some tombstones," said Cem, panting. "Till you've finished playing Romeo and Juliet. When's the death scene?"

"Olive oil," said Chas firmly. "How'd you get on, Sheila?"

"Not a bottle to be had, anywhere up in town. Even at under-the-counter prices."

"You rich people live off the black market," said Cem.

"So do you poor people," flared Sheila. "Like that seven-pound tin of butter your dad said fell off a lorry."

Cem turned to Chas, "You sent her round the Low Street shops, of course?"

"Not likely. Too dangerous for her."

"More dangerous for us. Now she's given the Maltese our names and addresses."

"I know who would know which shop sold Queen of Sheba," said Chas. "Deadly Ernest."

"Who's Deadly Ernest?" asked Sheila.

"Gauleiter of the Garmouth dust bins, Heil Hitler," said Cem. "Unfortunately. . . ."

"Let me *guess*," said Sheila. "You were *rude* to him? He is now your sworn enemy for *life*?"

Cem kicked a pebble so hard it must have landed in the middle of the Gar.

"Why don't we do our own refuse collection—along the Low Street?" suggested Sheila.

"How?" Both boys gaped.

"Salvage—collecting cardboard boxes for the war effort?"

"People wouldn't give *us* salvage."

"They would if we were in uniform."

"What uniform?"

"Well, I'm in the Guides. You in the Scouts?"

"I'm in Sea Scouts," said Cem. "*He* used to be in the *ordinary* Scouts, till they tied a knot in his woggle."

"It was the shorts. People used to wolf-whistle, like I was a girl."

"It was your sexy legs—"

"Shurrup!"

"But it is quite a good idea," said Cem patronizingly. "Especially if we only collect *hard* cardboard, like the Queen of Sheba box."

"Can you borrow the Sea Scout trek cart?" asked Chas.

"Only if you promise to wear your sexy shorts," said Cem. "This afternoon?"

Life was unfair. Sheila looked pretty in her uniform; Cem trim and naval in his. Chas felt ridiculous. His shorts had been too short when he left the Scouts a year ago. Now his long white legs seemed to go on forever. Already people were wolf-whistling. Calling him "Baden-Powell" or "Tom Mix the Cowboy." One drunk tried to embrace him, calling him "Florence Nightingale," but even Cem couldn't work that one out.

They had plastered the trek cart with homemade posters. *Choke Hitler with Cardboard. Save Cardboard and Save Soldiers' Lives.*

Cem tried insisting that Sheila go into the shops and ask for the cardboard, because it was her rotten idea. Chas wouldn't let her, so he had to go himself. And it was exhausting. Once you went through a dark shop door, past the tin notices for Woodbines and Fry's Chocolate Cream, you might find *anything*.

In one shop a little old woman was sitting, in her best hat and coat. All she would say, whatever you asked her, was that she was "keeping the shop for our Norah." But there wasn't a thing to sell. Nothing but huge fake packets of cigarettes, sun-faded and crumpling on every shelf.

Then there was the shop full of Chinese, who

grinned and couldn't speak a word of English. They kept sending into the back of the shop for more and more Chinese, but they couldn't understand English either. Every time one came through, a great waft of damp steam accompanied him. They all chattered frantically to one another like a cage of canaries. The steam and chatter made Chas's head spin. And they did so want to help; they wouldn't let Chas go, all pawing hands and gleaming teeth. Chas consigned Cem to the depths of hell. Because every time he came out of a shop, gasping for air, Cem would grab him by the woggle, half-strangling him, shouting, "What happened? What *happened?*"

But their bluff worked. The Low Street shopkeepers told them they were doing a grand job. Grinning yellow faces and brown faces offered them cups of tea, fruit gums, sugar-dusted Turkish Delight; and something brown and peculiar out of a packet that Cem held gingerly in his mouth for fifty yards, then spat out in the gutter.

"They're nice people," whispered Sheila. "Just like us. Patriotic. Why do you have all these *horrible* ideas about them?"

"The spy will be nicest of all," said Cem, with his craziest laugh.

The shopkeepers piled their trek cart high with Carnation Milk boxes, Bovril-Prevents-That-Sinking-Feeling boxes, even American dried-egg boxes. Cem noisily bashed boxes flat, rammed them inside each other, and there were still so many they were falling off the cart.

No Queen of Sheba.

" 'S a waste of time," said Cem. "Girls' ideas always are."

"It's my time that's being wasted," said Chas calmly; instead of hitting him.

Eventually they came to *S. X. Kallonas—Ships' Chandler and Spice Merchant*. Behind a dust-furred window, trails of dried vegetation like nibbled rats' tails hung from the ceiling. The window bottom was a wilderness of *Pasha* dates and obscene purple-mottled sausages, which the flies were using as landing strips.

Chas went in. The center of the floor was sawdust; the corners occupied by mountains of sacks and boxes, brass scales and Mr. Kallonas. Mr. Kallonas was another mountain, altitude about six feet six. Broad as an ape with hands like bunches of bananas dangling somewhere near his knees. He had an olive skin, with big open pores. His forehead was low and sloped back to blue-black hair. Blue-black eyebrows met above a broken nose. He looked like that boxer they called Primo Carnera, the Ambling Alp. The fact that he was wearing a clean white apron and a bowler hat made him look like something out of a chimps' tea party. . . .

Chas said his piece about *hard* cardboard for shell cartridges. He'd done it so often, it was getting singsong, like school prayers. But why was he talking so loud, so fast? Like a gramophone when someone's altering the speed? Was it because Mr. Kallonas was so big, and standing so close? Sweating so much? Nodding and winking so much? Mr. Kallonas had wet pleading eyes like a spaniel. In someone so massive, it was disgusting.

Chas finished at last. A toothpaste grin split Mr. Kallonas's face.

"Of course I help war effort! We must beat those Nazis quick! Every little helps! Come into the back and you can have all the cardboard you wish!" He led Chas through a door with one huge hand, patting him on the back with the other. Gabbling on as convincingly as a first-year kid in the school play. His hands were shaking; he smelled funny.

Mr. Kallonas was afraid.

The back room was stacked with boxes to the ceiling. Its contents would have filled the trek cart twenty times. Chas's eyes roamed the serried ranks in despair.

Then he saw the Queen of Sheba. Five boxes, right at the bottom. If he pulled them out, every box in the room would collapse to the floor. He gritted his teeth, closed his eyes and grabbed.

Only half the boxes collapsed on the floor. Mr. Kallonas gave an agonized yell.

"What you wanta take those for? Plenty besides those!" He tried to grab the Queen of Sheba box off Chas. A wrestling match developed.

"These are the sort the Army needs. Hard cardboard. *Hard* cardboard!"

"Oh, take them if you wish. But see the mess. Why you not take the ones on top? Two hours it will take to get straight."

"Sorry. We'll come back for the rest—our cart is full now. And we'll tidy up for you as well."

"I *hope!* Help the war effort? All I get is mess."

Chas bore the box out in triumph. The look on Sheila's face pleased him nearly as much as the look on Cem's.

"Let's go!"

It was agony, having to drag the cart the length of Low Street, before they could duck onto the Fish Quay, and search the Sheba box for a serial number.

It was 59873.

The box from the enamel bowl was 59875.

"We gotta go back," said Chas. "I knocked all his boxes down getting this, and I promised to go back and tidy up for him."

"Stuff that," said Cem. "He can tidy his own boxes up."

"Look, idiot! Tidying up will give us a chance to snoop round."

But there was no chance to snoop. Mr. Kallonas was in and out all the time, telling them how to do it, and proffering dates from gluey packs.

"He's dead worried," muttered Cem. "He's got *something* to hide."

"I think he's just trying to be friendly," said Sheila. "That olive oil box doesn't prove a thing. Maybe he gave it to somebody. He gave one to *us!*"

"After a struggle," said Chas.

"You're like the three wise monkeys, Sheila," said Cem. "Hear no evil, see no evil, speak no evil."

"I think you're both quite horrible," said Sheila. "I think you should stop this silly game now, before someone gets hurt."

"Oh, yeah," said Cem. "That's all it is to you—a game. But when we come up with *proof*, you don't like it. I mean, this is *England*, chaps. If Hitler landed in Whitley Bay, they wouldn't *speak* to him. Common little house paintah!"

"I think the box is no proof at all; I think you are quite foul, Cem; and I think I want you to take me home, Chas."

Just then, Mr. Kallonas came back and noticed the quarrel.

"What is matter? Are we downhearted—*no!* Here is

some figs for you to take home." He also insisted on them loading the cart with more of his lovely boxes; for the war effort.

"What shall we *do* with them all?" groaned Sheila, as they tipped the second load down beside the first onto the Sands.

"Can't leave 'em," said Cem. "He might see them and get suspicious. Let's have a bonfire!"

So they made a great bonfire, sparing only the Sheba boxes 59873, 59874 and 59876 for evidence. Cem forgot Sheila, and Sheila forgave Cem, and they spent a long happy time watching the charring cardboard twist and writhe inside the flames, and the black smoke drifting across the river.

"It seems such a waste," sighed Sheila, comfy with Chas's arm around her. "Those boxes really would've helped the war effort."

"If it keeps the infant happy," said Chas tolerantly, watching Cem farther along the beach, whirling a burning box on a stick round his head.

But Cem stopped suddenly, and the burning box flopped into the river with a hiss. Cem was staring up the beach.

"Who's that?" shouted Cem, and pointed.

They glanced in the direction he was pointing. It was growing dark, away from the glow of the fire.

"We can't see anything," shouted Chas. "Stop kidding!"

"Wasn't kidding," said Cem, coming over to them rather quickly. "There was a feller watching us from behind those piles of lobster pots."

"Don't believe a word he says," said Chas.

"I think it was Kallonas," said Cem.

12 Garmouth Church chimed one A.M. The music and laughing had died in the last of the Maltese cafés. Drunken footsteps going back to the ships.

"Cheeroh, Stan!"

"Cheeroh, marrer. See you after the war."

"If we're lucky."

The Low Street was left to the waning moon and the tomcats. The moon glistened on the cobbles of Wooden Dolly Quay, leaving the tall overhanging buildings in shadow. The Dolly threw her own shadow; kept her own counsel.

In the deepest shadow, a whispered fight was going on that had nothing to do with tomcats.

"You're bloody crackers," hissed Chas. "If you get caught, it's burglary. Kid down our street got sent away for that."

"Rather be sent away than dead. Kallonas *knows* we're onto him. He's not going to sit twiddling his thumbs. He'll be Gestapo-trained; they can stab you through the heart with a long hat pin without leaving a trace of blood. People think you've died of a heart attack."

"Go *on*. . . ."

"It says here. . . ." Cem was fishing another newspaper cutting out of his pocket. He'd been doing it all evening, in a frantic sort of way. Rather as if the world of the cuttings had finally caught up with him. Maybe he really *had* seen Kallonas at the Sands. Or was it all kidology? Another attempt to set up a no-guts situation?

"If you did break into his shop, what d'you hope to find?"

"Batteries. Oscillators. Maybe a German code book."

"Lying among the grocery orders?"

"Got a better idea?"

"Yeah—I'm going home."

"No guts."

Chas sighed with relief. So it *was* only a no-guts situation. Well, he'd go along and watch Cem make a fool of himself. Cem'd slink round Kallonas's back-yard, then come away with some lame excuse. *Most* enjoyable. . . .

They crept down the alley onto the river steps, and unlocked the chain on Sven's old boat. The chain was threaded through the oars too, so no one could pinch them. It was hard getting the chain off silently, and laying it in the bottom of the boat.

"I'll row," hissed Cem. "I'm good at rowing." His rowing was about as silent as a Mississippi paddle-steamer going full out. Chas had heard of people rowing with muffled oars. But who could ever muffle Cem? Thank God the moon had gone behind a cloud.

"Count the chimney stacks," said Cem, in his big master-spy voice. "Kallonas's joint is seven chimneys down-river from the alley."

"Where's the alley?" asked Chas, because the big master spy had traced several interesting circles on the broad bosom of the Gar. But the moon glimmered briefly, and they saw the seventh chimney. They knew it was the right one, because it had a funny whirling cowl on top.

They tied up; the moon died. Chas felt Cem leap from the boat like an ill-trained kangaroo; heard him slip and fall on the weedy steps. Then he walked into a crate of bottles at the top. Chas wondered if there was anyone in the whole Low Street still asleep. If someone phoned the River Police, a launch would be here in five minutes. . . . Still, it wasn't a crime to sit in a boat on the river, even in the middle of the night.

"I came to watch over my lunatic friend, officer. See he didn't do himself any harm. . . ."

"Hey, c'mon," vouchsafed Cem, in a muffled bellow. "It's a piece of cake."

"You go ahead. I'll come if you get the back door open." Chas didn't bother to hide the mockery in his voice. He sat waiting for Cem to fail; and Cem's big convincing explanation; which he could pull to bits all the way home.

"Hey. Got the back door open. Piece of cake." And Chas could tell from the sound of his voice that he had, too. Chas sat silent, full of sick hollow excitement.

"No guts."

Silence, all along the Low Street. Ears. Listening.

"C'mon. We ain't got all night."

Chas climbed the steps like a traitor going through Traitor's gate at the Tower of London. Suppose Sheila's father was the magistrate when they came up for trial?

They closed the back door behind them. Chas shone his torch, shading it with his hand. Beetles scuttled across the floor. Something bigger scrambled to safety behind the piled cardboard boxes.

"Here's the safe," muttered Cem. "Pretty wonky. Shall I try—?"

"No!" said Chas in a panic. Safes meant Borstal for sure. "Let's try this desk."

The desk was huge, old and unlocked. As Chas

rolled up the lid, an avalanche of papers fell on the floor. He began messing through them. Just invoices for margarine, huge envelopes leaking canceled ration coupons.

He tried one of the desk drawers. This was better. A certificate stating that Xenophon Kallonas was a member of the Grand Order of Buffaloes. Another saying that Xenophon Kallonas was a naturalized British citizen. A letter from the Royal Navy, rejecting the services of Xenophon Kallonas because he had varicose veins; dated September 1939. Pretty odd that, an enemy agent volunteering for the Navy!

Then came leaflets, offering to cure inferiority complexes and stammering; to teach public speaking.

"Cem, he can't be a spy." The whole thing felt indecent, like going through somebody's underwear drawer.

"It's all cover-up," spat Cem. "To fool nignogs like you."

Why was Cem breathing so heavily? Like an old man? Was he panicking?

No, it wasn't Cem. It was coming from the wrong place. Was it an echo of his own breathing? He stopped breathing, but the noise went on.

"Cem, there's somebody else in here. Scram!" Chas blundered for the door, and fell full-length over a box of Vim. Next second, the light went on. Mr. Kallonas stood by the back door, huge in striped pajamas. He had a meat cleaver in his hand.

There was a long silence, except for everybody panting.

Cem reached into a box and took out a full lemonade bottle; with a loud clink. Then everything was still again.

"Want more cardboard boxes?" asked Mr. Kallonas. "Put down that bottle, boy, before you get hurt."

"Make me," said Cem, face white as bone. Looking even nastier than Mr. Kallonas. Chas just went on lying on the floor, sure that if he moved a muscle something horrible was going to happen.

"You bloody funny burglars," said Mr. Kallonas. "You want my money? No! You steal my lard for the black market? No! Why you steal my British passport? My letter from Navy? What for you want take my British-hood away?"

"Because you're a spy!" said Cem quietly, getting a better grip on his bottle.

Goodbye Borstal, thought Chas, sweet safe Borstal.

But Mr. Kallonas did not strike out with Gestapo venom. He put the meat cleaver down, seemed to shrink.

"I tell Mama you are not Low Street boys who steal. I tell her you are decent boys from the town." Mr. Kallonas sat down heavily, and at that moment a tiny figure in a white nightdress flitted from behind some crates, and put an arm round his shoulders. A gray-haired woman, with a face like a walnut.

"Why you do this thing?" she raged. "He is good man; does no harm. He is Britisher for thirty years. But ever since War, children throw stones and call him Mussolini. He is British as you. Look, he has serve his country." She pulled a faded photo from the wall and thrust it in their faces. It was Mr. Kallonas, in uniform and very much younger, sitting cross-legged with his shipmates on the deck of some battleship.

"He is on the *H.M.S. Lion*—he is fighting in the Battle of the Jutland. Admiral say he do well—fire many shells at Germans—save comrade who is wounded. Look, here is *Lion*."

She pulled another picture off the wall, and there indeed was the British flagship of 1916, showing slight damage from German shells, and much greater damage received since from rising-damp and fly-droppings.

"I was in Last War," said Mr. Kallonas despondently. "They no let me in this one."

"I'm sorry we thought you were a spy," said Chas.

Why you think I a spy?" asked Mr. Kallonas. And burst into tears. Chas stared hot-faced at the boxes of Vim. A spy would have been easier to cope with.

It was Mrs. Kallonas who saved the day, shepherding them all into a sitting room, where sad-moustached Greeks in frilly skirts stared down from the walls. She made some super-smelling coffee that turned out to be nearly as thick as toothpaste. Only there were glasses of water to go with it.

It was a relief when old Kallonas dried up. Chas thought it was only decent to tell him the whole story; it was nice to feel an honest citizen again, but he was awfully tired of telling that story.

When he had finished, Mrs. Kallonas, who had been listening with her head cocked like a bird, said: "The lard, Papa, the lard."

Mr. Kallonas brightened. "Is true. One gross of lard stolen last Thursday night. Only lard. We thought black marketers, so I am having ear cocked every night. Only you make too much noise for burglars."

Chas laughed at Cem. "I *told* you!"

"Shurrup!"

"Now we know," said Mr. Kallonas, "why he wanted lard—to waterproof box. I think he steal box same night. Only *we* sell Queen of Sheba. My brother Nikkos send it from Cyprus."

Chas let out a deep breath. Suddenly, the spy was real. A week ago, he had been in this house. Stealing a gross of lard in the middle of the night could not possibly be kids fooling about.

"I will help catch spy," announced Mr. Kallonas, jumping about with excitement.

"Sit *down*, Xenophon! Who can think while you are dancing the dance? British boys do not like the fusses you make—they are embarrassed."

Xenophon sat down, like a well-trained St. Bernard.

"Now," said Mrs. Kallonas. "Tell me exactly what was in the bowl when you found it. And the bowl itself. New? Old?"

When they told her, she nodded.

"You were not wrong to trace the olive oil box. Now you must trace other things. The bowl was mended with a washer still shiny. Such things go dull very quick—it must have been bought recently. Perhaps they remember in some shop who buys such a thing. And American battery. Black market! Xenophon will ask. Many black marketers known to us. Someone will know. Most important, the watch. You say a good watch—gold. No man will use his own watch for such a purpose. He may have bought it. And since it was not new, you must ask at the pawnshop.

"We do all these things, then we see. Now it is time for British boys to be in bed, before their mothers come to wake them up. And Xenophon—tomorrow you buy new lock for back door. How many times have I told you old one was no good?"

They walked home thoughtfully up Tanner's Bank. Chas's pajamas were doing funny things under his trousers, and he paused to hitch them up.

"He's not the spy, is he?"

"I can believe a lot," said Cem, "but a henpecked spy, *never!*"

"Mevve *she's* the spy?"

"Give yer brain a rest."

13 Sheila went into the dark little shop at the top of Tanner's Bank, and took the washer out of her handbag for the tenth time. Her feet ached.

"Do you sell washers like this?"

The woman behind the counter rummaged in a drawer. "You're just too late, hinny. Sold me last set a week ago. You can't get them for love nor money. It's the war. People can't get new washers, so they have to buy whole new bowls. I don't see how *that* saves steel for the war effort. Except you can't buy new bowls either."

Sheila's heart missed a beat. Every other ironmonger's in the town hadn't had washers for months. And this shop was the nearest to the Low Street.

"I think it must have been my brother who bought your last set. Only he lost them on the way home. . . ."

The woman looked her up and down; shoes, suit, handbag. "I don't think it can have been *your* brother, hinny. Live in Whitley Bay, don't you? This man wasn't your sort. He was a working man, a seaman."

"Oh, my brother dresses that way sometimes—when he goes yachting."

The woman smiled inwardly, at some secret adult joke. *"No, hinny."*

"I'm sure it was my brother," said Sheila desperately. "Had he got red hair?"

"Couldn't see, hinny. He had his sailor's cap on."

"What color were his eyes?"

The woman looked at her sharply, all humor gone. "I don't know what your game is, miss. But if I was your mam, *I* wouldn't want you chasing after a man like that. Come to that, I don't see what your sort's doing in these parts. . . ."

Sheila fled.

The pawnshop sign said *Loans secured. Old gold bought.*

Chas hung undecided, staring in the window. It was full of amazing things. Brown riding boots with a brass telescope sticking out of one leg. A blue pin-stripe suit, with a Bakelite radio sitting on top. A fox fur draped over a picture of Queen Victoria. Both fox head and Queen surveyed him with contempt, only the fox had yellow glass eyes and the Queen washed-out blue ones. Nearby was a chamber pot, full of broken watches. Beyond lay impenetrable darkness; even when he held his hand against the window glass and peered under it.

Chas felt paralyzed. Inside his head, his whole family was watching. What Satan was to Catholics, and drink to Methodists, the pawnshop was to the McGills.

Mam always said, "First the pub, then the pawnshop, then the workhouse."

Every time Chas broke a window, Dad said bitterly, "You'll have us down the pawnshop yet."

Dad said all pawnshop keepers were bloodsuckers. Once they got you in their clutches, you never got out. He never said how they got you in their clutches, and somehow Chas never dared ask.

If he went into the pawnshop, he knew he would come out feeling dirty; but people were making bigger sacrifices than that for the war effort.

He went in. A bell rang somewhere in the back of the shop. It was dark, but he could see piled-up objects on his right. Each with a label attached. On his left was a row of cubbyholes, each with a metal grille at the back. Like the Post Office, only deeper.

"Yes?" It was a woman's voice, confident and slow, coming from the nearest cubbyhole. He plunged in, like a mouse going into a trap.

The woman's hair was so black, it shone blue. It was piled in great coils round her head. Her face and arms were round and smooth, and she was wearing a white lace blouse over a swelling bosom. He tried not to look at the bosom, but his eyes kept coming back to it.

She noticed; it amused her.

"Yes, sir?" she said, mockingly. Chas blushed, and that amused her too. "Do you wish to pawn something?"

"No!" said Chas, so violently his voice seemed to echo and echo in the silence. He blushed again.

She watched it, unblinking, then let her eyes travel lazily up and down him. "So what can a nice boy like you be doing in a place like this?"

He snatched his eyes again from her bosom, and stared at the watch tightly clutched in his hand instead.

"So, let me see it," she said, putting a smooth hand

through the grille. Helplessly Chas put the watch into the hand, and saw it drawn away out of his reach.

The woman opened the watch, and screwed a shiny black tube into her eye. Suddenly, she was neither smiling nor playing.

"This is a good watch. Have you stolen it?"

"Found it."

"That is called 'stealing by finding.' "

"I'm not keeping it. I'm trying to find the owner. I thought perhaps . . . you would know who he was. . . . I mean—if he's ever pawned it."

"Why not hand it in to the police station? If no one claims it after three months, the police will give it back to you, and then it will be yours honestly."

"He *won't* claim it, and I *must* find him."

"Won't? Must? Such words. They spoil your *beautiful* manners. In pawnshops, we are not used to such manners." She was laughing at him again. "But you don't want to pawn; you want to *know*. This shop is for pawning; if you want to *know*, you must come round the back."

Her face vanished from the grille, and the watch with it. Then a door opened in the back, letting in a blaze of sunlight.

"Come!" She was standing in the door, and he noticed the swell of one breast and hip. Why did he keep *noticing* her like that? He didn't notice Sheila like that. . . .

"Come. We can have a drink." Chas broke out in a cold sweat. Dad said people slipped things in your drink down the Low Street, and when you wakened up you could be on a ship going anywhere. Shanghaiing it was called. Was that how moneylenders got you in their clutches?

But his body took him through the door of its own accord.

"Sit down, *Liebling*." She closed the door behind him, and patted the couch next to her, as she sat down. Her legs were curvy too, inside dark nylon stockings. . . . Jeepers! He stared round the room. Bamboo tables, stuffed tropical fish, stone hot-water bottles. It was nearly as cluttered as the shop. Probably the stuff trickled back from there.

"Would you like tea—or lemonade?"

"Nothing—thanks."

She smiled and got up, pausing in front of an old fly-blown mirror to pin up a straying lock of her heavy hair. All the time studying him out of the corner of her dark expressionless eyes.

"So all you want is a name and address?"

"Yes," he said flatly.

"You are such a beautiful boy—but you have the soul of a policeman. That is all they ever want—names and addresses." She turned and laid a finger on his arm. "So what will you give me for a name and address? Will you give me a kiss, as you kiss your aunts?"

Chas remembered the guys who had won the V.C. posthumously, and said, "Yes."

"So *gallant!*" she laughed aloud, and took her finger away. Chas felt relieved, and yet sorry. His heart thumped and he felt a bit sick, as if he was waiting to get a prize in front of the whole school.

But the woman had turned her attention back to the watch. She screwed the black thing back into her eyes, wrote down a number, and then reached for a great leather-bound ledger. The ledger seemed too heavy for her. She crossed her legs to support its weight. She leaned forward to run her finger down a column of numbers, and her breasts almost touched the pages. Now her attention was elsewhere, Chas just stared and stared.

"Here we are: *William Mason, 5, Bankside Cottages.* You know I shouldn't be doing this? Mr. Mason would be very angry if he knew. You will be discreet? Protect my good name?"

"Yeah," said Chas, breathlessly.

She came across with the address on a piece of paper. She folded the paper four times, and then pushed it down into Chas's shirt pocket.

He got up quickly, but that brought him much nearer to her; brought him inside the circle of her perfume.

"Now pay me, beautiful boy."

He tried to peck her cheek, like he did with Mam. But she placed both her arms around him, and they were strong. For a moment he felt totally enclosed; trapped for ever. Then he was staggering back, taking deep breaths. And she was sitting down and crossing her legs, and smiling at him again.

"Goodbye, beautiful boy."

He got the door open after a struggle with the handle, then dared look back. She was laughing openly.

"Come and see me again. Perhaps one day you will marry me! I am *very* rich."

14

Bankside Cottages was a terrace overlooking the river; well-painted and respectable, even after four years of war. Number Five was in the middle, with gleaming knocker and doorstep scrubbed white.

"Funny place for a spy," said Cem.

"What you expect—a haunted mansion?"

"What do *we* do?" asked Sheila.

"Don't hang around being obvious. Cem, you pretend to mend your bike at one end of the back lane. Audrey, you wait for a bus at the other. If anyone comes out, follow him. Sheila, you come as far as the front gate, and stand like you're waiting for me. Then he won't get funny ideas about knocking me on the head."

Chas was sweating, and beginning to need the lav. He wanted to get started before nature overtook him.

"Bet the guy's at work," said Audrey, "or on the night shift and in bed. You won't get anywhere, you know."

"Thanks." Chas walked with Sheila to the garden gate. The garden was all weeds, which didn't match the gleaming knocker. Sheila gave his hand a last squeeze.

"Best of luck, darling. Yell if you want me."

"Seeyaround!"

The garden gate squeaked loudly. Perhaps a curtain would twitch . . . a gun. . . .

It was hard to knock on the front door, because it was half open. There was another door, with red stained glass, behind. Chas held the front door with one hand, and used the knocker with the other. No reply.

Chas glanced at the bay window, out of the corner of his eye. The curtains were drawn; he could see nothing. He knocked again.

A female voice called faintly, but he couldn't hear what it said. He knocked a third time.

"Come in." The voice *was* faint; and weary. He took a last glance back at Sheila and the blue sky. He walked in.

The room was dark, because of the drawn curtains. A clock ticked, unnaturally loud. There was a smell of elderly aunts.

"Hello," he said, too loud. Something moved, in the rocking chair by the fireplace.

"Shut the door, hinny. It's cold." Heavens, the day outside was a scorcher, for April.

As he got used to the darkness, he could see the fire had been laid, with paper, sticks and coal. If the woman was cold, why didn't she light the fire?

"Sit down," said the woman. "It's good of you to come. It's Norman, isn't it? Our Benny's youngest?" Her voice was uninterested.

Chas sat down. He could see everything in the room now. Brass ornaments hung round the fireplace, gleaming like silver. The whole room was spotless as a new pin. There was a black-and-white cat, that got up to lick itself every few seconds. It didn't seem able to settle, but screwed itself round and round, with furrowed forehead.

The woman never stopped rocking. "I'll make us some tea in a bit," she said. "I think I've got some seedy-cake left. How's your mother?" But she didn't really want to know. There was a long silence, full of the sound of rocking.

"I'm not Norman. My name's Chas."

"Chas? Chas? There's so many bairns in your family, I forget."

The woman's pinny had flowers on it. Her hands were clenched in her lap; her hair pulled back tight in a bun. As she rocked, her blue eyes swung up and down, watching something above Chas's head that wasn't really there.

"I'm not part of your family. I think I've found your husband's watch." Chas offered it to her. She did not reach out for it, so he had to press it into her hand. Only then did she look at it.

"Aye, that's Billy's watch. He had it off his da."

Rock, rock, rock.

Chas peered round frantically. What the hell was going on?

There was a photo on the mantelpiece: a bald man with a wrinkly forehead and knowing grin. He had a pint of beer in one hand, and was giving the thumbs-up sign with the other. He looked the sort who would go to the pub with no collar and tie; the sort who told filthy stories and laughed at them himself. It wasn't hard to imagine him being a spy; he'd spend the money on booze and not give two buggers for anybody.

"Is that Bill?"

"Aye, that's our Billy."

Rock, rock, rock. The tick of the clock got louder. The cat stirred again. Chas felt the muscles of his legs and belly getting tighter and tighter. He was really scared; but not of Bill coming home and catching him. Why *was* the room so cold?

"The days are long once I finish my housework," said the woman. "But the cat's company, and everyone's been very kind."

"Is Bill on shiftwork?"

"Billy's dead, hinny. He's been gone eight months, two weeks and six days. But I keep on listening for his step. Daft, isn't it? People keep on telling me I ought to gan out more. But I cannit. I just keep on listening for his step. Them's his slippers, there. He was always so cheery—used to keep me going. But it's the cheery ones that's taken, and the others left. I wish God would let me go to him."

Chas wanted to jump up and run out into the sunshine. The cold in the room was the cold you felt at funerals. But he didn't run away. He asked the question he'd often heard his mother ask.

"How did he come . . . to pass away?"

"He was on the Russian convoys, hinny. He was *that* feared of the cold and dark . . . used to wake up in the night shouting. But he still went. He was the cox'n, and he had to steer the ship. So the captain couldn't ha' done without him, could he? Every trip Billy made was going to be the last—just one more, he'd say, and that's me lot. But the U-boats finished him in the end. He got the crew in the boat, mind, an' got the sail up, but. . . ."

"What happened?" Chas didn't want to know but he had to ask.

"When the convoy was coming back from Russia—weeks later—they found the boat. Billy's hand was still on the tiller, but he was steering north, into the ice. They were all stark frozen stiff. The commodore wrote that Billy was a brave man, who died trying to save his mates. . . . I think I knew it was going to happen. Every other trip Billy pawned his da's watch for a last good booze-up. But that last trip he wouldn't—said he might need it. The commodore sent it back wi' his letter. It had stopped at half-past three."

"Please keep it now, to remember him by."

"*No*, hinny. It was me sold it to the pawnshop. I wouldn't have it in the house. That's not how I want to remember Billy, frozen like a side of beef. I want to remember him singing, after a good booze-up." She raised her cracked voice.

> *"I saw the old homestead and faces I loved*
> *I saw England's valleys and dells*
> *I listened with joy, as I did when a boy*
> *To the sound of the old village bells.*
> *The moon was shining brightly*
> *'Twas a night that would banish all sin*
> *For the bells were ringing the Old Year out*
> *And the New Year in."*

She was silent, rocking. Then she said:

"I'm waiting for God to take me. Then I'll see Billy again."

She stirred herself.

"I'll make some tea, Norman. How's your mother?"

Chas shivered. "I must be going. No thanks."

"Keep the watch, Norman, to remember your Uncle Billy by. And come again. It's company keeps me going. Everyone's been very good. . . ."

The sun was hot on his face, and Sheila's hand was warm. But he couldn't stop shivering as he told them all.

"I must get back to the office," said Audrey, giving Chas a peculiar look. "You going to be all right?"

"Must go and weed tombstones for me dad," said Cem.

Sheila took him for a brisk walk up to the Monument; he was glad she hadn't run away and left him too. But the walk didn't get the cold of the Arctic out of his bones. She put her arms round him, and they watched a flight of Spitfires, and the armed trawlers putting out to sea.

"What a pointless way to die!"

"I don't think there's any way that's not pointless," said Sheila in a low voice, "unless you're very old."

"But what'll *she* do now?"

"Perhaps she'll die soon. Some widows do. It might be best, if it's what she wants."

"But suppose when she does die, he's not *there*?"

"My granny always said love was stronger than the grave. She died three days after my grandpa. She lived her whole life for him. Some women are like that. One day I might start feeling that way about you."

He let her kiss him. It helped a bit, but it didn't drive out the cold. Would he ever be warm again?

Then a little flame lit up inside him. Not love. Hate. *Hate* was stronger than anything. He let it rage through his body, like the only time he had ever drunk whisky.

The woman in the pawnshop had sent him to Bankside Cottages . . . she must have known Billy Mason was dead. . . . He was going to *see* her.

But it wasn't enough to hate a woman who played spiteful tricks . . . the spy . . . the U-boat. Someone was going to pay for Billy Mason. Someone was going to pay, so Chas could forget Billy Mason. The world was full of things to hate, and he was alive again.

Now he knew how Sven felt about the Nazis.

He stood up abruptly.

"Where you going, darling?"

"Back to the pawnshop. For the truth this time."

"And I'm coming with you," said Sheila.

15

"Back so soon, beautiful boy?" Chas could tell from the purr in her voice that she'd been expecting him back. Then she saw Sheila holding Chas's hand. "And brought your nursemaid. Scared?"

"We want to talk to you—in the back!"

"And the manners are not so beautiful now. Orders, suddenly. But this is my home, you know."

"If you don't stop messing, we're going to the *police*."

The woman's enigmatic gaze rested on Sheila's face, then returned to his. A slight smile.

"So, come round."

Chas and Sheila sat side by side on the horsehair sofa.

"That William Mason you told me about—he's been dead eight months."

The woman inclined her head without speaking.

"His wife sold you the watch, after he was dead. You *knew*."

Again a slow mocking nod.

"So why did you send me?"

"Perhaps I thought a beautiful boy would cheer her up? You cheered me up. . . ."

Sheila shot her a look like a dagger. The woman laughed.

"Or perhaps," she added, putting a hand to her hair, "I thought that if I gave you the wrong name you'd come back and see me again, *Liebling*."

"*Liebling* is a German word," said Sheila.

"Yes, I was born in Germany. That is why the police come and inspect me every month, as if I were some cow. I did not have the privilege of being born English."

"That man you sold the watch to—he's a spy."

The woman's dark gaze hardened; all mockery gone.

"Why? Because he is a foreigner too? Are you bored with your school holidays? Tired of tennis? Riding ponies? This is an exciting new game. The Nazi children had similar ones."

"If you really are patriotic British, you would want to help us catch a Nazi."

"I will speak to my father; it was he who sold the watch."

They listened, as she creaked her way upstairs, and across the ceiling overhead. There was a sound of bedsprings, and fretful murmuring. When she came downstairs, her face had changed.

"My father remembers the man. He was a foreigner—a seaman. He was not a good man. He was nervous—he pulled at his ear and watched the door. My father thought he was going to be robbed—but the man paid for three watches and went away."

"What was his name?"

"People do not give their names when they *buy* things."

"What did he *look* like?"

"My father does not know. The man kept his face back in the shadows—it was night. But when he paid, my father noticed he had a ring on the third finger of his right hand. A silver ring—not English. And the man was not a Frenchman, or a Belgian."

"How d'you know that?"

"My father and I had a little time in Belgium, until

the Germans came." The woman played with the bracelets on her wrist.

"My father says you must leave this man alone . . . if he is frightened he may do bad things."

"How can your father *know* that?"

"He has been lending money for fifty years. If he did not watch people, know people, he could not be a pawnbroker."

"Thanks," said Chas, and suddenly smiled at her. Now she'd stopped messing about, he liked her a lot. She was . . . hidden—like a bird you can hear fluttering inside a bush. She must know so many foreign places. He wanted very much to see her again. He felt a curious hot wave of excitement.

"Let me know if he . . . comes back. I'll give you my address."

"Do you trust me then? I might give your address to the spy."

But the heart had gone out of her teasing. Something had broken. He knew he would never see her again. He scribbled his name and address on a piece of paper; and remembered how she had tucked *her* piece of paper into his shirt pocket. . . .

"Goodbye," she said, already retiring into the shadows.

Outside, Chas said awkwardly, "What a strange woman. Thought she might be in with the spy, but she's not. Can't make out what she wanted."

Sheila sniffed. "I can. And it wasn't shipping secrets."

Chas pushed away his cup of British Restaurant tea, half drunk. "So we know he's a working man, a sailor. Not British, or Belgian or French."

"A great pit-ee," said Cem. "Ze French—zey are so sex-ee." He wriggled seductively on his hard chair.

"Sit down, Charles Boyer," said Audrey.

"To continue," said Chas. "He wears a peaked cap, and a silver ring, not English."

"If that lady is to be *believed*," said Cem. "Maybe she was messing you about again."

"I believe her."

"Have you got a soft spot for *her* as well? You're a raving sex maniac, you are."

"I believe her too," said Sheila, icily.

Chas did not look at her. He just blundered on. "He can't be a *real* sailor. Not off the big ships. Or he'd be away from Garmouth six months at a time."

"He could be off the trawler fleet," said Audrey. "Or work at Smith's Dock. Or just hang around the Low Street living off some woman."

"He must have a job," said Sheila. "Or he'd be called up in the Army, or directed to work of national importance. There's an Act of Parliament. . . ."

Audrey sniggered vulgarly. "What do they care in the Low Street about Acts of Parliament? The police don't know half what goes on down Low Street. That lot stick together."

"There are so many secret doors between the houses," said Cem, "that you can go from one end of Low Street to the other, without ever having to see the light of day. . . ."

"And you've got a newspaper cutting to prove it?" asked Audrey.

"It's a rabbit warren," said Cem.

"Munch, *munch!*"

"We must search," said Chas firmly. "For the guy with the silver ring."

"But there's nobody about down there during the day, except ordinary people. That lot only come out after dark."

"Then we go and search after dark."

"In the *blackout*? You won't see your own hand in front of your face."

"Then we'll go in the pubs. That's where the spy gets his info—off drunken sailors."

Audrey turned pale. "You must be out of your mind. Even our chief reporter won't go into those pubs alone after dark." She finished off her coffee, and began gathering her things together. "Besides," she added, comfortably, as if that settled the matter, "you two would just get chucked out as under age."

"Oh, go *on*," exploded Cem. "We don't look *that* young. If I didn't shave for a week. . . ."

Audrey inspected his chin. "Thirty-two hairs. My granny's got a better beard."

"Cem and I could go as greasers," said Chas.

"You mean . . . with big sombreros?" asked Cem, starting to dance the Mexican hat dance, clicking his fingers like castanets.

The couple at the next table paid up and left quickly.

"No, fool. Greasers are the men who grease ships' engines. Dad says they never wash from one week's end to another. Black as pitmen. I could lend you a pair of Dad's old overalls. . . ."

Audrey looked at Sheila. "These two lunatics are going to do it, you know. Whether we come or not. The blind leading the blind."

Sheila looked distinctly worried.

Audrey sat down with a bump and lit another fag. "Be *reasonable*, Chas. Look at the trouble you've caused already. Getting that bunch of dockers into trouble over the *Esperanza*. Frightening that poor Greek half out of his wits. You've nearly been had up in court for burglary. You've nearly been drowned. Just how long d'you think your luck's going to last? Third time's catchy time. . . . Lay off."

"But what if there is a spy?"

"Then it's none of your bloody business. Leave it to the police, before somebody *really* gets hurt."

Something in her voice got through to Chas. He hesitated.

Then Cem sniggered.

"Right!" roared Chas. "We're going. *Right?*"

"All right," said Audrey wearily. "I suppose I'd better come with you. But this is the very last time I keep you out of trouble. Right?"

"Right."

"I'm coming too," said Sheila.

"It's not . . . your kind of place," said Audrey.

"Try and stop me."

"You two could go dressed as tarts," said Cem. "If you put your hair up and paint your faces with that muck you use, who'll know the difference?"

"Thanks. I'm glad you can't tell me from Nelly Stagg."

"Some of the young tarts aren't bad-looking."

"Flattery will get you nowhere." But, slowly, the idea of dressing up as tarts took the girls' fancy. They began working out what clothes to wear with increasing enthusiasm.

"When do we do this, big shot?" asked Audrey. "I mean, Sheila's mother is going to *adore* her wandering round the Low Street at midnight, picking up lascars. Quite the in thing this season, darling. . . ."

"We could pretend to go to the Essoldo, second-house Friday night. That would cover us till half-past ten."

"Does your mother let you go to the pictures late?" asked Audrey.

"If I'm with a girlfriend she knows."

"I'll come round to your house tonight. I'll even wear my old school blazer and pigtails. Buttah won't melt in my mouth."

Sheila flinched, then said:

"Don't you think all this is a bit silly?"

"Oh, the *spy* bit's ridiculous. But I've always wanted to see how the other half lives. Sodom and Gomorrah revisited. By our own girl reporter."

The Gents at the Essoldo was gleaming and deserted. The main movie had just started. Chas finished tucking his jerkin inside his dad's overalls and handed Cem a tin of black gungy mess.

"What's this?"

"Mixture of soot and lard."

"If we get hot, we'll *fry*." Cem applied it liberally to face and hands, stuck Mr. McGill's oldest cap on his head, and peered in the mirror. "What do I look like?"

"Al Jolson, working on munitions."

That was a mistake. Cem started a big song-and-dance number, up and down the long mirror over the wash basins.

A well-dressed man came into the Gents, said, "Excuse me," and dived into the nearest WC like a frightened rabbit.

"Hey, mister," shouted Cem. "You like buy feelthy postcards—very cheap to you, mister?"

The WC flushed in outraged protest.

Normally Chas would have laughed; but tonight he didn't. His stomach felt heavy with fear, like a cannon ball. He had a nasty feeling he'd started something he couldn't control. There was going to be something terrible happen. . . . "C'mon," he said abruptly. "Let's see if the girls are ready."

Out in the foyer, the commissionaire glowered. When the girls arrived, he turned his back with an expressive "Humph."

No wonder. Audrey had achieved miracles with bra straps. Sheila's once-discreet bosom stuck out like a pair of Spitfire nosecones. Her hair, swept up on top of her head with innumerable hairpins, left her slender white neck disturbingly bare. Her sequined dress must have played the star part in many a jumble sale, and her coat was draped loose across her shoulders.

Chas could hardly recognize her face. Black-penciled eyebrows tilted up in a look of permanent stupid surprise. Her mouth was a scarlet Lana Turner gash. She looked every inch the tart who went out with American soldiers.

If anything, Audrey looked worse.

"Rubbish!" said the commissionaire loudly, as they passed him going out.

Chas didn't like feeling like rubbish. But the girls were in a high old mood; almost Cem-ish.

"Here, carry our suitcase, little Chas," said Audrey, in the transatlantic drawl certain girls used. "Want some gum, Sheel?"

"Yeah, Aud!"

"Let's hurry," said Chas. But it was hard to get them to hurry, as they teetered down Tanner's Bank in unaccustomed high heels. And they wouldn't stop giggling.

"What do I do with this suitcase? It'll look daft in a pub."

"You're on leave from your ship, little Chas," said Audrey. "Seeing the bright lights of Garmouth. *Home is the sailor.* . . ."

The girls giggled afresh.

But it seemed to Chas that they slithered down the cobbles into a great gulf of dark, only broken by the fireflies of dimmed car headlights moving on the far side of the river; and out to sea, the intermittent stars of the lighthouses. No air-raid warden could put them out. They might help bombers and U-boats, but without *them*, ships would just sink on the rocks anyway. But in the otherwise total dark, the lighthouse stars seemed dangerously bright, casting four walking shadows like intermittent ghosts on the blitz-stripped walls and chimneys of Tanner's Bank. A cold wind off the sea made the girls yelp as it curled round their nyloned legs. A wind from Norway and Denmark; a German wind. . . .

In front, the girls suddenly hesitated, making him bump into them with the suitcase.

"What the—?" Then he saw why they'd stopped.

Through the eerie lighthouse flickers, a solitary figure was climbing up toward them. As Chas watched, the figure suddenly transferred itself from the left-hand pavement to the right. Then back to the left, stumbling over the curb and mumbling incoherently.

"Mind out—a drunk," said Audrey, and laughed.

They went on cautiously.

Ten yards off, the figure lifted his white blur of a face and noticed them. "Are you Sally Army lasses? Aah must talk to a Sally Army lass." He came on at a shambling run.

"We're not Sally Army," said Audrey sharply. The drunk paused, looking from one girl to the other.

"No, Aah can see that," said the drunk bitterly. "Ye're a pair of young hoo-ers." But he still came on, arms groping.

Chas got in the way, just in time. The drunk wrapped both arms round him, swinging him round and round in a dizzying waltz. Chas tried in vain to hold him still. "All right, mate, you're all right. You're all right."

"Where's them two young hoo-ers?"

"Gone," said Chas soothingly. Audrey and Sheila were safe, twenty yards down the pavement. Cem lingered half-way.

"Good," said the drunk. "Good. Ye're a good mate, Nobby. A good mate te me." He was trying to burrow closer into Chas's body, like a baby does. "Aah've got to tell ye, Nobby. Aah've been a bad bugger. Aah've done terrible things, *terrible* things. . . ."

"You're all right," insisted Chas, trying to break away.

But the drunk clung tighter. His whisky breath kept hitting Chas in the face, warm, sweet and horrible. "Aah'm not all right. Aah've done terrible things. Aah'm damned, Nobby. Aah'm going to Hell. An' Aah'll tell ye something else, Nobby."

He held Chas at arm's length, nodding with great conviction. "Hell's doon under the sea, Nobby. It comes up at night, when ye're just sailing along in a flat calm. Devil's waiting. Then there's flames, Nobby, spreadin' all over the water an' a hundred foot high. An' ye can hear the screamin' doon there. Ye never heard screamin' like it, Nobby. Tommy Jones is down there, Nobby—remember Tommy Jones, the donkey-man? An' little Jock Spivey an' our Steve . . . ?"

"You'd better get back to your ship," said Chas desperately.

"Aye—me ship. Where *is* me ship, Nobby?"

"What ship you on?"

"The *Cleveland*—no, she's gone. The *Bay of Malta*—no, she's gone an' all . . . the *Clifton* . . . the *Hettie?* Aah cannit remember. . . . Aah's on *your* ship, Nobby. Ye knaa which ship . . . divven't kid us, Nobby. Take us back to our ship. . . ."

Cem hovered nearer. Chas called, "Give me a hand with him!"

"Not bloody likely. He'll just grab me an' all."

"What shall I do?"

"Shove him off and leave him. He's only tight. Come on, you're wasting time."

"*Help* us, Nobby . . . back to the ship. . . ."

"*Leave* him—we haven't got all bloody night."

The drunk heard. He clung tighter, started to cry. "Don't leave us, Nobby, don't leave us, don't leave us."

"Tata," said Cem, walking away.

Chas panicked, pushed the drunk with all his strength. The drunk fell into the gutter.

Chas ran. At a safe distance, he turned. The drunk was still lying in the gutter, sobbing. "Don't leave us, Nobby. Aah'm going down te Hell."

"It's a cold night," said Chas.

"All the more reason for us to keep moving," said Cem. "Cops'll pick him up—drunk and incapable."

"He wanted help. . . ."

"Just the booze talking."

"Hard sod." But he followed Cem, arms and legs jumping with nerves; sweat drying on him, freezing. So wet he thought for an awful moment the drunk had. . . . But it was OK, the outside of his overalls was dry. Just his own sweat.

"You all right, Chas?" called Sheila.

"We'll try the Old Hundred first," said Audrey. "I'll get the drinks. You lot wouldn't know what to ask for."

They pushed through the blackout curtain over the door.

Their first glimpse of Sodom was a letdown. Three middle-aged shipyard riveters drinking steadily before going home. Discussing tomorrow's football at Newcastle.

They made the most of Audrey's hip-swinging as she walked across to the bar. Enjoyed Sheila's first attempt to cross her legs in a tarty way. Then they pronounced loudly that it was *disgusting*. The girls were young enough to be their daughters. If *they*'d had daughters who behaved like that, they'd have put a strap across their backsides. What were things coming to? It was all the fault of the war.

Then they returned to the more pressing problem of whether Andy Dudgeon was the center-half Gateshead really needed.

Others in the bar were keener in their scrutiny. The barman, sporting a George Raft hairstyle with sideburns, kept peering at Chas and Cem, trying to make out how old they were, under the soot and lard. Cem tried a string of Glaswegian oaths; but his throat seized up after three, and he was reduced to helpless coughing. Chas lit up a fag and blew a vigorous smoke screen.

Audrey returned with the drinks.

"Beer!" called a spiteful female voice. "Must be amateur night tonight, girls. I might be getting past it, but I wouldn't do it on *beer*."

A pair of what Cem always called *"les demoiselles de la nuit"* were sitting in the far corner. They'd obviously abandoned any hope of trade from the shipyard workers, because one was doing her hair and the other was reading the *Sporting Pink*.

Chas covered his confusion with a large swig of beer. It tasted like old cycle inner tubes.

"Where you from, dear?" called the nearest *demoiselle*. In spite of her jet-black hair, Chas could have sworn she was older than his Aunt Aggie. She sat in the same despairing sag-thighed way.

"The *Alaska Pine*," said Chas gruffly.

"Funny. Could have sworn the *Pine* sailed yesterday. Jumped ship, 'ave yer? No wonder you can only afford *beer*. Anyway," she swiveled her eyes malevolently, "I was referring to the *ladies* wiv' yer. Bit off your patch, dears, ain't you? Police getting keen at Newcastle?"

"Get lost," said Audrey.

"Get lost, is it?" The *demoiselle* heaved herself to her feet and advanced. "You come on our patch and tell *us* to get lost?" She tried staring Audrey out and failed.

"Talking to me like that, and me old enough to be your mother."

"Grandmother," corrected Audrey nastily. What on earth had got into her?

"Ey," said George Raft. "Women fighting I draw the line at."

The *demoiselle* came to heel like a well-trained dog.

"And drink up, you lot. Before the police gets wind of yer; or Nelly."

"He means us," said Cem, swallowing his half-pint without pausing to draw breath. Chas and Sheila abandoned theirs, but Audrey drank hers very slowly, eyeing the *demoiselle*; until the *demoiselle* swept past them and went out of the door, as if she had suddenly made up her mind to do something, urgently.

Outside in the blackout, Cem said, "I feel sick."

"Serve you right for swallowing so quick," spat Audrey. "You were hopeless, all of you. Convincing as a pack of Brownies."

"None of those men wore a silver ring," said Sheila.

"I don't think this idea is going to work," said Chas.

Audrey turned on him in a fury. "It was *your* idea. *I* spend hours getting us ready. *I* spend *my* money on beer. Now you want to back out, after the first pub."

"That one was so *ordinary*."

"Right," said Audrey. "We'll try the Bullring then."

The others gasped. The Duke of Westminster was known as the Bullring from Hong Kong to Buenos Aires. Once a Georgian customs house, its huge Ionic columns were now black as soot, except where bombs had chipped sandy-colored lumps off them. It was splattered with yellow signs saying *S.P. Here and Fire Hydrant 4 Ft.* One end, now discreetly dark and silent, housed the Ministry of Ag and Fish. The rest, with a sound like a football crowd leaking out through its tattered blackout curtains, was Sin HQ, Garmouth.

As they opened the swinging door, the noise hit them like a bomb. The place seemed on fire, but it was only the blue whirl of fag smoke. It was jammed to the doors. People kept sticking their elbows into

Chas and shouting "Mind your back." Missing him by inches with tin trays on which pint glasses were practically afloat in loose swilling beer that spouted to the floor with every joggle of the barmaid's plump elbows. Every so often there would be a thump that would shake the sawdusted floor; and a scream from some woman hidden by the thronging heads of the crowd.

Above the heads, the walls were hung with stuffed flying fish, ships' lifebelts, Spanish bullfight posters, the tattered tricolors of Holland and France, and notices saying:

Customers are requested to expectorate in the spittoons provided.

Careless talk costs lives—be like Dad, keep Mum, and,

Do not request credit, as a refusal can only offend.

From the chandeliers hung the shriveled red-white-and-blue corpses of Christmas balloons, and a homemade banner reading:

GOD HELP OUR KING!

A plump ginger lady in backless evening dress was sitting at the piano, pounding out "The White Cliffs of Dover" for the third time, by request. Her pet terrier sat on the piano top, drinking beer out of a selection of pint pots, and slopping most of it down the piano's exposed wires. But her playing was better than the singing. Two hundred foreign sailors' heads were thrown back, exposing shining teeth, stumps of teeth or none.

The Duke of Westminster was Sodom indeed. There was much sitting on knees, and changing to other knees, and every so often a woman would take a sailor by the hand and lead him upstairs, saying to her friend:

"Keep me seat, Doris, I won't be long."

But it was the hands that hypnotized Chas, when

he could keep his watering eyes open against the fag smoke. Hands drifting up women's skirts, lifting beer mugs, lighting fags, scratching under armpits, beckoning barmaids, reaching in trouser pockets and counting out currency notes of twenty different countries. Hands that wriggled like a bed of maggots; hands that were never still, so you couldn't make out if they were wearing rings or not. But there *were* rings; a lot of rings. Death's-head rings, wedding rings, engagement rings and gold rings half an inch thick.

It was at that point that Chas despaired. He *knew* it had been a mistake to come—a horrible mistake.

Audrey thrust another mug of beer into his hand, and he sipped it miserably. He hugged Sheila to him for comfort, only to find that another, thicker arm was already round her waist.

"'Allo! What you want to trink wid little boys for? You come drink wid big sailor. I buy you gin!"

A huge blond creature with close-cropped hair was nuzzling into Sheila's white neck, and Sheila was standing frozen like a terrified rabbit.

"You nice girl. You ver' priddy girl. Come to my table, huh?"

Sheila mumbled something inaudible, blinking helplessly. The huge sailor threw Chas's arms off, and began to drag Sheila away, almost picking her up bodily.

Chas followed, clawing his way through the crowd, wondering frantically what to do.

"Put my girl *down!*"

The sailor turned, smiled good-humoredly, and put a huge hand against Chas's chest. Then he pushed, sending Chas flying to the floor ten yards away, among the legs of the crowd.

There was a great unfair roar of laughter. Blind with

rage, Chas ran back, reached out a foot and tripped the sailor up. The sailor fell on top of Sheila, making the sawdust jump as he hit the floorboards.

There was instant silence. People began moving subtly sideways, until a solid ring had formed around Chas and the sailor.

The sailor got up.

Chas got up.

The sailor reached for a beer bottle, and broke it on the bar counter. The tinkle of glass seemed to last an eternity in the silence. The barman said:

"No trouble, Dirk. I don't want the police in here *again* tonight." But his voice was despairing.

Chas was able to study the sailor in great detail, because the sailor was not in any great hurry. He looked like a pig, with blond bristles round his snout. No ring on *his* finger. . . .

Surely, thought Chas, there is some way in which a highly intelligent human being can outwit this human pig? But he couldn't think of anything. Meanwhile, the sharp ends of the bottle waved slowly closer.

Then Sheila stepped forward. Her elaborate hairdo had collapsed in the scuffle. Most of her make up had wiped off onto the sailor's jacket.

"Stop this ridiculous nonsense at *once*. This is absolutely *disgraceful*."

More than any police whistle, the voice cut through the tension in the bar. The voice of outraged middle-class morality; of the woman magistrate and the lady from the Welfare. . . .

"Who *are* you, miss?" said the barman.

"My name is Smythson!"

"Your dad *Councillor* Smythson?" A sigh of horror broke from the crowd. Smythson, Chairman of the

Watch Committee; Smythson, the hardest beak north of the river. The crowd shrank back. All except the sailor with the bottle, who shook his head in bafflement, and shambled forward again.

"Stop him, for Gawd's sake!" screeched the barman. "I'll lose me license!"

A hundred hands grabbed for the sailor. He struggled. Then somebody invisible behind the crowd hit him twice with something small and brown. He collapsed and was borne away on many willing shoulders.

"For Gawd's sake," pleaded the barman, "take your friends away from here, miss. Whatever ye're up to, just take them away and don't *never* bring them back."

16 Face burning, Sheila followed Chas through the blackout curtain. Outside, the night enveloped her like black velvet. She stood still, waiting for her breathing to quieten, and her eyes to get used to the dark.

Audrey bumped into her back, said, "Oops," and giggled. For some reason, she grabbed Audrey's hand.

"Chas?" she called. There was a sound in the darkness, like someone hitting a tennis ball hard. Then a sigh that she somehow knew was Chas; and a rustle of clothing, like someone sitting down.

"Chas!" she screamed.

As if in answer, hands grabbed her arms. Small hands, almost children's hands. The hands thrust her forward into blackness. She dug in her feet and opened her mouth to scream again. Something hard crashed into her ribs, and after that all she could think about was trying to breathe. Her legs moved loosely beneath her, of their own accord.

By the time she was taking notice again, they were walking along Low Street. On her left, Bank Top stretched up and away, long grass glimmering under a touch of moonlight.

Three people were walking in front, close together. Two were little men in belted raincoats and trilby hats. Between them, sobbing and gasping, was Audrey.

She seemed in a bad way; swaying from side to side. The little men, who hardly came up to her ears, were having a terrible time holding her up.

Then Audrey's legs gave way completely.

The little men hauled her doggedly onward. Her toes scraped along the cobbles, and one of her shoes came off. Sheila could hear the little men panting.

Given Audrey's solid nine stone, there was only one possible end. The whole group collapsed to the ground, one of the little men underneath. The other bent over Audrey, shaking her. Audrey's nyloned leg flashed out in one tremendous kick, and the man collapsed on the cobbles, making heartrending noises.

Next second, Audrey had leaped up, kicked off her remaining shoe, and was streaking up Bank Top.

The little men picked themselves up and set off in pursuit. But one was limping badly, and the other seemed reluctant to get too far ahead. Audrey had twenty yards clear lead as she reached the top and vanished from view.

"Don't you get any ideas, Mary," said the little man on Sheila's right arm. "When they catch her, she's *sorry*. Yes-no?" They pushed Sheila forward again, their fingers digging into her arms more cruelly than ever.

"Please stop it—you're hurting," gasped Sheila.

They giggled, as if they were playing with a kitten or a puppy.

"We not hurt—Nelly wants you nice."

Then they stopped again.

"Police," said the one on the left.

A hundred yards ahead, two policemen were lighting up fags in a shop doorway. The flame of the match outlined their pointed helmets. Sheila opened her mouth to scream. A fist banged into her ribs again. She couldn't breathe, and at the same time she felt sick.

One of the men took a little bottle out of his pocket, and splashed something round Sheila's neck. The reek of whisky came up, making her retch helplessly. Then the little men were dragging her forward again.

The policemen stepped out, not bothering to throw away their cigarettes.

"What's going on?" The bigger policeman sounded nastier than any policeman Sheila had ever met. Nasty and bullying.

"She have too much to drink, sir!" said the little man on Sheila's right.

"We are taking her back to Nelly's," said the little man on the left.

Sheila tried to say something, but her tongue was paralyzed. She couldn't even lift her head. The bigger policeman grabbed her hair, and pulled her head back. She began to be sick.

"Disgusting," said the policeman. "And she can't be a day over eighteen. You ought to keep closer tabs on these young'uns, Louis. I could run this one in for being drunk and incapable; little cow."

He let go of Sheila's hair, and her head flopped back on her chest. Why couldn't she *speak?*

"We take her straight home, sir," said Louis. "And next time I see you, I give you bottle whisky for favor."

"See you bloody do. Now run along." The policemen retired to their doorway to finish their cigarettes.

At last the little men turned up an alley, to a door where a red light showed, no bigger than a torch bulb. Through the blackout curtain was a narrow corridor: wooden-boarded walls painted pink. There was a smell of cats and perfume. A lot of doors led off the corridor. One of the little men began knocking on them, and getting muffled angry answers. At last, he found one room unoccupied.

They pushed her through the door and locked it behind her. She stared around. The room seemed no bigger than a cupboard; just large enough to take a bed and a chair.

Next door, through the thin wooden partition, she heard bedsprings begin to creak.

Cem was right fed up. At first he'd been quite pleased with himself for remembering the suitcase they'd left behind in the Duke of Westminster. Daring to go back for it under the angry glowers of the boozers.

But when he got outside again, there was nobody about. He shouted Chas's name angrily; got no reply. Had they gone off and left him? Or were they hiding up some side alley, stuffing hankies in their stupid mouths to stop themselves giggling?

He set off along the Low Street. When they saw

him making off with the suitcase full of their clothes, they'd have to follow. Then the laugh'd be on them.

After he'd walked quite a way, and the case was hurting his hand, he heard them following him in the dark. They were pretty quiet, but he had good hearing. Every time he spun round and shouted at them, he could hear them ducking into some doorway. He yelled that he could see them; would they grow up and stop messing around, for God's sake; it was nearly time to go home?

No reply.

All right. Two could play at that game. He ran down Wooden Dolly Alley and settled in a nook at the far end, behind the suitcase. The nook was stacked with old beer bottles. Better keep very still, or the bottles would rattle and give him away.

There they were now, clever buggers, silhouetted against the moonlit bulk of Bank Top. But only two of them. Had Sheila gone home already? What about her clothes?

They came closer, muttering. In one second he'd jump out with a great yell. Frighten them out of their silly wits. . . .

Why were they wearing trilby hats?

Then the front one stepped into an especially clear patch of moonlight. He wore strange shoes. Dark sides and white tops. . . .

There was a wild animal inside Cem. It made him a superb scrum-half. It often scored ties in rugby matches before he realized he had the ball in his hands. It scared him a bit.

The animal acted now. Grabbed the neck of a beer bottle and threw it. Not at the men in trilbies. At the wall above their heads.

The bottle shattered. Cem heard the sharp fragments hitting the cobbles like shrapnel. The little men raised their arms above their heads to ward off the flying glass. Suddenly they looked like pathetic clowns.

Cem rose to his feet, throwing bottle after bottle with gleeful accuracy; missing them by inches.

The Maltese turned and ran. Clem lobbed a last bottle at the pavement just behind them. They jumped in the air like Laurel and Hardy, as the slivers of glass hit their ankles. They vanished round the corner, leaving Cem hooting derisively.

Until he looked at his feet.

There were only five bottles left.

It was Sven's boat or nothing. He always wore the key to it round his neck on a string, as Chas did.

He lobbed one bottle down the alley at random, just to let the Maltese know he hadn't forgotten them. Then he ran down the steps, threw the suitcase into the boat, undid the padlock and began to draw the chain out from the oars.

Instinct warned him it was time to run up the steps again. The Maltese were halfway up the alley, holding scarves over their faces to protect themselves against flying glass.

He gave them a salvo of three bottles. But his aim was poor, and they only ducked for cover into a doorway. And the moment he stopped throwing, they came on again. His last bottle didn't even make them pause.

Cem panicked and ran blindly down the steps. Tripped and landed headlong in the boat, his knees and shins a mindless agony. He crouched, unable to move. Heard shouting, and their feet on the steps. . . .

Then silence. He opened his eyes; looked back. The shore was twenty yards away and still receding.

The force of his arrival had been enough to slip the chain, and send the boat skimming out over the surface of the river.

The Maltese stood jabbering helplessly on the stair. Thank God they couldn't swim!

When he'd got his breath back, he unshipped the oars and started to row. But the moon had gone in, and it was infernally dark. He could see neither bank of the river. And when he did find one, he couldn't tell if it was the north bank or the south. Maybe he had rowed round in circles. Certainly he was completely lost.

It was then that he heard the sound of another boat's oars. Nobody said the Maltese couldn't row. . . .

The moment Chas wakened, he knew he wouldn't be going to school that day. His head was splitting. His face was all pins and needles. It was pitch dark and he was freezing. What terrible disease had he caught? Scarlet fever? Diphtheria? No, he'd been inoculated against diphtheria at school. Lockjaw?

He tried shouting to Mam in the other bedroom. But his voice wouldn't work. He tried pushing himself up on his mattress, then found it wasn't his mattress. He was lying on cobbles, and there were no blankets. A wind was blowing. He was outdoors. Or was it a bad dream?

He heard footsteps approaching, and a cheerful song.

"Glory us, glory us,
  One pint of beer between the four of us,
  Glory be to God there were no more of us. . . ."

The singer tripped over Chas, and fell with a curse. Then he sat up and struck a match.

"*Hallo*, Chas. What you doink heres?"

It was Sven. Chas tried telling him what had happened, but the words kept coming out funny.

"Alley Ooops," said Sven cheerfully, hauling Chas to his feet. "Hey!" he added, feeling the back of Chas's head. "Someone biffed you, hein? Bloody-damn odd. I buy you drink and you tell me about it." He began hauling Chas into the Duke of Westminster.

"*GOD!* Not in there. . . ."

"OK. We find quiet joint. Snack bar."

The snack bar contained nothing more threatening than tea-washed tables and plates of cold chips. Chas warmed his hands round a steaming mug of cocoa, and told Sven everything. It seemed to take forever.

"Perhaps your friends ran away, when the man hit you."

"Cem might. Sheila wouldn't. The spy's got 'em."

"Three is bit of handful for one spy!"

"Nico Mintoff's lot will be helping him," said Chas bitterly. "Funny thing is, I think I should *know* who the spy is, now. I feel I've got all the bits of the jigsaw in my mind, but I can't fit 'em together. . . . My head's so woozy. . . ."

Chas could tell Sven was worried, from the way he sat with furrowed forehead, hands clenched under the table.

"Look," said Sven at last, "this too difficult for me. Captain Burley will know best. The tug is at the harbor mouth—we are on duty tonight, in case ships gettink in trouble. Come and see captain. I row you out in jiffy!"

It was tempting. At that moment Dick Burley seemed

as big and safe as the Rock of Gibraltar. But what could Dick *do*, stuck out there on the river? The important thing was to find Sheila, and quick. Even if the spy hadn't got her. . . . The snack bar clock said ten P.M. The Essoldo would be coming out soon. How could he get Sheila home? Where was the suitcase with her clothes?

"Sorry, Sven. Can't come. *Must* find Sheila."

"No, no. You come out to boat. We must see to your poor head." Sven was getting all worked up. Why were foreigners so excitable? "Commink with me you must!"

But at that moment, the snack bar door opened. Andy, the *Hendon*'s engineer, shoved his whiskery face in.

"Hey, Sven, bloody come on! Got to get steam up. Where the hell you been? Looked everywhere for you. Don't you know what time it is?"

"Cheerio, Chas. Good luck," said Sven, jumping up.

"But . . . but . . . shall I come?"

"No—no time now," said Sven, and was gone.

Chas sat on. He ought to do something, but he couldn't think what. The snack bar was warm and quiet. His legs were far away and asleep. The peroxide-blond granny behind the counter said, "Want another cocoa, dear?" in a pointed way. That meant buy something or get out. Chas gave her his last sixpence, and sipped the cocoa. It tasted lousy, but it was hot.

"Like some music?" asked the blond granny, and switched on the old radio behind the counter, without waiting for an answer. The smooth rhythms of Victor Sylvester's Ballroom Orchestra filled the grease-laden air. Soothing. . . .

Until the crackling and buzzing started.

The woman banged the wireless on its left-hand side. "Bloody thing."

The crackling didn't stop. She banged the wireless on top instead. But the crackling persisted. Chas could have told her it would.

"Bloody atmospherics," said the woman. "The Government shouldn't allow it. What do we pay our wireless licenses for?"

But she looked up to find her snack bar empty. Chas was gone, running.

"Funny kid!" said the woman.

Chas ran and ran toward the harbor mouth. He kept bumping into parked fish carts and dust bins, tripping over the curb because he couldn't see very well out of his right eye. All that side was swimmy and vague. He tried closing his right eye. But the things on the right were still woozy. That knock on the head. . . . But the big throbbing bruise was over his left ear. . . .

He knew running like this wasn't logical. The enamel bowl he was running after was either stuck on Fish Quay Sands by now, or floating out between the piers. If it was stuck on the Sands, it could wait till morning. If it was already out between the piers. . . .

All along the Low Street, the sound of violins and crackles boomed out behind blackout curtains. Even the Maltese must be Victor Sylvester fans.

Then Chas stopped running.

Because the radios had stopped crackling. Sylvester's strict-tempo rhythms flowed on sweet and uninterrupted. Chas looked at his watch. The crackling had only lasted five minutes. The bowl's battery should have lasted at least an hour.

The U-boat must have picked it up.

Another ship was going to die.

Chas ran on toward the Lifeboat gangway, not knowing what he hoped to see, just unable to stand still.

Then he saw what he had hoped to see. *Hendon* steaming out between the piers, funnel shooting red sparks like a volcano. Dick had heard the crackle. Dick was keeping his word. Dick was looking into it.

Far too late, of course. But still *marvelous*. How could Britain lose, with men like Dick Burley? Chas felt close to tears, like a soft tart. He wiped one eye with the cuff of his overalls.

The red volcano faded to a dot, weaving back and forth across the sea. Then, clear over the water, came the *tacca-tacca-tacca* of a Lewis gun. Good old Sven. He'd *spotted* the bastards.

Or was he firing at shadows? The U-boat should have submerged long since. As Dick said, Jerry was no fool.

Or was the U-boat somehow stuck on the surface? No way of telling.

The sound of the Lewis gun stopped. The red spot of *Hendon*'s funnel weaved about the sea a little more; then the tug came back up-river and resumed station. No hooting; no celebrations. They'd drawn a blank.

He wished he could find out what had happened. But it seemed so far to where Sven's boat was tied up, and he was a worse rower even than Cem.

He sat down on the Lifeboat gangway, too tired to move. But the Sands reminded him of Sheila, and he grew frantic again. And—and—suppose the U-boat struck the same night it got its message? Somewhere at sea, at this very moment, some British ship. . . .

What could he do?

Tell the police? They wouldn't believe a word. Tell Mr. Kallonas? The police wouldn't believe Mr. Kallonas either. Anyway, he still had no proof that Mr. Kallonas wasn't the spy . . . a very clever spy playing with him like a cat plays with a mouse. Chas's head kept expanding and contracting like a balloon, as the waves of thought came faster and faster. He began to run again, because he couldn't sit still.

He ran through the open gate of the Fish Quay. It should have been empty; the herring fleet was down south. But it was full.

A long row of gray shapes, moored in ghostly moonlight. Moon-silvered glass domes of radar against the sky. Four-inch gun turrets. Depth charges ranged in deadly clusters. He peered at the name on the stern of the nearest ship.

Acanthus, Arbutus, Virago, Lord Grey and *Lord Coyne*.

Cousin Robert's East Coast Convoy escort group.

It was too good to be true. They were run-down, mind, stone-cold. Every funnel smokeless against the sky. In harbor for a boiler-clean. But Cousin Robert would be there. He would listen; he would know what to do. Radios crackling. Sailors piling ashore in white gaiters with rifles, enough to deal with every rotten spy and Maltese in the Low Street.

Chas took a deep breath and ran up the empty gangway of the *Virago*. A figure in white gaiters and holster belt moved out of the shadows. "What's your business, lad?"

"I've come to see Commander McGill," panted Chas.

*

The door opened. A Maltese came in, and flattened himself deferentially against the wall. Then looked expectantly toward the door.

A woman stood there, tall, straight as a ramrod. Harsh red hair done up with pins like a Japanese woman's. Hair gray at the roots. The face under the make up could have been any age; but the dark eyes were bright and sharp.

Sheila had an absurd desire to spring to her feet, like you would for a headmistress. But she made herself stay sitting down.

The eyes roamed over Sheila slowly: coat, dress, shoes, hair, face.

"You've not starved," said the woman. "Have you?"

Sheila shook her head mutely.

"Or worked for your living, either. Lady's hands. And a lady's coat. Right?"

"Yes." Sheila found her voice somehow.

"And never been with a feller in your life?"

"No."

"And you come from Whitley Bay?"

Sheila just nodded, amazed.

"You stupid young cow! What the hell you trying to do? Find out how the other half lives?"

Sheila nodded.

"Pity a Swede didn't get hold on you—you'd mevve have found out. What's your name?"

"Sheila Smythson."

The woman's hand tightened on the door handle—so much that Sheila expected the handle to snap off. "Smythson's daughter." It wasn't a question; it was a statement.

Sheila nodded a third time. Now there was so much violence in the room she was afraid to speak.

The Maltese wasn't so wise. "We didn't *know*, Nelly. Mary Kerr said. . . ."

Nelly hit him one blow, with her open hand. He was flung back against his wall like a doll. Slid down the wall to the floor, trilby hat tipping over his eyes.

It should have been comic; but it wasn't.

"Ye've done for yourself, Louis," said Nelly. "An' ye've done for me an' all. Tek her upstairs."

"Bugger off, kid," said the ship's sentry.

"*Please*," said Chas. "It's urgent family business. Somebody's died."

"Pull the other leg," said the sentry. "It's got bells on it."

Chas groped desperately through the hole in his overalls, into his trouser pocket. Had he got his identity card? Was he wearing the right trousers?

His hand closed over the card. He showed it to the sentry.

"*Charles McGill*," read out the sentry ponderously, by the light of a shaded torch. Then he surveyed Chas's appearance. "You're not one of the Old Man's family. You're not his sort."

"Please, he's my cousin. Only he's the posh end of the family, who live in Whitley Bay. But we've got the same granny, and she wants to see him before she dies."

"Thought you said she was *dead*," said the sentry.

"No . . . at least she might be dead by now, for all I know."

The sentry hesitated, impressed by the official document. The kid seemed genuinely frantic. . . . If he did the wrong thing now, it could mean trouble in the morning. . . .

"Regulating Petty Officer," bawled the sentry. After that, it wasn't his responsibility.

An imposing figure marched down the deck, inspected the identity card and heard the story.

"Christ," he said. "This is all the Old Man needs, after the trip *we*'ve had. Won't it wait, kid? Till morning, eh?"

"She's *dying*. The doctor's there. And the vicar. She keeps breathing funny, then waking up and asking for *him*."

The petty officer moved from foot to foot with indecision.

"It won't be any use, kid, you know. It's our first night back in port."

"Look!" screeched Chas. "My *dad* sent me."

The petty officer shrugged. "Come on, then. But you're wasting your time."

He led Chas up onto the bridge. The handrail on the ladder was all twisted, so that Chas slipped and nearly fell.

"Force nine gale off Yarmouth," explained the petty officer. "Watch your hand on the plating, there."

Chas gaped. The plates of the bridge had been opened up jaggedly, like a sardine tin.

"E-boat . . . ?"

"Well, it weren't mice, son."

He led Chas through a door with a wheel in the center of it. The next door said:

Comm. N. E. R. McGill, R.N.

Chas took a deep breath, preparing himself for the towering figure with jutting beard and rows of medals, so familiar from the *Evening News*. He hoped Cousin Robert would understand the reason he'd *had* to lie. . . .

The petty officer knocked on the door; again and again. A faint murmur replied. The petty officer opened the door and gabbled:

"Member of your family to see you, sir!" Then he pushed Chas through, and closed the door quickly behind him.

The stink was terrible. Mainly sweaty socks, but someone had been sick as well; and over all, the cloying hated smell of whisky. Wet clothes tossed in heaps. The white walls of the cabin were streaked red with rust; green mold grew in patches on the ceiling; moisture streamed everywhere.

A man sat at a desk covered with papers. Bottle in his left hand, glass in his right. Head drooping, nearly among the papers.

The man looked up at Chas, as if he was pulling his head up on wires. He wore a white polo-neck sweater, very dirty.

"Yes? What is it?"

This wasn't Cousin Robert. Cousin Robert was only thirty, and this man was older than Dad. Gray-haired, unshaven, deeply lined face with dirt ingrained in the lines. This was some mucky old sea cook . . . the petty officer had played a nasty joke.

But the uniform jacket that hung over the man's chair carried the commander's rings.

"Won't you sit down?" asked the man, with careful politeness. "Will you have a drink?"

Chas shook his head silently; the man returned to staring at the papers on his desk.

"We're going to lose, you know," he said, as if talking about the weather. "We've got to support groups, escort carriers, long-range Liberators now. Everything we thought we needed to win. But we're losing. It's not working. Jerry's building U-boats faster than we can sink them." He refilled his glass. A lot of whisky slopped onto his papers; ink began to run.

"Know how many ships we lost in March? Over a hundred. Faster than we can replace them. Six more months like March, and it's all over."

"I'm sorry," said Chas stiffly, as if the man had told him someone had died. Did they really have moaning misery guts like this in the Navy? Spreading alarm and despondence was a *crime*. . . .

"You know how many U-boats operated against SC 121? *Eighteen*. The last night we had fog and a gale. You'd have thought that would have kept Jerry's head down. I was working down the middle of the convoy, just trying to keep them on station. The masthead lookout reported a breaking sea to port . . . thought it was a torpedo . . . but it was a U-boat on the surface. Right in the middle of the convoy. Tried to ram, but he dodged. We were so close we could hear the Jerry captain giving helm orders. *That* close. . . . We missed him, and he sank two more. If we can't even keep 'em out of the middle of the convoys. . . ."

"Mr. Churchill said we're *winning* the Battle of the Atlantic!"

The man turned and stared at him. "Civ—civ—civilian morale must be preserved at all costs." Then he hiccuped, and went on hiccuping so it was awful to listen to. Holding a handkerchief to his face that was all dark-brown stains like nose bleeds.

"Sir?"

The man focused his attention with an effort. "Yes?"

"There's a U-boat off the Gar. . . ."

"Range? Bearing?" A change had come over the man.

He was no longer flopping, but rigidly upright, hands crushing the papers on his desk into tight balls.

"Range?" he called again. "Bearing?" He kept swallowing over and over, as if he had something stuck in his throat. And belching in between. Then he swung in his swivel chair, and pulled the plug out of the voice pipe at his elbow.

"Captain to bridge. Captain to bridge."

There was no reply. Chas knew the bridge was empty, save for the night wind. He listened with horror as the man talked in turn to an empty radar shack, a nonexistent Asdic operator. In a funny automatic repeating way, like the machine in the fairground that tells your weight.

Only this machine was running down. The man's head drooped, till his face rested among the papers.

Chas fled from the horrible mechanical man in his dripping rabbit hutch. Down the ladder, back the way he had come.

The petty officer was waiting; read the look on his face. "Hard luck, kid. I did warn you. First night in port. Come back in the morning."

When Chas was halfway down the gangplank, the petty officer called after him:

"And keep your mouth shut, kid. Our Old Man's the best there is."

Audrey wished she'd never started smoking.

The wide streets that led up toward Northumberland Square were deserted; the Georgian houses where the sea captains used to live were boarded up. Bombed in 1940. Nobody lived there anymore.

The moonlit pavements were cold beneath her

stockinged feet. Like a dream. All she could hear was her own breathing, getting more ragged. And the footsteps of the men behind.

They were waiting for her to make a mistake; to run up some side alley where they could pounce. So she stayed in the middle of the broadest streets, and prayed the moon wouldn't go behind a cloud.

The Maltese were nervous, here in the upper town. Because there were still a few people about. Courting couples in doorways; solitary men going on night shift. Audrey was tempted to ask for help. But people never interfered when the Maltese were after their women. Tarts only got what they deserved. Why should a decent man risk a knife for that sort?

But Audrey slowed as she passed the couples, getting a breather. As if in collusion, the Maltese slowed too. The couples knew damn well what was going on, but they kept their faces turned away.

What should she do? She hadn't the strength to run all the way home. Besides, home was down a little winding lane; just the place the Maltese would like. Her parents mightn't be in. . . .

Home was a trap.

Go to the police? The police station wasn't far. But the moment she went near it, the Maltese would fade away, and then what evidence did she have? No shoes; and bruised arms that could have been caused by anything.

All the police would see was one hysterical teenager. They'd give her a cup of tea, soothe her down, lecture her on the dangers of going down Low Street after dark, and send her on her way.

The Maltese would be waiting. . . .

The decision was suddenly taken out of her hands.

Her eyes full of sweat, she had been running more and more blind. Now, she misjudged a curb. Her left ankle turned under her, and she was frantically hopping on, on one good leg.

Twenty yards more, and she was cowering helplessly in a shop doorway. The Maltese walked up the far pavement, and hovered. What were they waiting for?

Heavy clinking footsteps. A policeman? The station was only fifty yards away, round the corner.

But it was only another workman, collar up and cap pulled down over his eyes, not taking a blind bit of notice of the world around. He would pass in a minute, and then that would be that.

She glanced round desperately. The doorway she was standing in belonged to a jeweler. Quite a posh jeweler, because he had a metal grille over his windows, to keep out burglars. Burglars? She glanced overhead. There, on the wall, was a small red dome. A burglar alarm.

Audrey swung her handbag at the metal grille, trying to set off the alarm. But her handbag just bounced off. She grabbed the grille, and wrenched at it with all her strength.

Silence.

The workman's footsteps faded. The Maltese were sidling across the road, worry starting to dawn on their faces.

Then she saw the half-brick in the gutter. Very carefully, she stepped forward on her good leg, and picked it up. She pretended to throw it at the Maltese. They separated, grinning. But it made them hesitate a second.

She turned, and threw the brick with all her strength

at the window. It struck the wooden window frame a glancing blow, and the paintwork splintered.

Silence. As she fell onto her back, helpless, the Maltese were bending over her. She closed her eyes. . . .

Then the burglar alarm went off. Its noise filled the street; it filled the town. It would have wakened the dead. Audrey, opening her eyes, could see the Maltese's mouths opening and shutting as they shouted to each other. But not a word could be heard.

Then the world went black.

Chas sat halfway up Bank Top, watching the moon on the river. Nothing was real any more. He no longer desired anything. But after a while, he saw *Hendon* on the move again.

Ten minutes later, a tremendous explosion lit the sea horizon, showing up every building and ship on the river, clear, like a flash of lightning. Then total darkness; and a rolling rumble of sound, like some giant coalman pouring one huge bag of coal into a giant coal cellar. Then a frantic rushing and flapping of wings as the seagulls, disturbed from their roosts on every windowsill and chimney, tried desperately to find their way back in the dark.

Searchlights came on at the Castle, waving like imbecile's arms. All along Low Street, doors flew open. Seamen emerged, buttoning their trousers; tarts, hugging themselves inside thin fringed shawls. Everyone asked what was up. One woman wondered, monotonously and loudly, whether there had been *another* landslide on the cliffs by the Castle. Then the air-raid siren went, and everyone sighed with relief and went back indoors. Nowadays, the occasional lone bomber the Germans could manage was no more than a joke.

Only Chas knew what it really was. Final proof that as a spy-catcher he was *the* great flop. And the proof was a torpedoed ship and thirty dead men. Real men, with real wives like Billy Mason's wife, who rocked and rocked and found the days long once her housework was finished. Thirty kids with no dads, or sixty kids or ninety kids. All staring at him, Chas McGill, because it was his fault. . . .

But he could no longer think of anything for very long. Sheila, Sheila's mother and the spy lying back in the shadows, pulling at his ear; they all went round and round in his head like a roundabout. The moment he tried to think sensibly about one, he began worrying about another.

Only one thing stayed constant. Cold though he was, chilled to the marrow, he didn't want tomorrow to come. It was sort of peaceful, sitting in the moonlight. He wished it could go on forever.

"You come with us, Chassy, yes-no?"

Chas looked round behind him. There were four of them; they had their hands in their pockets.

"Don't make trouble, Chassy. There's a good boy."

He went quietly with them, down the bankside to Low Street. He was so stiff he could hardly walk.

17 The Maltese took Sheila upstairs and pushed her through another door. She was shaking; frightened of being hit again.

But it wasn't a room for violence. Flowered wallpaper, and long red velvet curtains. Every available space filled with spindly tables and cabinets, loaded with tiny objects. There was a cigarette lighter, made from a brass cartridge case. Paperweights of the Crystal Palace. Pictures of Japanese ladies, made from iridescent butterfly wings. A porcelain boot, marked *A present from Hamburg*. Everywhere, presents from somewhere.

The walls were thick with photographs of sailors: embracing dusky girls and six-inch guns, giving the thumbs-up while sitting in rickshaws.

The tall red-haired woman was staring at the window. As if it was her habit to stand there, staring out at the river. As if she hadn't noticed it was night, and the blackout curtains drawn hours ago. She poured herself some yellow liquid out of a cut-glass decanter, drank it with a grimace as if it were medicine, then poured herself another.

"Aye, well, Aah've had a good innings." Her voice was low, and broader than it had been. As if she had given up pretending.

"May I sit down?" asked Sheila, before her legs collapsed under her.

"Aye," said the woman. "Butter wouldn't melt in your mouth, now you've done the damage." She swayed back and forward on her heels, as if to ease some pain. And she remained silent.

"How did you know I was from Whitley Bay?" asked Sheila. Anything to break the silence.

"Aah could tell you weren't bought at Woolworth's."

"You thought we were . . . prostitutes."

"*Louis* did."

"What would you have done if we had been?"

"Given you a hiding an' sent you packing. Or if

Aah'd liked the look of you, Aah'd have given ye a hiding and taken ye on."

Sheila looked round the room, at all the sailors' grinning faces. There was something else in a frame. Some kind of message with Union Jacks plastered all over it. She peered closer. A message from King George V. *About your husbands and to you, their wives.* Dated 1914.

"Was your husband in the First World War?"

"Aye. And he didn't come back. Left me wi' four to bring up."

"Is that when you . . . ?"

"Aye. Well, it was that or scrub floors. And Aah'd seen what scrubbing floors did to me mother. Aah suppose Aah'll get me share of scrubbing floors now."

"What do you mean?"

"Oh, Aah'll get ten years' hard labor for what Aah've just done. Kidnapping Smythson's daughter. White-slaving, the judge'll say. Let alone common assault. They'll throw the book at me. Aah'll be lucky not to get *twenty* years."

"For me? But that's not fair. I'm perfectly all right. I've had worse bruises playing hockey."

The woman laughed harshly. "Ye don't know your father, hinny. Nor the chief constable. They've been waiting to get me a long time. Now Aah've played right into their hands. They'll be licking their lips, once they get hold of you."

"What are you going to do?"

"Nothing. There's nothing Aah can do. Aah know when Aah'm beat."

"Not even try to hide me away?"

Nelly laughed again. "They'd search every ship in

the river; tear the Low Street apart brick by brick, to find *Smythson*'s daughter."

Sheila glanced round the walls again; at the Union Jacks and sailors' faces. The presents from Aden and Kowloon and Madagascar.

"Do you *like* . . . the sailors?"

"They're great lost lonely babbies. Somebody's got to take care of them, and it won't be nice young ladies from Whitley Bay." She sighed. "Why did you have to go and mess it all up? What in God's name were ye *doing* down here?"

Sheila made her mind up. "Looking for a spy."

"A *what*?" Nelly poured herself another drink. "God love you. Aah think ye'd better tell me what's going on. Afore the police come."

"Well, there's this boy . . . he's got it into his head there's a German spy operating down the Low Street. . . ."

"There would be a boy," said Nelly. "Aah might have guessed. Is there any daft thing women wouldn't do for men? Gan on. . . ."

Sheila told the whole story. When she had finished, she said lamely: "Does it all sound stupid?"

Nelly narrowed her eyes. "A bit far-fetched. But not stupid. D'you know who the best German spy in the last war was? An old granny who ran a lodging house for sailors. She sat there knitting them socks; writing letters for them to their wives, an' just listening. She sank a lot of ships, that one. *And* they never caught her. . . . Aah read the book."

"So there might be a spy?"

"There just might." She glanced at the worry on Sheila's face. "Don't fret, hinny. Police'll be here soon."

"It's not that. I'm worried about Chas. He keeps

mucking about with this spy thing, and he doesn't really know what he's doing. I'm afraid he'll get hurt."

"Aye. If he goes on messing around here, he *will* get hurt. Spy or not."

Sheila made her second great decision. She took a deep breath and said, "Can I make a bargain with you?"

"What?"

"I'll say *nothing* to the police. Not a word. If you . . . help Chas clear up this spy business, after I'm gone."

"By God, you're a cool 'un. But it's too late. Your girlfriend got to the police station. She's talking to them now."

"But what does *she* know? Two Maltese in the dark? *I* still don't have to say anything. . . ."

"What, when ye're up there in the police station, and yer da and ma and the chief constable are going on at ye? When they tell ye what a terrible old woman Aah am? That locking me up would be a public service? Aah'm Nelly Stagg, ye know; not yer dear old granny!"

"*Yes*," said Sheila. "I need someone to look after Chas. You're not the only one who's in danger of going to prison."

"What d'ye mean by that?"

But Sheila only shook her head. She held out her hand. "Is it a bargain?"

Nelly thought a long time. Then wiped her hand on her dress and took Sheila's, with a wry grin. "Aah do believe ye mean it. What have Aah got to lose? Anyway, there's no fool like an old fool." Then, briskly, "Where's this lad o' yours now?"

"He'll be hanging around looking for me. He's dark,

and about sixteen; very tall and thin. Dressed in his father's dungarees and he's made his face very dirty."

"We'll have him in," said Nelly. "Afore anything worse happens. Tidy the place up a bit. . . ." She went to the door and muttered instructions.

"But how can you find him?"

"There's not a cat has kittens doon the Low Street but Aah get to know about it. Give me a quarter of an hour. . . ."

Chas hadn't a clue what was going on; except that he was in a strange room, and holding Sheila's hand, and drinking something that burned his throat but made him feel good and warm and sleepy inside. Nelly Stagg was there, and she and Sheila were somehow getting on like a house on fire, so it must be all right *really*.

At that moment, the door opened, and another dungareed figure was flung in, flailing wildly.

"You ask us find one, Nelly—we find you two," said Louis, his brown bun-face splitting into a grin of pride.

"Cem!"

"This is just not my night," said Nelly.

Once Cem had convinced himself he wasn't going to be murdered, he got very loquacious. Chas listened, as from a great distance.

"I rowed round for a bit, having a scout-round like, till I heard this boat coming up in the dark. I nearly wet myself, thinking it was the Maltos, till they shouted. It was Sven, and Andy the engineer. I went out to the *Hendon* with them. I didn't fancy going back and facing the Maltos. . . ."

Chas wished Cem would stop saying "Maltos," especially with the Maltese standing listening. Didn't he realize they were on *our* side now? But there was no holding Cem.

"Dick was getting steam up to go on duty. They had the radio on—Victor Sylvester. Then it began to crackle and buzz. Dick dropped his mug of tea and went down the harbor like a rocket, with Sven hanging over the bows looking for the enamel bowl. We were getting nearer. The crackle was getting louder and louder, when it suddenly stopped.

" 'That's it,' says Dick. 'If there is an enamel bowl, Jerry's got it. He'll be under water faster than a dropped brick.' But he kept on a bit farther, just to please Sven, who was dancing round those Lewis guns like a dervish. Dick was just going to turn back when Sven gives the old Viking war cry and starts blazing away over the port bow. I couldn't see a thing—Sven must have eyes like a cat. He must live on carrots like those night-fighter pilots.

" 'Stop wasting good ammo,' says Dick. But Sven reckoned there was a periscope and he hit it.

"Dick says, 'Well, at least ye've let off yer feelings about Jerry,' and comes back into harbor.

"But he was all jumpy. 'Cause apparently there *was* an important ship due. He kept blowing through his whiskers like an old walrus.

"Then, to crown it all, Sven gashes his hand changing·magazines on the Lewis guns. Dick says it will put Sven in dock for a week, and who's going to handle the towing cables meanwhile? They had a right nasty barney.

"Then Dick says he'll just take a look down Sunderland way, for the important ship that's coming. Sven says it's a waste of fuel, an' Dick says it's his fuel to waste. You should have heard them going on.

"Anyway, we went out and were stooging about in the dark, and Sven says he can see a ship when . . . *blooey* . . . I felt the heat on my face a mile away. Dick goes belting in, but we couldn't find anything but bits of wood like firewood, all over the sea for miles and miles. No survivors. Dick said he didn't expect any, it being an ammunition ship and full of detonators."

Chas noticed a note of gruey enjoyment creeping into Cem's voice, and braced himself. . . . Again, he wondered if Cem was really normal.

"Then they spotted something in the water, an' Dick ordered me below. When he let me up again, we were headed for harbor. But there was something on the deck under a tarpaulin. I edged in while Dick wasn't looking, and lifted the tarpaulin. . . ."

But Cem was denied his big thrill. There was a thunderous knocking on the door downstairs.

Nelly took a long deep breath.

"Police," she said.

Why did it feel like an enemy coming?

Chas sat on the bench in the entrance hall of the police station, between Mam and Dad. A lot had been said, in savage whispers. There was nothing more to say. But that didn't stop Mam saying it.

"I've never been in a police station in me life, and I never thought I would be. I told you if you didn't take this lad in hand, Jack. . . ."

"You needn't wait," said Dad patiently. "Aah told you Aah'd pay for a taxi to take you home."

"If my bairn's in trouble, d'you expect me not to stand by him?"

Chas sighed. They'd had this conversation five times already. His head drooped.

Mam nudged him. "Wake up! You ought to be thinking about what you've done; bringing disgrace on your family like this. What you want to get that girl into trouble for?"

"Haven't got her into trouble."

"Have you seen her poor face?"

"Her father's a stuck-up gyet," said Dad heavily. "I expect he's busy in there, airing his opinions, while we have to wait out here. That's money talking."

"What you want to get involved with *her* sort for?" hissed Mam. "Why can't you stick to your *own* sort? That sixth form. . . . Well, you can go out to work and earn your living after this. That'll knock these grand ideas out of your head. University. . . ."

The chief constable's door was opened by a bowing and scraping sergeant, and Sheila and her mother came out.

Everybody froze. The adults looked daggers. Sheila's mother stuck her nose in the air.

"Don't worry, missus," Dad said to her. "The dust bin men are coming to clear us away, directly."

Sheila giggled. Her mother grabbed her by the arm and thrust her toward the door. As Sheila passed, she gave Chas a smile, and a tiny nod. She had beaten the chief constable; even if she was as white as a sheet, with big blue shadows under her eyes.

Chas turned his head to watch, as her mother led her to the polished swing doors that gave onto the street.

At the door, Sheila paused and turned, resisting the pressure of her mother's arm.

"Goodbye, Chas." Suddenly her face was sad.

Then she was gone. The swing doors slowly ceased their swinging.

"That's a bonny lass," said Dad. "And a canny lass. You could do a lot worse, Chas. . . ."

Mam opened her mouth . . . but at that moment a sergeant called:

"Charles McGill!"

Chas got up and walked across. Dad went with him. But the sergeant said Dad couldn't go in; Chas was sixteen and the age of criminal responsibility. Dad began going on about one law for the rich and one for the poor. But Mam pulled him away, saying *one* McGill in trouble with the police was *quite* enough for one night.

The chief constable had shoulders as wide as his desk. He was aggressively clean; badges like silver and a collar like snow. Cropped gray hair, like some rotten Prussian.

He was angry. His rage was making everyone in the room nervous. The sergeant stood rigidly to attention; spoke in nervous bursts, like a machine gun. Two constables twitched in the corner, till the chief roared them into stillness. Chas had never seen grown men this frightened before.

The chief's eyes were golden, and glared horribly. Chas wondered if he was insane; no *sane* man could be this angry. What happened if chief constables went potty? Nobody would dare arrest them. . . .

"Let's have it, McGill. All of it."

Chas tried staring the chief constable out. But he

couldn't hold up his eye for even ten seconds, though he tried the old trick of staring at the bridge of the chief constable's nose. The man gave out rage like a furnace.

So Chas glanced sideways instead. Sheila's father was sitting back behind the chief constable, watching and listening quietly. He was the only one who didn't jump when the chief constable roared. He had a highly intelligent face, and a very expensive camel's-hair coat. He looked as though he was trying to be fair.

"Look at *me*, McGill!" The roar made the pencils and pens on the desk rattle. But Sheila had managed to outface the sod, so he couldn't be all *that* marvelous. . . .

So Chas shrugged and said, "We went down the Low Street. We went in two pubs. People got nasty, so we came out. Then somebody hit me on the head and knocked me out. When I came round I went to look for Sheila. A Maltese told me she was at Nelly Stagg's and took me there. Then the police came."

The chief constable seemed to swell even bigger.

"Don't try messing *me* about, lad!"

"It's the truth!" Chas even managed a squeak of indignation.

"Part of it. Now tell me the rest."

"I saw the *Hendon* putting out to sea, and I saw that ship blow up. . . ."

There was a long nasty silence. What did you do if a chief constable hit you? Call the cops?

"What about Nelly Stagg?"

"She gave me a drink 'cause my head was hurting. I wasn't noticing things much, 'cause of my headache."

"Look, McGill. You're in trouble—*real* trouble. You

lure Miss Smythson down the Low Street—take her into a pub under age—get her drunk—then she's assaulted—kidnapped—and now you're obstructing the police in the course of their inquiries, which is a serious offense in itself. You could get sent away. . . ."

Terror gripped Chas, but it also held him still. And even in his panic he couldn't help noticing that behind the chief's back, Mr. Smythson was showing signs of discomfort. Frowning, pursing his lips. Ever so slightly dissociating himself from the chief's remarks.

"Bring me a charge sheet," said the chief. One appeared instantly. He began filling it in, with slow and ponderous hand. One charge, two, three, four. Chas watched fascinated, hands clammy with sweat.

But still he said nothing.

"Once I read these charges out," observed the chief, without looking up, "they become official, and even I cannot stop the law taking its due course."

He wrote down two more charges, then paused a long time.

Chas found his mouth was starting to quiver; he couldn't control it. Soon, he mightn't be able to control anything.

Then he remembered when his mouth had quivered like that before. In first year, when Old Monty the headmaster had had him on the carpet. Monty played a game with kids who'd been annoying but not enough to warrant caning. He asked impossible questions, like, "Do you think I am insane, boy?" and badgered and badgered till you gave some stupid answer. Then he tore your answer to ribbons. In between questions, he kept you waiting in silence. It really broke the young kids up; they left Monty's study squalling, even though he'd never laid a hand on them.

The chief was playing the same trick now.

It suddenly cut him down to Monty's despicable size.

The chief constable waited.

Chas was content to wait too.

Finally, the chief looked up.

"Six charges. Anything you want to say before I read them out?"

Chas shook his head.

The chief began to read the first charge out. Long boomy words that meant little to Chas.

"Chief constable, . . ." said Mr. Smythson, in a low calm voice, which still cut through the chief's like a knife through butter. The reading of the charge stopped. "Chief constable, I must point out to you that three of your charges simply won't hold water. This young man did not take my daughter down the Low Street, or into a pub, against her will. And she will say so in court. Nor do I believe that this young man had any hand in her kidnapping. And if you intend to charge him with entering a public house and drinking under age, you must charge my daughter also. . . ."

Chief constable and chairman of the Watch Committee glared at each other.

"I say who's charged in this town, sir. *I* am the law."

"No. You are the police. I and my fellow magistrates are the law. Do you wish to charge my daughter?"

The chief tore up the charge sheets, very slowly, into very small pieces.

Chas looked at Mr. Smythson in admiration. Mr. Smythson looked back with utter coldness.

"Master McGill," he said, "has been extremely *fool-*

ish, but not very criminal. We do not sent *children* to prison for being *foolish.*"

"But he's no better than . . . than. . . ."

"I advise you to be careful, chief constable. I would dislike giving evidence against you in a slander action."

The chief constable opened his mouth, and then thought better of it. Another sergeant knocked and came in.

"We got nothing out of the other lad, sir. Don't think he knows much. Seems to have been aboard the *Hendon* most of the evening. We've been in radio contact with the *Hendon,* and Burley confirms it.

"As for the other girl. . . . We had a line-up of Maltese . . . she couldn't tell one from another."

"Get *out!* Get out, *all* of you!"

His minions fled.

The chief pulled a pipe out of his uniform pocket, and twisted it viciously, lion-eyes on Chas again. "D'you know what venereal disease is? Syphilis? Sailors' lives wrecked? D'you know what you've *done* tonight?"

Mr. Smythson wrinkled his nose in distaste, and stood up to go. "You won't be needing me further? I'd better drive my family home."

When he'd gone, the chief returned to the attack. "Twenty years I've been trying to nail that woman. Twenty bastard years. And you know enough to put her away for life, don't you? DON'T YOU?"

Chas was careful not even to move his head. Not in the very slightest. But he wasn't scared of the chief anymore. He'd seen Mr. Smythson call the chief to heel. As Dad would have said, the chief was just a monkey up another man's stick.

"What did you go down the Low Street *for?*" The chief was hoarse, giving up. It made him sound oddly more reasonable.

For a moment, Chas was tempted to mention the spy. But the chief would just go on like a lunatic again.

"We were just having a bit of fun," said Chas.

But he was already worrying about something else. Why had Sheila looked so sad, when she said goodbye?

18 Chas couldn't get to school quick enough, first day of the summer term. He'd spent the last week of the holiday throwing stones in the Gar. Waiting. Every hour of daylight. Even missing meals.

She hadn't come.

He'd told himself, be reasonable. Of course her parents would ride shotgun on her at first. But they'd get tired. She'd turn up.

She hadn't come.

The sixth-form room filled up. People making the old stupid joke about a pair of tennis balls. Had he heard that Russy Miller had made a century for Garmouth Seconds on Saturday? He didn't listen; he watched the door.

She hadn't come by the time the lesson bell went. She wasn't in double geography after break. . . .

She didn't turn up on Tuesday or Wednesday either. Maybe she was ill? None of the other girls knew anything about her; none of them had known her that well. He thought of asking Audrey to go to her house;

but Audrey's name would be mud at Brinchdene Avenue as well.

On Thursday, he waited after school till the form room emptied. Then he asked the form master, Stan Liddell, if she was ill. Stan was OK. He didn't mock you, even when you blushed and stammered.

Stan said gently, "Leave it, McGill. Don't you think you've done yourself enough damage?"

"What do you mean, sir?"

Stan closed his eyes with a sigh. "I'm a bit tired of hearing about McGill at the moment. First I have to argue your own parents out of taking you away from school. Then I have to talk the Head out of expelling you because someone else's parents have complained. It went to the Governors, you know."

Chas felt sick. "But it all happened *out* of school. I'm not even in trouble with the police."

"By the grace of God. But the Smythsons have a lot of influence . . . the only thing that saved you was that I told the Head you were our first chance of an Oxford Open for years."

"But where *is* she, sir?"

Stan looked at him with an awful quiet pity. "She's not coming back here. And there's no point to your hanging round Whitley Grammar either."

"But . . . her Higher School Certificate?"

"There are other schools, Chas. If you have the money."

"But I must see her!"

"No!" Stan sounded suddenly frightened. Frightened for Chas. "If there's one more complaint, *I* shan't be able to save you. You've got a big future. Don't throw it away for a passing fancy. I know . . . these things hurt when you're sixteen. I can remember, even if I'm a graybeard now. Believe me, it'll pass. There'll be other girls.''

He might have saved his breath. Chas spent Thursday evening cycling round and round Whitley Bay. Getting nearer and nearer Brinchdene. When he finally ventured down it, he got in a terrible shouting match with one of the bald-headed old hedge-clippers, who called him a young blackguard, and told him he should be in the Army serving his country.

Next morning, the Head summoned him. *One* more complaint and he'd be expelled, Oxford Open or not.

After that came black despair. He ignored his schoolwork. After a bit, the teachers stopped bothering, and left him to sulk. He turned up at one school tennis practice, and played with a crazy viciousness that left the school champion on the verge of tears. The staff put him on the team, thinking it might help. First match he hardly hit the ball and lost 6-0, 6-0.

Otherwise he rode himself to exhaustion on his bike, round and round a town he suddenly hated. Because she was not there. Or he walked along North Pier on stormy nights, when the waves broke over and soaked him. It fitted his mood. The only God was the God of rock and wave; uncaring as rock, violent as wave. Men were poor flies, who spent their lives just trying to dodge getting hurt. But you got hurt just the same, no matter how cunningly you dodged. Even the most successful guys, who drove big cars round on black market petrol, smoking big cigars—life got them in the end. They only had bigger funerals than anybody else.

One night he nearly chucked himself down from the piers, onto the rocks and waves. Might as well finish the farce; get it over with.

Then he remembered there was homemade meat pie for supper. Might as well eat the meat pie first. . . .

He hadn't even got a photo of her. He began to forget what she looked like. He haunted the Sands, the Monument. All the places they'd been together. It hurt at first, but even there the memory of her faded, faded.

At home, he conversed in grunts. Mam took him to the doctor. He chattered to the doctor cheerfully about everything under the sun, till the doctor began giving Mam funny looks . . . but the joke soon wore off and everything was black again.

He didn't *want* to see Audrey; he didn't *want* to see Cem. He *wanted* to feel alone in the world. Because that was the truth, really.

One evening, he glowered so much Mam went to bed early with the spaniel for company. Chas could feel Dad watching him, from behind the pages of the *Daily Express*. Chas went on flicking over the pages of an American comic, pointlessly.

"If ye go on like this much longer, ye'll do yourself a damage."

"What you mean?"

"Broodin'. Your face'd turn the bloody milk sour. You're a right bloody pain in the neck. What's the matter wi' ye? Ye're young. Ye've got your whole life in front of ye."

"That's the trouble."

"So ye've lost her. Never lost anything afore? Ye *must* have led a sheltered life."

"You never lost anybody. You don't know what it's like."

"Only me father and me mother."

"That's different."

"Why?"

" 'Cause they were old."

"So they don't matter?"

"No . . . but they're *dead*. I could accept it if she was *dead*. But she's not."

"Fat lot you know about dead. But you can accept she's dead as far as you're concerned. Ye'll never see her again. An' Aah'm glad in a way. Though she seemed a canny enough lass."

"How do you know I'll never see her again? They can't keep her prisoner forever. They'll have to let her out of the house sometime."

"Ye don't think she's still at home, do you? She could be anywhere by this time. London. America. When you got money, the world's your oyster. Her dad'll gan doon to London quicker than Aah'd think of cycling to Percy Main. . . ."

Chas thought; and had to nod. "But there's no need for you to be glad about it."

"Well, Aah am glad, Aah'll tell ye straight."

"Why?"

"Well, suppose them Smythsons had been a bit kinder to you? Had ye round to tea, and fed you bits like a little lapdog. Who'd'a become more important to ye—them, or yer mam and me?"

"Never," said Chas. But he remembered the grand piano, and the shelves of books behind glass doors, and the people you could talk to about T. S. Eliot. . . .

"Aye, ye can say that now," said Dad, a bit kinder. "But they're clever, that lot. Clever at tekking *our* bright kids an' mekkin' them into little lapdogs. World's full o' little lapdogs. That's how that lot survives, an' keeps their power. . . ."

"But that's *wrong*."

"There's a lot in the world that's wrong. But ye won't find it in *their* poetry books. Ye ought to try reading *men's* books . . . like them. They'll tell ye how it was . . . and how it is." He pointed to his own bookcase; went over and took out a book. It was marked *Left Book Club*. "That's the truth about the workers in the Spanish Civil War, for a start. By the time ye've worked your way along that shelf, Aah'll guarantee ye'll be cured o' the Smythsons. Ye'll see them for what they *really* are."

Chas went along that bookshelf nonstop. He had never learned so many new facts in his life, and he liked facts. It didn't cure the pain about Sheila, but it certainly opened his eyes. Riding round the town, whenever he saw slummy places or slummy kids, he didn't despise them anymore—he saw them as the victims of the Smythsons. Once, he even got off his bike to help an old woman push home a sack of coal in her rusty pram. She got very embarrassed and kept saying not to bother, sir, she could manage. She kept on thanking him in a smarmy way and told him he was a proper young gentleman.

It only struck him when he got back to his bike that to her, *he* was a boss. . . .

But the pain of Sheila only really began to fade when, one fine May evening, he heard a girl's voice calling him. He fell off his bike in surprise. A car had to swerve, missing his head by inches.

The girl bent over and stared down at him. Not Sheila. Audrey.

"Get up, you silly sod. You might've been killed."

"And a good thing too."

"Rubbish!"

She took him to the British Restaurant for coffee. Let him tell her all about Sheila. Once. After that, she refused to listen.

But she said she was taking him on. She was between fellers, and bored. They went to the pictures once or twice. She let him put his arm round her, in the back row of the circle. It wasn't like Sheila, but it was vaguely comforting.

Only once did she mention the spy. He wasn't interested. As far as he was concerned, the spy could blow up the whole of Tyneside, starting with Brinchdene Avenue.

Then, one evening at half-term, she said archly she had a message from You-know-who. Via another old girlfriend of You-know-who, who was the only person in Garmouth who You-know-who was allowed to write to, by You-know-who's very strict new headmistress.

Chas's stomach turned to jelly.

"What?" he asked hoarsely. It was like getting a message from beyond the grave.

"Be on the 2:15 from Newcastle to Hexham, next Monday afternoon."

"But I'll be in school!"

"After the trouble you've been in, what's playing truant?"

"Haven't got the fare!"

"I'll lend it to you. God knows why. I never knew a more ungrateful guy. Some guys would give their eyeteeth to go out with *me*. All you do is moan about another girl. Lucky I'm not in love with you, isn't it?"

"Yeah. Thanks."

Audrey gave him the money. "Sheila says get to the station early, and get into the compartment next to the engine as soon as the train pulls in. And wear something over your school uniform. Got it?"

"Yeah," said Chas, jubilant.

"Don't know why I bother," sniffed Audrey.

19 Chas sat in the compartment next to the engine, wearing a fawn raincoat and Dad's oldest trilby, rather bent from traveling in his school satchel. Hiding his face inside a cop comic he knew by heart. He felt ridiculous. In the wrong place, at the wrong time, in the wrong life. And missing double games. . . .

The sun was shining. If he kicked the seat opposite, a cloud of golden dust motes flew in the air. The minute hand of the station clock moved like a caterpillar with arthritis. On the compartment wall opposite were prints of Peterborough Cathedral and Old Yarmouth. He had learned every detail off by heart, bombed them, rebuilt them and had no desire to see either place again as long as he lived.

She had not come.

The minute hand of the clock made it, in the end. The train played its intricate symphony of throbs, thrums and jerks, and they were moving out of Newcastle Central.

She had not come. It was the kind of absurd joke that Life was so fond of. . . . Perhaps the train would crash as well, and his body would be charred to a cinder and never identified. Perhaps he'd be buried in Hexham Churchyard, and become famous as "The Unknown Traveler." Ghoulish tourists would flock to his graveside; perhaps even his own uncomprehending parents.

Meanwhile, the fields of cows passing the carriage window seemed masterpieces of pointless stupidity.

The compartment door opened, and a school kid in floppy hat and ginger blazer got in. She wore horrible woolly ginger stockings too . . . and probably horrible ginger knickers. A real passion-killer. That was all he needed. He stared hard at the floor, in case she was the chattery sort.

"Hello, Chas," said the ginger kid.

It was Sheila. God, what a mess. The ginger uniform made her face look faintly green, and her lips were as pale as her face. Her nose was shiny and her hair screwed back into pigtails. A voluminous gym tunic hid her bosom, and made her neck look pale and chopped off like a plucked chicken's.

"How do I look, Chas?"

"Great. *Great!*"

"Liar!"

"You look like a soldier."

"Sexless!" She laughed. "This is the finest antisex uniform in the world. Elmhurst College, Keswick. That's what Daddy's paying for, and that's why Mummy's escorting me there. To keep me away from the likes of you. You can hold my hand, if you like."

He glanced round, panic-stricken. Sheila laughed again.

"It's all right. Mummy's three compartments away. She thinks I'm at the loo. I've got *terrible* diarrhea."

Chas took her hand, remembering the blue-veined slimness. Her eyes were shining so bright, he could hardly bear to look at her. Her eyes made him ashamed, somehow.

"What's the college like?"

She pulled a face. *"Boring.* Ponies, ponies all the way, and never a hint of men. The girls are so *wet.* The headmistress is the sniffy sort—always got a cold. Washes out her own hankies in her bedroom, and hangs them in her window to dry in the sun. They make a different pattern every day, and do you know what those *wet* girls think?"

"No."

"That she's a German spy, signaling to a confederate in the hills."

"Oh."

"Makes *our* spy seem quite *real.*"

"Yeah," said Chas uncomfortably.

"Any luck with Nelly?"

"No."

"What does she say?"

"I haven't seen her."

"Oh, Chas. Why *not?"*

He shrugged. "Seemed no point after you went away."

All the joy went out of Sheila's face. Chas felt doubly rotten.

"Chas, you must go and see Nelly. She's the sort that keeps her word. She must have gone to all sorts of bother."

"Suppose so."

Sheila held his hand tightly between both of hers. "Chas, you must go. Even if there isn't a spy, you must finish what you started. If you give up things halfway, nobody will ever take you seriously. People will go on thinking you're an idiot."

"People meaning your precious daddy?"

"Yes—if you like. People who matter. I want *you* to be someone people take seriously. You must see that."

Chas closed his eyes. He was seeing only too well. What life with Sheila would be like.

He'd always known that life would be fighting your way upward. But he'd thought it would be like flying. Free; like a bird. Suddenly, Sheila made it seem like a hill you *had* to climb. And on top, already arrived, were all the people who mattered. Even if you climbed really well, they still wouldn't let you join the club. And if you climbed badly, they'd kick you down the hill again. Right in the teeth.

"Chas?"

He opened his eyes and eyed Sheila coldly. "Who says your father's somebody who matters?"

Sheila didn't look at him.

"My dad says that when your dad talks, it's really his money talking."

Tears glistened in Sheila's eyes. "Oh, Chas! Oh, I must go. Mummy will be looking for me." She jumped up, hand on the door handle.

He couldn't let her go off like that. Not after all the trouble she'd gone to.

"OK," he said. "I'll go and see Nelly."

Sheila smiled again. But her smile was only the ghost of its former self. "That's my Chas. . . ."

"Will you write?"

"Don't know. It's difficult. There's a cleaning woman who smuggles letters out of school. But she charges the earth, and we only get seven-and-six pocket money, and we have to buy toothpaste and soap out of that. . . . I'll try."

"See you in July, anyway."

Her smile faded completely. "No. You won't. Mummy's taking me to Cornwall for the whole summer."

"I'll hitch-hike down. Meet you on the beach."

"The hotel's got private grounds. And a private beach."

It was like a punch in the face. Chas shook with rage. Money, money, money. Smythson used his money like a fist. Like Dad's books said.

Her lips might have gently touched his cheek, then she was gone. Leaving only a whiff of posh soap to prove that the ancient, dusty railway compartment hadn't sprouted an illusion.

He got off at Hexham, keeping his back turned and examining a fire bucket on the platform till the train rolled out. He had two hours' wait for a train back to Newcastle. He spent them thinking about everything, and trying to kick something out of a chocolate machine that had given up the ghost in September 1939.

But he didn't change his mind. He *would* go and see Nelly for Sheila's sake. Or in Sheila's memory. . . .

20 "More tea, Chas?" asked Nelly, pouring the dregs from his cup with her little finger cocked genteelly.

"Yes, please," said Chas, sitting upright in a straight-backed Victorian chair and wearing his best trousers. He always wore his best trousers for Nelly's. It was like visiting Gran, only grander.

Nelly dressed up too. A new dress every time he came. Well, not exactly *new*. They were long-skirted with lace at the collar and ponged of mothballs.

"Get down, Caesar!" said Nelly sharply. "You'll ruin Chas's trousers." The little brown-and-white spaniel was begging for cake again, eyes and mouth brimming with hope. Nelly gave it a piece, on a rosebud saucer in the corner.

Nelly still baffled Chas. She was two women. Long before he'd dared visit her, he'd watched her parading the Low Street, from the brothel to the Black Ox. Parading was the word; she walked down the middle of the cobbles with her girls straggling behind. Somehow, every time, the Low Street people gathered to watch, from curb and window. It was like the procession of a foul-mouthed queen.

"Where do you scratch, Nelly?"

"Where do *you* itch, Ernie?"

"Going home to get your knees up, Nelly?"

"Why—you coming calling, Jim Green?" The crowd laughed, as Jim Green turned away, under the glower of his wife.

"Here's the chief constable coming for ye, Nelly."

"He'll ha' to wait his turn, like everybody else."

Chas couldn't tell if the Low Street people loved or hated her; but they couldn't ignore her; she was the big daily event of their lives.

Alone with Chas, she was different.

She wouldn't let him use the brothel entrance in the alley. He had to walk right through the alley, onto the quayside. And then turn left and climb an outside stair, up to her private door. Once, she had caught one of her younger girls talking to Chas in the alley.

She'd slapped the girl's face; and Chas had never seen that girl again. After that, the other girls left Chas strictly alone.

Inside Nelly's sitting room, you'd never guess the brothel existed. The walls were lined with books, and Nelly had read them all. Even *Jane's Fighting Ships*. She tried to lend Chas some books, but he was afraid to take them home. She didn't offer books again. But she asked about his schoolwork; advised him not to marry too early, and always wear wool next to his skin.

They were cozy visits. The hour fled, with scurrilous tales of the Boer War, and the private life of Earl Haig. Chas was always tempted not to mention the spy business at all. But he was getting desperate. June was past and there was still no word from Sheila.

So Chas asked. Nelly sighed.

"I suppose if we catch your spy, you won't come and see me anymore?"

" 'Course I will!" But that didn't fool either of them. There was a wide gap between the Low Street and Garmouth, but gossip would cross it sooner or later. Then some kind person would mention the matter to Dad.

"I wish I had grandchildren," said Nelly.

"Haven't you got any?"

"Oh, aye. I send them presents, Christmas and birthdays. But they're never brought to see me." Nelly closed her eyes for a minute, and looked as old as anyone else's granny. Then she opened her eyes again, and their sparkle took twenty years off her age.

"Spy!" she said briskly, gathering her thoughts. "I don't think there *can* be one, Chas. I don't see how he could get the sort of secrets you think he's getting.

I've offered fifty pound reward to anybody who can tell me of one ship that's *coming* to the Gar, an' what it's carrying. The girls have been working like beavers for a month. Aye, and the Maltese. I've learned quite a bit. . . . I know what any ship is carrying—an hour *after* it's docked. I know who the captains' fancy women are—I could break a dozen marriages. I know what's being smuggled in and what's being smuggled out—that'd surprise ye. But nobody seems to know beforehand what ships are *due*. Except a few bigwigs at the naval base, mevve. And they never come near the Low Street."

"What about the sailor with the silver ring?"

"If he exists, he's taken it off. And it's left no mark on his hand. Or else he's done a bunk. There's been no more ships sunk, while we've been watching for him. Mevve we've stopped him after all."

"Yeah," said Chas. But that wouldn't show Sheila's father where he got off.

Nelly's harsh face softened. "You love that bonny lass, don't you? And she loves you. She'll wait for you."

"She'll have to," said Chas glumly. "They won't let her see me—till she's twenty-one and they can't stop her. I'll be in the Army before then. I could be dead. Or else she'll have forgotten me, and they'll marry her off to somebody with money."

"She'll wait. I woulda done, at her age."

"Why? What's so marvelous about me?"

Nelly smiled. "You've got a way with you. I only saw it once before . . . my little sublieutenant . . . he was killed at the Battle of the Dogger Bank. Here's his photo." She produced something gold from her handbag.

Chas stared at the sepia face in the oval frame. Young, handsome, eager—and thirty years dead.

"He looks . . . nice."

"Aye, I shan't forget him, though we were only together twice. He came from the West Country— Devonport. I read his name in the casualty lists and wrote to his mother. She never replied."

There was a long silence, full of dead time and the ticking of the clock. Chas played with the spaniel's ears, thinking of the face that looked as young as his own, and was buried at sea, or in Nelly's heart, or in the cheap oval frame.

The silence went on too long.

"I'd better be going," said Chas. He knew he would never come again. If there was no spy, he was just hanging round a brothel, and he was in enough trouble already.

"Look," said Nelly. "If I catch your spy—and you see your bonny lass—will you fetch her to see me, just once?"

Chas swallowed with shame. Nelly was the nicest person he knew. Nelly was on his side, like nobody else was. Why *should* he care what his parents thought? They weren't on his side, like Nelly was. Nor the rotten neighbors. Nor the rotten chief constable. Why should you have to hurt people who cared about you, just to please people who didn't give two damns about you?

He hated Garmouth. But you couldn't fight all of it. Not yet. Not till you'd been to University. . . .

But Nelly had asked him a question.

"Yes," he said. "Yes, I'll bring her lots of times."

"Once will do," said Nelly dryly. "It's just that I like to see *somebody* happy."

"But how can you catch the spy, if he doesn't exist?"

Nelly's eyes were glinting with sudden excitement. "There's one last trick I can play, win or lose. A trick that's as old as the hills; but it's a good 'un. If he exists, it'll fetch him."

"What trick?" asked Chas.

"That's *my* business," said Nelly, savoring her secret. "Now you better go—I'm going to be busy." Nelly's voice was gruff; perhaps because her eyes were shining too brightly. She reached into a china cabinet and brought out a brass model cannon that had become Chas's particular favorite. She pressed it into his hand.

"But Nelly, it's valuable. . . ."

"Tek it," said Nelly. "It's no use to me." She gave him a hug and kiss that forced the cannon against his chest, until it hurt. "Look after it. Now off you go. I've got work to do." And she bundled him out of the door.

He stood on the outside staircase, watching a sunlit corvette making its way up-river, and rubbing his cheek where she'd kissed him. She hadn't kissed him like a granny. . . .

He cycled home, working out ways of hiding the cannon from Mam. Everyone he passed on the Low Street spoke to him, or nodded respectfully. He was a friend of Nelly Stagg's now. He was the boy who was going to catch the spy. . . .

21 "Let's go down and chuck bricks at bottles," said Cem.

"Let's not," said Chas, yawning and leaning back against the sun-warmed stones of the Monument.

It was the first evening of the summer holiday. All July had been sunny, and lazy with the end of term. The sun had been a balm to Chas. Washing away pain; leaving only the smell of mown playing fields, the sweat of tennis and the ice of cold drinks.

His mind had returned to schoolwork. He'd done so well in exams that his teachers were disgusted. His report was shrill with their indignation.

He hadn't been back to see Nelly. That last kiss, and the gift of the cannon. . . . He'd put off calling on her from day to day, and finally given up thinking about it. Thank God no gossip had reached Dad!

The spy was only an embarrassing memory. You had to grow up sometime. Dad was using the famous enamel bowl to hold fertilizer.

Even Sheila had shrunk to a daydream; in between taking Audrey to the pictures.

"Aw, c'mon," said Cem. He was likely to go on saying "Aw, c'mon" for the next three hours, with all the wit and erudition of a hungry mosquito.

Chas looked down on the Fish Quay and the Sands; the Low Street. Under the westering sun they looked as small and harmless as Dinky Toys. "My dad always says let sleeping dogs lie."

"Aw, c'mon," said Cem. "No one will notice us."

So it was embarrassing, as they swooped down on their bikes, warm air stroking their faces, to have Mr.

Kallonas run out in his white apron, waving his arms with excitement. They screeched to a stop, slewed all over the road.

"Come! Come see! I have it for you! At last I have it!" He led them into his back room, rubbing his great hands together. And there was an American battery; just like the one out of the enamel basin. "You cannot dream what search I have had—I have done the impossible. There have been none in Garmouth at any price."

"How'd you get this one?"

"My cousin at Portsmouth. It is off the American destroyer. Only American ships have them. No Americans come to Gar—so no batteries. Have I not done the miracle?"

They agreed. But it wasn't a very *useful* miracle.

"Have there been *no* Americans in the Gar?"

"One only. An American destroyer of the British Navy!"

The boys looked at him, baffled.

"She is what you call louse-lend destroyer!"

"Lease-lend?"

"Yes. Louse-lend. Old ship with four funnel. She was called *U.S.S. Clarksburg*, but we British called her *H.M.S. Kirkcudbright*. She came here for repairs after the commando raid on the Liftens."

"The Lofoten Islands?"

"Yes, the Liften Islands."

"Hey," said Cem. "Sven was on that trip. That's when he was rescued from the Jerries. He'd know who else was on the *Kirkcudbright*. It might be a lead."

"It might," said Chas flatly. It was all too long ago and far away.

Mr. Kallonas peered anxiously from one boy to the other. "I have helped? Like I promised?"

"Yeah, yeah. Super!"

"You have not found spy yet?"

"No," said Chas, "but we're still working at it. We're going to the Sands to check . . . something now."

"Well—I not hold you up. Keeping me in touch? Take battery—do not forget it!"

Chas lifted the battery, feeling guilty as a thief.

"Goodbye, Mr. Kallonas. Thanks ever so!"

They parked their bikes, and sat on the Lifeboat gangway. The smell of rotting fish was strong in the warm air.

"It's embarrassing," Chas burst out. "They still believe in the spy, down the Low Street."

"*Really?*" said Cem, yawning and stretching.

"We must have been *mad*. Burgling old Kallonas's place."

"It was a giggle."

"And that raft."

"Wouldn't mind making another raft."

"Too hot!"

"Still got the key for Sven's boat?"

"Sent it back by post. Wonder how they're all getting on? I did go to see Nelly Stagg, you know." Chas hadn't mentioned it before; Cem had a big mouth.

"Crafty sod. What happened?"

"She said there was no spy. But she gave me tea, and a brass cannon."

"Lucky dog. Let's bomb some bottles."

They bombed, but were sweating within minutes. They sat down again.

"Hey," said Cem. "What's that brown-and-white

thing, floating in the water, under the gangway supports?"

"Something dead. It's all bloated."

"I'm going to have a look," said Cem, and began climbing out along the wet timbers.

"Gruey sod!" shouted Chas after him, but without conviction.

"Hey," called Cem. "It's a dog."

"What sort?"

"Spaniel. Little brown-and-white spaniel. . . . Eeurgh! The heartless bastard!"

"*What?*"

"Somebody stuck a knife into it—you can see the place."

Chas climbed out along the gangway. Slipping all over the place, because his legs had turned to putty. When he reached Cem, he didn't want to look at the thing in the water. But in the end he looked, and was promptly sick.

"What's up wi' you? Never seen a dead dog before?"

"It's Caesar—Nelly's dog."

"*Somebody* must have it in for her. Bet she'll get her own back, though; set Nico onto them. Hey, what's this?"

Chas looked again. It was a handbag, floating. He picked it up, and water streamed from one corner. He opened it.

Inside were keys, a soggy ration book, and an oval frame containing the photograph of a young naval officer. The one who'd drowned at Dogger Bank. Now he'd been drowned again.

The oval frame came apart in Chas's hand. The photo fell in the water and dissolved to pulp.

"Let's go and tell Nelly about the dog." Cem sounded excited. Chas hated him for it. Because Chas had suddenly been seized by a terrible thought.

"I think . . . Nelly might be dead."

"What—'cause of an old dog? Rubbish."

" 'Cause of that photo. She'd never have let it out of her sight."

"Let's go and find out—hey, watch it, you'll fall in!"

Chas made it back to the shore with Cem's help. As they walked to Nelly's, the front wheel of his bike kept twisting round and tripping him up.

The brothel door was locked, the windows shuttered. Chas tried knocking on Nelly's private door, up the outside stair. That was locked too, and no one answered.

But as they were going back down the alley, the brothel door opened. Louis poked his head out. He was still wearing his brown-and-white shoes, but they were filthy now. So was his vest; and he smelled of drink and armpits. In fact, he looked bloody miserable, but his face lightened as he saw the boys.

"Hi, Chas! Hi, Cem! Good to see you, yes-no?"

"Louis, what's happened? Where is everybody?"

"All closed down. Nelly go away."

"When?"

Louis counted on his fingers in a fuddled way. "T'ree weeks ago. We try stay open, but girls are running wild, so Nico close us down. Make me caretaker."

"Where's Nelly gone to?"

Louis shrugged. "No one knows. She has done it before. Gone for a month. Then come back. Say nothing. You know what Nelly's like, yes-no? Maybe she go see grandchildren."

"Where do her grandchildren live?"

Louis shrugged. "We just know she gone. Take dog, ration books, money from her hidey-hole. Nelly had thousand pound in hidey-hole. That is first thing Nico checked. That is why we know she is gone. Hey." His face lit up. "Did she write to you?"

"No. Why?"

"She has good news for you. All the week before she go, she tell everybody she has good news for you. Make you happy. But you not come see her. We try t'ink of ways of letting you know. T'ink of writing, but that upset your mama, getting letter from Nelly. I say I will wait for you and speak to you outside your school. But Nelly say that embarrass you, in front of other boys. We will wait, say Nelly, he will come. But you no come."

"What was the good news?"

"She tell nobody—very secret. But we t'ink it about spy."

"Oh my God," said Chas. He broke out in sweat all over: a cold sweat, in spite of the heat of the day. He could see it all now. This was Nelly's trick to catch the spy. The oldest trick in the world, she'd said. But it would fetch him, if he existed. Word trickling over all the Low Street that Nelly Stagg had news that would make Chas McGill happy. Gossip in every bar and brothel. And the spy *did* exist; he had heard; he had come to see Nelly.

"Nelly's dead," said Chas. The words just jumped out of his mouth. He handed the sodden handbag to Louis.

"What's this?" said Louis. But he knew. He motioned with his head for the boys to follow him.

The passageway between the little rooms only seemed darker for the single naked light bulb. They went upstairs to Nelly's room. Louis pulled the shutters half back, to let in a ray of sunlight. It showed the difference a month had made. Several of the ornaments were gone, or broken. There were cigarette burns on the furniture, and a heap of blankets at one end of the sofa, where Louis had been kipping down.

Louis looked at the handbag in his hand.

"We pulled it out of the river," explained Cem.

"Lotsa handbags in river. Lotsa everything in river."

"It's got her ration card inside."

Louis shrugged again. "Nelly had lotsa ration cards. You can buy them on black market—three quid. Maybe Nelly want to change her name. Easy. Throw old ration book away."

Chas handed him the oval picture frame. Louis recognized it. His hand shook slightly, but it could have been his hangover.

"No picture. . . ."

"It fell out," said Chas. "And we found Caesar in the river as well. Stabbed to death."

"Lotsa dogs in river," said Louis doubtfully.

"It's Caesar, I tell you!" yelled Chas. "Come and see for yourself."

They got Louis along to the Lifeboat gangway in the end. They had to half-drag him. He kept shading his eyes against the sun. He really had a bad hangover.

But when they got him there, the tide was running strongly in. The whole pattern of floating sticks and bottles, sawdust and filth, had changed. And Caesar's body had gone.

Louis just stood staring at the river, as if he would stand there forever. It was quite clear he was going to do nothing at all.

His awful inertia spread to Chas. Chas just stood staring and staring at the gap between the piers. Where Nelly had gone, along with the cods' heads and fish-boxes, the tin cans from Newcastle, and branches of trees that had fallen in the water as far upstream as Hexham. All carried away by the strong brown waters of the Gar. Nelly, who'd loved him. While all he, Chas, cared about was school exams and tennis. . . .

That awful Shakespeare poem came into his mind. The one Stan Liddell had made him learn, though he hated it so much.

> *Full fathom five thy father lies;*
> *Of his bones are coral made;*
> *Those are pearls that were his eyes;*
> *Nothing of him that doth fade,*
> *But doth suffer a sea-change*
> *Into something rich and strange.*

Rich and strange nothing. Sewage. Seagulls scream-ing, feeding.

Chas was sick again. Not that he had much left to be sick with. But he felt better afterward. He accepted that he had killed Nelly, just as much as the spy had killed her. In some funny way, the spy and he were alone, now. "I want to see Nico," he said to Louis.

Louis led the way without a word.

"Nico will not see you," said Louis.

"Did you show him the handbag?" asked Cem ea-gerly.

Chas thought how much Cem was enjoying him-self.

"Yes," said Louis. "I told him all. He say there is

nothing he can do. If you are wrong, Nelly will come back. If you are right, is too late."

"We'll go to the police. Show them the hand-bag. . . ."

"Nico keep handbag. Not want police down Low Street."

"Not if he's covering for a German spy. . . ." Chas was screaming out of control.

"Don't you say that thing," said Louis, suddenly frightened. "Nico lose father, mother, brothers, all . . . when Germans bomb Malta. Nico never help Germans. Go way. Nico in very bad temper." He glanced round nervously, back into the entrance of the Blue Café. It quietened Chas wonderfully.

"Well . . . just go back and ask him one thing. Who was the last person to see Nelly?"

"*I* know that," said Louis. "If I tell you, will you go away?"

"Yeah."

"Annie Parkes, the cleaner. She lives at Colling-wood Street."

Collingwood Street was just off the top of the Bank Top. They pushed their bikes, because Chas still didn't feel up to riding. Cem chattered and chattered. Why hadn't Nico wanted to see them? Had there been some kind of quarrel between Nelly and Nico that had nothing to do with any spy? He talked about them like they were something out of a crime film he'd just seen.

Chas supposed people were like chocolates; there were soft centers and hard centers. Cem was a hard center; nothing ever hurt him. Nothing ever got through *his* thick skin.

"What you looking at me like that for?" said Cem. "*I* didn't kill her. If you'd gone to see her. . . ."

"Shut your stupid face!" said Chas. And for once he really meant it.

Just for a second, something showed on Cem's face. Something that wasn't a laugh; or a desire to do somebody down. But the something only made Chas's mood worse.

"Shut your *stupid* face," he repeated. "Stupid, stupid, *stupid*."

Cem's sneery mask returned.

"Suit yourself," he said, putting one leg over his bike. "Go and play the great detective. You'll probably get yourself killed next. See you at the funeral."

And he rode off whistling.

Next minute, Chas wanted to call him back. Had an awful feeling that he *ought* to call him back. He got as far as calling "Cem," but it came out as a useless croak. Next minute, Cem turned a corner and was out of sight.

Chas trudged on. The sun was shining warmly, and the people he passed looked cheerful. More hard centers.

Annie Parkes's front room smelled of mothballs, just like Nelly's. What was more, it seemed full of Nelly's cast-offs: presents from Shanghai and Aberdeen.

But Annie was pleased to see him. Perhaps old people were pleased to see *anybody*.

"Nelly was very kind to me," said Annie. "The soul of kindness itself."

"*Was?*" asked Chas.

"Nelly's gone, isn't she? It's all very well Nico Mintoff saying she'll be back. But she won't. He's a great fat bladder o' lard, that feller—Aah reckon he's scared o' what happened to Nelly. Aye, we seen the last of Nelly. Aah feel it in me bones." She clutched the knobbles of her scrawny neck as if to confirm that feeling. She was genuinely grieving, yet Chas had a nasty suspicion she was also enjoying it; squeezing the last ounce of pleasure out of death. Were old people so empty they had to squeeze pleasure out of death as if it were a football match?

"When did you last see her?"

"That Wednesday night. Aah went up to see if she wanted anything before Aah went to the Black Ox wi' the girls."

"Didn't Nelly go?"

"Usually. But she said she had some business to see to, and she'd follow on." There was a smirk, a simper, a secret coming through the grief.

"She was waiting to see . . . a man?"

"Mevve. She kept on a few old friends. . . ."

"Nobody . . . young?"

"No, hinny. Young 'uns is rough."

"What happened after that?"

"Just the pub. Afterward, the girls was busy, and so was Aah."

"No Nelly?"

"No, she sometimes turned in early. She was no chicken, you know. In the morning, when Aah took her tea, she was gone."

"Is that all?"

"Nothing else happened, hinny." There was a long silence, and then Annie said, "Oh!"

"Yes?"

"You could ask Captain Burley."

"Captain *Burley?*"

"Me an' the girls met him, as we was going to the Black Ox. We had a bit crack."

"Why should he know anything?"

"He was an old friend of Nelly's. We thought *he* might be calling. . . ."

Chas got himself away somehow, in spite of offers of tea, biscuits, seedy-cake. He walked to the Bank Top railings and looked down-river. The *Hendon* was moored out between the piers, only a thin trace of smoke coming from her funnel.

The thought hit him like a cold wind.

Both nights when ships had been torpedoed, *Hendon* had been duty-tug. Both nights, Dick Burley alone had known that some special war cargo was expected.

What had Cem said, the night the last ship was sunk? Dick Burley was "jumpy."

Another thought hit him.

That day they'd tried launching the enamel bowls from the raft—the only bowl that had floated out between the piers was Number Five: the bowl that had drifted away while the *Hendon* was rescuing them *in the middle of the river*.

Only bowls launched in the middle of the river got through the piers. And the *Hendon*, moored as she was now, was the ideal launching place for enamel bowls. . . .

Dick Burley had known the captains of German ships before the war; had admired the clean, tight way they ran their ships. *Hitler's* ships, even then. . . .

Dick Burley was Nelly's old friend. Who could visit Nelly unseen at her private door, up the outside stair. Without arousing her suspicions.

It all fitted.

Dick Burley was the spy. Dick had killed Nelly.

He must find Sven. Sven would know what to do.

22

Chas did not like going to Sven's house. For a long time he had not realized that Sven *had* a house. He had imagined Sven living a tough life aboard the *Hendon,* or perhaps in some garret above the Duke of Westminster.

But no. Sven lived down the Low Street, with the widow of a soldier who'd been killed at Dunkirk.

That sounded all right. Except that the widow was only about twenty, and rather pretty in a plump way, and not at all sad about her dead husband. And Sven sat around her kitchen in his collarless shirt, and her eyes followed him everywhere. Her name was Dolly, and when she was slopping about in carpet slippers and a sweater with no bra, she embarrassed Chas silly.

It was Dolly who opened the door now, carrying her cat wrapped up in an old woolly shawl. Chas stared at the cat disapprovingly. Dolly put the cat down.

"Aah know Aah'm daft, but Aah've got to have something to cuddle. It's not having any bairns. . . ."

"Sven in?"

"He's just gone down to me mother's for a cup o' sugar. Sit down, Chas. Like some tea?"

Chas perched on the corner of an armchair. As far from a pile of clean but unironed panties as he could get.

Dolly made his mug of tea; generous with thick

creamy condensed milk. Liking condensed milk was the only thing he and Dolly had in common.

"Aah'm pregnant," announced Dolly triumphantly.

"Oh." Such a pregnancy would have been as welcome in the McGill clan as the Fall of Singapore. Chas blushed furiously, then made himself look Dolly full in the face and say, "Congratulations."

Dolly pushed back a strand of newly washed hair, cheeks glowing, green eyes shining.

"Sven'll have to marry me now."

"Yeah."

Sven *married*. An unbearable thought; like Thor or Superman settling down in a council house and taking up gardening. What an end for a guy who tackled a U-boat with only a couple of Lewis guns. . . .

Yet he couldn't be angry with Dolly. Her happiness painfully reminded him of Sheila's.

Sven solved the problem by returning with his cup of sugar.

"Hi, Chas!" His hand was still heavily bandaged.

"Your hand not better yet?" asked Chas, for want of something better to say.

"It septic has gone. I poisoned-thumb have, like fisherman."

"Hard luck!"

"Nothings. Nearly better."

"I've found the spy."

Sven's eyes flew to Dolly who, noisily slopping tea leaves down the sink, didn't seem to have heard.

"Hey, missus! Making bed, eh?"

Dolly blushed, smiled, and departed upstairs. Chas told his story. Sven turned very pale.

"Rubbish," he said mulishly. "Captain Burley good man is. Like father to me."

"But it all fits together. Don't you see?"

"Clever guessings. No proof."

"There could be proof aboard the *Hendon*."

Sven struggled with himself, in long painful silence.

"You say little smoke from *Hendon*'s funnel?"

Chas nodded.

"Captain ashore will be. On duty tonight, maybe. I do not see him much, since my thumb hurt. OK. We *Hendon* will search. If nossing, Captain Dick we will see. Sorting things out. OK?"

"OK." Chas's belief was already beginning to waver. They took Sven's boat.

"Shall I row?" asked Chas.

"You better than Cem?" Sven laughed. "If not, *I* row. We are not all day having. My hand not bother me now."

It didn't. They soon bumped alongside the *Hendon*. The tug was full of creakings, as she swung and tossed on the choppy waves. The mast threw moving shadows on the bridge. A pencil rolled to and fro across the chart table. But there was no one aboard.

Sven turned to a mahogany locker, with a brass keyhole. "Captain always keep this locked."

Chas noticed some little wavering scratches round the keyhole. "Hey, that's funny. Someone's picked this lock before."

"They easily picked," said Sven, taking a piece of wire from his pocket.

Inside the locker was a bundle of Admiralty forms, all clipped together. Forecasts of arrivals of ships. The *Corwen Star* was among them; and the *Esperanza*. There was also a sealed buff envelope, marked *O.H.M.S.* and *Confidential*.

"Captain Dick open those," said Sven. "But only after we have sailed on duty."

"Shall we open it?"

"*We* are not spies," said Sven. He put it firmly back in the locker. There was nothing else, except invoices for coal and rope. Sven was careful to relock the locker.

"There must be other hiding places," said Chas.

"Thousands," said Sven, smiling. "Search where you like. But you only an hour have."

They searched the engine room, where the great yellow-greased pistons stood silent. They searched the coal bunkers of the stinking-hot boiler room, where the furnaces were banked with coal dust, and steam hissed gently. They searched behind lagged pipes, up ventilators.

"It's a nightmare," gasped Chas.

"A smuggler's paradise," agreed Sven. "Would you like the shop chest to try?"

They went down a companionway. There was a rusty white door in the for'ard bulkhead, with a big wheel in the center. Sven turned the wheel, and flung the door open, with a showman's gesture.

It was an incredible place; full of the rubbish of years. Worn-out mops. Oilskins that cracked and split as you lifted them. A box of old knives and forks, including a huge old bread knife. Cardboard boxes by the dozen.

Sven groped through the boxes, and withdrew his hands with a sharp whistle.

In one hand he held a gray cylinder, about as big as a can of peas. In the other, an American battery.

Chas leaped on the cardboard boxes, throwing them all over the place. There were two more oscillators; two more batteries.

"Sven. Proof! We've *got* him."

But there was no answer. Chas turned in time to see the white door shutting. He heard the wheel turning on the other side of the door.

There was no wheel his side.

Too late, he knew who the spy was.

Even then, he almost shouted "Sven." Till he remembered Caesar floating in the river. . . .

Instead, he grabbed the big bread knife. He felt slightly ridiculous, brandishing it like a kid playing soldiers. But the blade was nearly a foot long, with a vicious saw edge. It was a comfort.

He began piling the contents of the slop chest against the door: brooms, mops, boxes. They made a poor barricade. But they might trip Sven up, or at least make him look down. . . .

But Sven had lost interest, it seemed. Chas heard him walking on the deck above, mounting the ladder to the bridge. . . .

As the minutes passed, Chas saw clearer and clearer what a fool he'd been.

So Sven's dad had been shot by the Germans. Whose word did they have for that, besides Sven's?

So Sven was a slave-worker? More likely a spy sent to watch the slave-workers. He must have found it *very* funny, when the commandos liberated him. . . .

So Sven had machine-gunned the U-boat? Very impressive, in the dark, when no one could see where the bullets were falling!

But worst of all, Chas remembered pouring out his every thought to Sven, that night in the snack bar. All about the spy with the silver ring. And Sven listening, with his hands clasped under the table. Sven going out straight afterward and pretending to cut his hand on the Lewis guns, so he could bury that damning ring under a mass of bandages.

And that same night, Sven had asked him to go out to the *Hendon*. Alone with Sven in a rowboat, on a dark river. . . . He knew now he would never have reached *Hendon* alive. But Andy the engineer had come past by chance. . . .

I *deserve* to be dead, he thought bitterly. But he clutched the bread knife tighter, and kicked more objects against the door.

Sven's footsteps came back across the deck, and down the engine room ladder.

Chas tensed up, ready. He would drive the bread knife at Sven's face, the moment Sven trod on something and looked down. It probably wouldn't work, but it was better than dying helpless like Caesar. Like Nelly. "Take one with you when you go" is what Mr. Churchill said.

But Sven still wasn't interested. He began hammering at something farther astern. Then he ran up on deck again, and there was the sound of the dinghy grating against the tug's hull. Was Sven leaving?

Chas ran across to the single porthole, and peered out through the grimy-green, inch-thick glass.

Sven was rowing vigorously for the shore. He was already fifty yards away.

Chas's knees went weak with relief. He looked at his watch. In forty minutes, Dick Burley would come aboard, and it would all be over.

Sven would be away by then, of course. Catching a train at Garmouth Station; getting on the bus for Newcastle, cool as a cucumber. Or would he hitchhike some army lorry? He'd better be a long way off, before the police circulated his description. There'd be no hiding that Norwegian accent. . . .

A sudden urgency seized Chas. He must get out and warn people.

The door was useless. Half-inch steel. But the port-hole was only fastened with screws. If only he had a screwdriver. . . .

He realized he was still holding the bread knife.

The porthole screws were embedded in black grease, and moved easily. In ten minutes, he had the port-hole open. The sea breeze made him feel better. After a day of sun, the slop chest was like an oven.

He considered squeezing out of the porthole. The mooring rope that held the *Hendon* to her buoy hung tantalizingly just beyond.

He tried it. He soon wished he hadn't. He got his head and shoulders through, then the porthole fastened round his ribs like a vise, and for a horrible moment he thought he was stuck, half-in, half-out. He finally got back with a torn shirt and the loss of a fair amount of skin.

He tried shouting. Waving his hanky through the porthole on the end of a broomstick. Neither worked. The *Hendon* was a hundred yards out in the river. There was only one bloke in sight on the shore, and he was too busy throwing sticks for his dog.

Chas sat down sweating and thought again. Sven was getting farther and farther away. . . .

The tug gave a sudden lurch. He must have dozed off, because it made him jump. When he looked at his watch, he saw nearly an hour had passed. Where was Dick Burley?

Something about the tug was different. The sound

of water flowing past the hull was different. It made him uneasy.

Then he realized. The tide had turned as he slept. It was running out now, quite strongly. It had slewed the tug round on her mooring. The mooring rope was now hard across the porthole, blocking off the light. Or was it already growing dark?

Tide going out at dusk. Enamel-bowl time in the old days, before he'd sent Sven on the run.

But hey—what about that sealed confidential envelope in the bridge locker? And Sven had had an oscillator and a battery in his hands, just before he locked Chas in.

Chas groaned. There must be an enamel bowl floating out between the piers at this very moment.

What could he do?

Nig-nog! There were other oscillators and batteries beneath his very feet. He'd had a crude radio transmitter in his hands for the last hour. How *stupid* could you get?

He wired battery and oscillator together with feverish fingers. Touched the wires and felt the old faint familiar vibration.

Slowly and methodically, he began to send Morse.

S.O.S. . . . S.O.S. . . . T.R.A.P.P.E.D . . . A.B.O.A.R.D H.E.N.D.O.N. . . .

The cabin darkened more, as the sun began to set. It made him quite unreasonably panicky. An hour and a half had passed, and still no Captain Burley. He had to concentrate hard to keep his Morse-coding steady. He tried sending different messages. Each sounded less convincing than the last. Wasn't *anyone* listening to the radio? Or did they all think it was some kid messing about?

Still nobody came. At last he threw buzzer and battery away in disgust.

Then the tug lurched again. The deck seemed to slope upward to the door. All the brooms and boxes came tumbling down on top of him.

Surely the tide couldn't be *that* strong?

The tug gave another lurch, and returned to even keel. But she felt different again. Sluggish. Not riding the waves easily any more.

He shoved his head through the porthole. He could just squeeze it past the great mooring rope. He could feel the rope vibrating against his cheek, with every surge of the tide.

He looked down.

The water was much nearer the porthole than it had been before.

The *Hendon* was sinking. . . .

Now he knew why Sven had been content to row away and leave him. Now he knew what the hammering astern had been. Drowned boys told no tales. All the time he'd been waiting and messing about, water had been rising inside the hull.

Panic swept over him. He wanted to throw himself clawing at the steel door. But when people did that in shipwreck movies, they always died screaming soon after.

The porthole was a better bet. He'd drag himself through if it meant leaving *all* his skin behind. But the tug's mooring rope lay right across the porthole, blocking it.

He snatched up the bread knife and began hacking at the rope. The rope was two inches thick, and hard as iron with the salt water. The knife twisted in his sweating hands.

But it was a good old massive knife, with a huge saw edge. Little strands of the rope gave way, making star shapes because the rope was under strain. Bright new rope showed beneath.

The tug lurched again, and now his feet were sploshing and sliding in water. But he hacked on and on like a maniac. He was a quarter through the rope; half. The water was over his ankles.

Then a blow knocked the knife from his hand; set it clattering against the far bulkhead. His hands hurt; his eyes were blinded with grit. He staggered to and fro, struggling to keep his feet, trampling on a tangle of objects under water. He knew it was the end.

Then he realized the water was still not up to his knees. He managed to get his eyes open. The mooring rope was snapped, gone. The porthole was unblocked.

Beyond, the whole world was on the move. A line of cranes swung by, in quick succession. To be replaced by an oil tanker. Then the piers swept into view.

Of course. He'd cut the mooring rope, and the *Hendon* was spinning wildly down-river on the ebb tide.

Somebody had noticed, because there was the frantic *yip-yip-yipping* of another tug. Other ships began hooting. Chas stuck his head out of the porthole, then pulled it in again quickly. The tug was heading straight for the gray guardship at the end of the defense boom.

There was an almighty crunching and scraping. The porthole went dark. Then footsteps on the deck above, and men shouting and swearing.

But at the same time there was another rush of water under the door, nearly up to his waist. Then he really was screaming and clawing, trying to get out.

It was the last thing he remembered.

*

He opened his eyes.

He could see the masthead against the darkening sky, with a gull sitting on top.

"Why doesn't it sway?" he asked dreamily. "The mast?"

" 'Cause we're agroond on South Shields beach." Dick Burley was bending over him, cigar protruding from gray whiskers. A ring of warm cigar ash fell on Chas's face. "What the hell's being going on in ma ship? Who locked ye in the slop chest? Who turned the seacocks on? They coulda drooned ye."

"Sven."

"*Sven?* Aah thowt it was kids. . . . Why should Sven do a thing like that?"

"He was trying to drown me. He's the spy."

"Hey, Inspector. Come and listen!"

Another peaked cap joined Dick's. River Police inspector. "Can you answer a few questions, lad?"

Chas nodded. As long as he didn't have to *move*.

The next bit was muddling. Three times the sky went dark, but each time when Chas reopened his eyes, it was still pale dusk. People kept piling more and more blankets on him, till he felt suffocated. Dick poured something down his throat that warmed him to the toes. But Chas still didn't feel like moving.

Then a toffee-nosed voice saying, "This youth is suffering from shock and cold. He's soaked to the skin—he could catch pneumonia. He should be home in bed, or I won't be medically responsible."

"Ha'd steady, doctor," said Dick. "There's more lives than his at stake tonight."

So they carried Chas up onto *Hendon*'s bridge; huffing and straining and knocking his head on the bridge telegraph in the process.

But it didn't seem to matter.

They asked him the same questions, over and over. In between, they ignored him as he lay on the chart room bunk. Almost as if he was a bit of the furniture. So he lay with his eyes shut and listened. The voices kept coming and fading, like a defective radio.

"He never went back to his lodgings."

"The Army's got roadblocks on the Morpeth and Durham roads. The police are covering Newcastle Station."

"Waste of time. He'll be a hundred miles away by now."

"What about neutral ships?"

"There's a Swedish iron-ore boat lying at Hebburn. They're searching it now."

So they hadn't caught Sven. . . .

Then a Scots voice. Andy the engineer. "The pumps is winning. We'll be bone-dry an' ready tae move in half an hour. Lucky the water didn't reach the boilers."

"Lucky the whole bloody ship didn't sink."

"The seacock's blocked wi' floatin' rubbish. The Gar's a dirty old river. . . ."

But for floating rubbish, thought Chas, I'd be drowned by now, and Sven would have won. Hard luck, Sven. . . .

Chas must have really dozed off then. Because the next voice he heard was new; a voice of crisp authority. Only it kept breaking off into bouts of coughing.

"That special cargo due tonight—aero-engines— we've diverted to the West Hartlepool."

"That's one Jerry won't get," said Dick.

"I've got a favor to ask you, Captain Burley."

"Ask away," said Dick.

"Do you know a coaster called the *Pelaw Main?*"

"Aye—a floating scrapyard. Engine's solid rust. Been tied up at Seaham Staithes since 1937. She'll never sail again."

"We've had a quick survey done on her—she'd float—she could be towed."

"Mevve—in a calm sea. A force three breeze'd sink her."

"We *want* the U-boat to sink her. We want to use her as a decoy."

Dick laughed with sudden excitement. "Like the old Q-ships in the last war?"

"Exactly. Flag officer, East Coast, has authorized the requisition of the *Pelaw*. But we need someone to tow her. . . ."

"Try and stop me. How much time Aah got?"

"Plenty—seven hours. Special cargo wasn't due till 0400. My group will slip out at midnight, darkened ship. We'd just tied up, and we hadn't begun to blow down boilers, so there'll be no need to flash up."

It all sounded so fascinating that Chas sat up, though it made his head swim.

The men grouped at the chart table looked round, startled. Dick and the inspector and. . . .

Cousin Robert. The Cousin Robert of the newspapers. Jutting beard, gold braid, white scarf at throat. Immaculate. Except he looked so . . . faded. With networks of lines at the corners of his mouth and eyes, like old ladies have. And angry spots of red color in his cheeks.

"Damn! How much have you heard, you young monkey?" asked Cousin Robert.

"Everything," said Chas.

"Oh, dear," said Cousin Robert. "Then on grounds of national security, the next move is to get you tucked up in bed, in charge of your mother."

"Oh, *hell*," said Chas. "We take all the risks—you get all the fun."

"What fun?" asked Cousin Robert. He suddenly looked a hundred years old, and started coughing again. He walked out into the dusk, along the wing of the bridge. They watched him double up over the bridge telegraph, hanky to mouth.

"You mustn't worry the commander," whispered Dick. "He's got TB, bad."

"But I thought the sea was a healthy life."

"Not four days nonstop, wi'out sleep or a change of clothes."

Cousin Robert recovered himself, and came back. "We haven't shaken hands yet, Chas. They told me you'd called at the ship. I'm sorry. . . ."

"Don't mention it," said Chas fiercely. It wasn't right that heroes should be embarrassed.

"I think you've done rather well," said Cousin Robert, shaking his hand. "I'll take you home."

It was high, grand and scary, riding home in the jeep, behind the bulled-up naval driver. The ground whizzed past either side, and there wasn't much to hang on to as they went round corners. Cousin Robert sat beside him, steadying him. All the streets to home looked unfamiliar, and people stared, impressed. So this is how it felt to have power. . . .

As the jeep pulled up at the front gate, he said quickly:

"S'pose I couldn't come with you . . . tonight?"

Cousin Robert sighed. "I was afraid you'd ask. No. Do you know how many forms I have to fill in before I can ship an *authorized* civilian? Even if he's over twenty-one? Anything else. . . ."

Chas's heart leaped. "There's a guy called Smythson, and he thinks I'm a fool. . . ."

Cousin Robert listened with great sympathy. Then he said, "No can do, old son. I can't tell him, and neither can you. Ever."

" 'Cause of the rotten Official Secrets Act?"

" 'Cause of the rotten Official Secrets Act."

23

Chas wakened in darkness, wanting the lav. He had a splitting head; his ribs ached. But he was awake. So much for doctors' sleeping powders. . . .

Out in the living room, the clock said half-past two. Chas sat on the couch, playing with the sleeping spaniel's ears, remembering his homecoming. In spite of Cousin Robert, it had not been triumphal. Mam. . . .

Cousin Robert had been contented to sit by the living room fire. But no, Mam had insisted he go into the front room, usually reserved for the vicar and funerals.

The front room fire had not been lit since the War. It smoked abominably. Robert sat bravely on, coughing discreetly, till his white scarf was covered in smuts.

The best china had to come out of the china cabinet. Then Mam noticed how dusty it was. So it all had to be washed. . . .

Cousin Robert had said no less than five times that Chas had done very well, and was a credit to his country.

Mam replied five times that Chas wasn't a bad boy really, and would soon grow out of it. It was all that sixth form . . . Chas wouldn't be had up by the police again, would he?

Cousin Robert tried hard to reassure her, but since he couldn't tell her exactly what Chas was supposed to have *done*. . . .

Chas sat and writhed. Robert took despairing peeps at his watch and worried about the U-boat.

Finally Dad settled matters by asking if Robert had any interest in tomato plants. The two men fled to the greenhouse, by the light of a shaded torch. Chas was bundled into the bath, had his hair forcibly washed, got soap in his eyes and was sent to bed like some kid. Cousin Robert came to say goodbye, with a huge bag of tomatoes in either hand. The crew of the *Virago* would never die of scurvy. . . .

The family doctor arrived. He also assured Mam that Chas would not be had up by the police. And prescribed the sleeping powder that had just worn off. Chas fell asleep to the sound of Mam at the back door, repelling neighbors' inquiries about the jeep and the naval gentleman.

Thank God it was over.

Except it wasn't. Even now Dick Burley would be creeping up the coast with the *Pelaw Main* in tow. Robert's escort group, the U-boat, the spy—all on the move. Except Chas, tucked up like a baby.

It wasn't to be borne. Tiptoeing between the floorboards that creaked, he dressed and made for the back door.

A light clicked on.

Dad, in his old checked dressing gown. "Where d'ye think you're off to?"

"Robert's after that U-boat. . . ."

"Off the piers?" Dad's eyes lit up.

"Want to come?" asked Chas. It was worth a try.

Dad sighed. "No—Aah'm on the morning shift. But," he added, softening, "ye'd better not go down there on an empty belly. Cup o' tea?"

"Yes . . . please."

Mam called out, from the bedroom. She *must* have been tired, not to have heard before.

"It's all right, hinny," shouted Dad. "It's just the bairn—he can't sleep. Aah'm givin' him tea an' aspirin."

"Aah'll get up."

"Divven't disturb yourself. We're just talking."

"What about?"

"Men's talk." It was as if Dad had softly closed a door. They heard Mam turn over, in muted protest.

"Robert seemed pleased," said Dad. "Though by, he looks poorly. . . ."

"Shall I tell you about it?"

Dad hesitated. "No—ye've sworn to keep a secret, an' ye'll keep your word. But Robert reckoned you deserve a medal, though ye won't get one."

"Just doing me bit," said Chas, embarrassed. "Like Churchill says."

"Aye, Churchill," said Dad, a strange bitterness creeping into his voice.

"Don't you *like* Churchill?"

"He's just another boss."

"You mean he's running the war for the sake of the bosses?"

Dad sipped tea from his pint pot, considering. "No—this gyet Hitler has got to be stopped—and Aah suppose Churchill's the man to do it. But the last war was a bosses' war. There was no quarrel between the German workers an' the British. Christmas, 1914, the Tommies and Jerries got oot of their trenches an' shook hands in no-man's-land. Swapped presents—played football. Yer grandfather saw it. But the bosses soon stopped that, and ten million working lads died for nowt. And what did them that survived come back to? A land fit for heroes? Unemployment an' the dole, an' watching their bairns starve. While the bosses drove round in motorcars."

"But Churchill saved us in 1940. . . ."

"*Aah* remember Churchill in 1926. When he was Home Secretary in the General Strike. The miners held a rally in the Bigg Market at Newcastle. Churchill set the cavalry at them wi' drawn swords. People diven't forget. Hitlers come an' Hitlers go. But the *real* war, between workers an' bosses, that never ends."

"But bosses are just people," said Chas, thinking of Sheila's face.

"Try telling *them* that," said Dad. "Anyway," he glanced at the clock, "ye'd better get moving, if you're going."

Outside, the moon was high. Thin clouds moving toward Germany. Just like the last time, four months ago; except Chas's legs ached more.

The Monument was deserted, and the harbor. No

maroons tonight. Chas sat by Collingwood's cannon. Collingwood had been a boss. And Nelson. And Richard the Lionheart and King Alfred. How many workers died to make *them* famous? It was confusing; it seemed to turn all history inside out.

But Cousin Robert was a boss, too . . . and Dad seemed to like him well enough.

A clink of heel caps climbed the Monument. A figure towered over him.

" 'Allo, Chas! Chin up, eh?"

Kallonas.

"What—what are you doing up here?"

"I hear something is up. About U-boat."

"Who told *you*?"

"Is all over Low Street."

So much for Official Secrecy.

"Why isn't everybody up here, then?" asked Chas, suddenly suspicious.

"Oh . . . they are knowing nothings for certain. Only I am putting twos and twos together. Come to see Royal Navy in action for last time, eh? I am old boy, now." He sat down with an over-heavy sigh. "What do you think is going to happen?"

"Dunno," said Chas. Kallonas seemed too damned keen to know.

"I t'ink Captain Burley is mixed up in it," said Kallonas, wheedling. "I hear *Hendon* is duty tug tonight, but I not see *Hendon* in harbor. . . ."

"Mevve," said Chas. He noticed that Kallonas was carrying a satchel on his shoulder, and there was something big, round and heavy in it. Like a Morse code signaling lamp? That could still flash a warning to the U-boat, as it lay at periscope depth, miles out to sea?

Sven had been the spy, but had he been the only spy? Spies worked in rings. . . .

Oh, balls! Kallonas a spy, with his wrinkled wife and membership in the Grand Order of Buffaloes?

But Sven had lived with harmless Dolly, who was going to have his baby. Spies were very, very ordinary; otherwise they wouldn't last long. Like the old granny who knitted socks for sailors . . . Tubby Tolliver.

Kallonas noticed Chas glancing at his satchel. "I have coffee—you like coffee? Is nice and hot—will do you good. You not look well."

He put a huge arm round Chas's shoulders; it was hard not to cringe. The coffee might be drugged. What Dad called a Mickey Finn. They knew all about Mickey Finns down the Low Street.

Kallonas removed his gorilla-like arm. "I *insist* you have coffee!" He thrust the steaming top of a vacuum flask in Chas's face. Chas took it. Kallonas was too big; the Monument was a lonely place.

He sipped the coffee gingerly. It didn't taste funny; it tasted great. But who'd drink a Mickey Finn if it *did* taste funny?

He tipped the cup and managed to spill some; mainly down his trousers.

"Hey, steady," said Kallonas, putting his great hand round Chas's and the cup together. "Hey, you are shaking! Drink up quick—make you feel better!"

He didn't let go of Chas's hand till the last drop was drunk.

Ten minutes passed. Chas still felt OK. Better, if anything. But he couldn't help looking south. There was a smudge on the moonlit sea; and it was twenty to four. . . .

"What can you see?" asked Kallonas. "Why you not use binoculars?" He tapped the pink opera glasses that hung round Chas's neck.

Chas used them, reluctantly. As he got them into focus, he saw *Hendon*. She had a little single-funneled collier in tow. Dick had managed to get smoke coming out of the collier's funnel, but it still looked pathetic. That would never fool Jerry. . . .

"May I look?" asked Kallonas, politely. Chas passed the glasses over. "The cheese to catch the mouse, I t'ink. Is Captain Dick, no?"

"Mevve."

"I t'ink you do know. I t'ink you don't trust me no more!"

"Don't trust anybody."

Kallonas sighed gustily. "Is a wicked world."

Chas squinted at his watch again. Four o'clock exactly. How could Dick bear to do it? Sail into a trap like that? Tug and collier were so close . . . the U-boat would fire its torpedoes in a fan shape, set to run shallow. One could easily blow *Hendon* to matchwood.

Chas kept the glasses tight to his eyes. He could even see Dick, or somebody who might be Dick, on *Hendon*'s bridge. The little bow wave of the tug; the little bow wave of the *Pelaw Main*.

The night sky cracked with indescribably orange violence. The flash, seen through the opera glasses, blinded Chas.

But while his ears were still ringing, he heard *Hendon*'s siren whooping with indignation. Dick was safe.

When he looked again, the *Pelaw Main* had vanished; an old tired ship, gone without a fight. *Hendon* was heading for harbor with every ounce of speed.

It was nothing like that other night. When the Castle searchlights came on, they didn't wave round the sky like idiot's arms. They searched a very narrow sector of the sea. When the Castle guns fired together, night became day as star shells floated overhead.

And there, two miles out, was the U-boat's conning tower, clear as a pea on a drum.

Tiny white lights winked all round the seward horizon. There was an approaching sighing on the air; and a forest of shell bursts grew where the U-boat had been.

"Hundred yards short," said Mr. Kallonas, with the air of a man who had fought at Jutland.

The U-boat had gone under.

The star shells died and were not replaced. But there were ships out there now; searchlights lengthening and shortening, making skimming pools of light on the surface of the sea.

The ships reminded Chas of a pack of farm dogs he had seen once, hunting rabbits in a field of corn. One collie had plunged wildly through the corn, scaring the rabbits to the edge, where the other collies waited with ready teeth. The dogs had hunted till they had a rabbit each. Dad had said they were old hands.

Robert's ships were old hands too. Prowling, sniffing, methodical. Performing intricate white circles, but never getting in each other's way. Every so often, a row of depth charges stitched the sea with foam. Chas almost pitied the poor steel rabbit, desperately twisting and turning on the sea bed.

But all so far away. The bangs came a perceptible time after the flashes, and they were not loud. All the same, back in Garmouth, for the last ridiculous time the air-raid siren sounded.

Slowly, the sniffing ships moved northward and shoreward.

"Jerry is trying to lose them among coastal sand-banks," said Mr. Kallonas. "I t'ink he playing very dangerous game."

As if old Kallonas had been a conjuror pulling a rabbit from a hat, the black conning tower broke surface, less than half a mile from the Long Sands beach.

One of the hunting ships came tearing in, bow wave rising, Oerlikons throwing slow red lines of tracer shells at the black conning tower.

"Ram! Ram!" shouted Mr. Kallonas. Chas clenched his teeth, waiting for the clang of metal on metal.

It never came. Suddenly, the ship's bow reared out of the water, and she came to a grinding, rumbling halt.

"She is aground on sandbanks," said Mr. Kallonas. "They both aground."

It looked absurd. Like a glass case full of stuffed animals Chas remembered. A cowering rabbit; a snarling fox poised for the kill. But both dead and stuffed a hundred years ago.

In the searchlights' glare, a white cloth fluttered from the black conning tower. The guns stopped firing.

"End of party," said Mr. Kallonas, stuffing his Thermos flask back into his satchel.

"Aren't you going round to see it?"

"What more is to see? They do nothing else till morning. I go tell Mama—she pleased. Come and see us for tea on Sunday, eh?"

"Yeah, thanks," said Chas. "Sorry I suspected. . . ."

"I used to it." Mr. Kallonas clinked off down the Monument steps.

24

By the time Chas got round to Long Sands, the ships had gone. All but the stranded ship, which still played her searchlight on the U-boat. Which still displayed the white flag.

The stranded ship had only one funnel. *Acanthus* or *Arbutus*. Chas was glad it wasn't Robert's ship, for the tide was going out; both ship and U-boat were farther out of the water and starting to look absurd.

A soldier from the Castle was guarding the stairway to the beach.

"Bugger off, kid. This is secret."

"*What's* secret?"

"What's secret . . . is . . . what's secret!" said the sentry, overcome by his own wit.

"You must be Bob Hope," said Chas. "I thought you'd be in the *American* army."

"Bugger off or I'll call a policeman."

Chas retreated twenty yards and sat on the seafront railings. The threat of police was idle; the soldier daren't leave his post. He passed the time calling to the soldier. Was he a lance corporal? Corporal? Sergeant? Ending up with field marshal.

The sentry pulled up his collar, lit a fag and ignored him. Time passed; very slowly. After the sentry's fourth fag, shouting broke out between ship and U-boat.

German seamen came out on the conning tower for a breath of air. Yellow lights flickered. The Germans were smoking fags as well.

After the sentry's sixth fag (Chas considered reporting him for smoking on duty in the blackout) dawn broke. The tide was now right out; nearly to the stranded vessels. The whole of the U-boat's deck was uncovered and *Acanthus* looked as big and square as a house.

After the sentry's eighth fag (*they* didn't go without smokes, even if civilians had to) Chas heard footsteps coming along the seafront. He swiveled round, stiff as an old horse, and got his backside soaked with dew.

The approaching figure wore a camel's-hair coat.

Smythson.

Cousin Robert must have told him after all. Happy endings weren't just in storybooks. Suddenly Chas noticed the sun was up and all the birds were singing. Suddenly he loved everybody.

Mr. Smythson drew nearer. He was walking briskly; it was impossible to judge the expression on his face.

Chas wished he felt more respectable. Important occasions always caught you wearing the wrong clothes.

He wouldn't be hard on Mr. Smythson. Let bygones be bygones. As he drew near, Chas jumped off the railings to greet him.

Mr. Smythson paused in mid-stride. They stared at each other.

Chas noticed again the blond hair swept back in a smooth wave, the straight nose and piercing blue eyes, the spotless white collar. Mr. Smythson was a very handsome man.

Mr. Smythson first looked baffled, as if Chas was a

total stranger. Then his eyebrows shot up in surprise. Then he looked at the pavement, his mouth and nose curling in delicate disgust.

He swept straight past. Cousin Robert had told him nothing.

The sentry came awake with a start and, impressed by the camel's-hair coat, sketched a sloppy salute.

Smythson descended the stair and stood waiting on the lower prom, as if afraid to get his highly polished shoes dirty on the beach.

Chas hovered, baffled. If Cousin Robert had told Smythson nothing, why was Smythson *here*?

The question was soon answered. Cars began pulling up, disgorging men in posh tweed overcoats, who called each other Harold and William loudly across the quiet morning air. Faces familiar from the *Garmouth Evening News*. Councillor This and Alderman That. J.P., M.B.E., D.S.O., V.D. and bar. . . .

Bosses. They ignored Chas and went down to join Smythson.

A jeep-load of army officers arrived from the Castle, important with revolvers in unbuttoned holsters.

More soldiers arrived in a three-ton truck, were told to look lively by their sergeant, and leaped down to the road with a stamping clatter.

What did they expect? The U-boat to make a last stand on the bloody beach?

Everyone but Chas went down to Smythson.

Cousin Robert arrived, in jeep and camel's-hair duffle coat.

"He wouldn't let *me* past," said Chas, nodding at the sentry, "but he let all *them*."

"C'mon," said Robert, soothingly, "you're with me, now."

The sentry managed a superb present-arms. Robert flipped the brim of his cap casually, as they swept past in turn and descended the stair.

For the second time Chas felt how it was to be a boss.

On the lower prom, Smythson gave them a nasty look. Muttered to the other bosses, who also gave nasty looks. But they didn't *say* anything. Probably got through their thick skulls that both Chas and Cousin Robert were called *McGill*.

"Can we proceed, Commander?" asked an alderman meekly.

"Pray do," said Robert, with a grin in his voice that only Chas noticed.

The party moved off, across ribs of hard sand that still dribbled water toward the sea. Bosses on the left in a straggling line; soldiers on the right at a respectful distance.

"Tide's gone out a long way," said Chas.

"It's spring tide—very high and very low," explained Robert.

The bosses looked back over their shoulders, irritated by the sound of Chas's voice.

"*They* think I shouldn't be here," said Chas loudly. "But it's them that shouldn't be here. What have they done that's so bloody marvelous?"

Meaning Smythson.

Cousin Robert said nothing.

"Even if he knew what I'd done," raged Chas, "it wouldn't make any difference. *He* wouldn't say sorry. *He* wouldn't fetch Sheila home. He'd still think I was a lunatic. . . ."

"If you don't shut up," said Robert, "you'll have to go home."

"Meaning you think I'm a lunatic too?"

"No—but then I haven't got a teenage daughter."

"But it was Sheila's idea as well. . . ."

"Do you want to see the U-boat or not?"

"Rotten Tory pigs," said Chas, extra-loud, to the world in general. He knew he was behaving badly. But feelings were breaking loose inside him and he didn't really want to stop them.

Then Robert started a bout of coughing, and Chas felt sorry. It wasn't Robert's fault.

By the time they reached the water's edge, shallow waves were just swirling round the U-boat's bulging flanks. It was a monstrous thing, leaning gently, red with rust and thick with weed.

"Just remember," said Robert, "if it hadn't been for you, this heap of junk wouldn't be here."

"Will it be in the papers?"

Robert looked uncomfortable. "It will. Eventually. You won't be."

"Official secrets?"

"Official secrets."

"You mean too many official red faces!"

"Yes, if you like."

"That's not fair!"

"Life's not fair. But," Robert grinned, "I'll get you a souvenir if you like."

"Oh. . . . OK. I mean . . . yes, please."

Robert walked away toward the U-boat's conning tower, where the soldiers were putting up a builder's ladder. Bosses kept on appearing out of nowhere, like maggots out of cheese. The chief constable. Even the mayor of Garmouth, ridiculously carrying his chain of office in his hand, though he hadn't quite got the nerve to wear it.

The telephone lines must be red-hot.

They all seemed to know each other, "Harolding" and "Williaming" like mad.

But they didn't seem to like each other much; kept talking each other down, trying to be clever. Smythson's voice was raised in *expert* comment.

"They say it's the smaller coastal type of U-boat— absolutely useless for the Battle of the Atlantic—obsolescent, really. . . ."

Then someone asked the chief constable a question. All the other bosses looked at him, and fell silent.

The chief constable said, "I shouldn't say anything really—it's hush-hush." But Chas knew he would. He couldn't resist; not with all the other bosses hanging on his every word.

"We haven't caught the spy, yet. But it's only a matter of time. And we've got his accomplice—the tart he was living with. We've been giving her a going-over all night at the police station, I can tell you. She'll crack and blab, sooner or later."

Dolly.

What were they doing to her, up there in the police station?

"A whore like that," said the chief constable. "She probably slipped him most of his information."

Chas wanted to run across and shout she wasn't a whore; she was the widow of a soldier killed at Dunkirk.

But who'd have listened?

Then the crowd swirled with new excitement. The press had arrived, complete with photographer. The photographer took a few shots of the U-boat; then the bosses moved in. Bosses posed in groups, pointing at bits of the U-boat they knew bugger-all about, and saying "Cheese" while flashbulbs exploded. Just like at a garden party or the mayor's ball. Everybody ordering enlargements as fast as the photographer could write the names down. Though why they wanted pictures of their great fat backsides, balding heads and wrinkled necks, God only knew. . . .

While from the U-boat's deck, the German sailors stared down indifferently.

Then, just like at a garden party, someone made an incomprehensible announcement, and the crowd drew back expectantly.

German sailors began coming down the ladder, carrying kitbags and little attaché cases. They wore floppy berets, and badly creased greatcoats that obviously hadn't been worn for weeks. They lined up three-deep, looking cold, bored, but glad to be alive.

Chas moved nearer. The sailors seemed so ordinary. The fat one, who scratched his bum. The boy with terrible spots on his face, that his fingers wouldn't leave alone. The dark flashy one with a thin moustache, who kept eyeing the legs of the girl reporter from the *Newcastle Journal*. *He* wouldn't enjoy an all-male prison camp.

And then there was. . . .

Sven.

It couldn't be. This bloke was wearing German naval uniform. Standing to attention like the rest. In the rear rank. Any resemblance to Sven must be pure coincidence. . . .

Chas sidled down the German lines, keeping a wary eye on the British, who had gone back to posing round the U-boat's hydroplanes, sunbathing in flashbulbs and public fame.

He must catch the German sailor's eye. That would prove it wasn't Sven.

But the sailor wouldn't look at Chas. All the others did; angrily, sneeringly or with dull indifference. But the one that might be Sven kept his eyes on the cliff-top, above Chas's head.

"Sven?"

The man still didn't turn his eyes, but he began to shake. His mouth trembled. His knuckles were clenched white, against the dark blue of his greatcoat.

Then, under his open greatcoat, the inside of his trouser leg darkened suddenly.

The man had wet himself.

It *was* Sven. He hadn't sent his last message by enamel bowl. He'd delivered it personally. Must've rowed out between the piers. Lurked in some bay till nightfall, pretending to fish, or repair his boat. Then headed out to sea and called up the U-boat with battery and buzzer.

Chas stood paralyzed. One word, and Sven was a dead man. Oh, there'd be long interrogations; the farce of a trial. But one morning, Sven would be dragged, trembling and wetting himself, to. . . . Just like Duncan Alexander Croall Scott-Ford.

Well, he deserved it. He'd killed Nelly; Caesar.

But he didn't look like a murderer, standing there. He looked like an ordinary working lad caught in a terrible trap.

Besides, *was* Nelly dead? What if she turned up? She had before, Nico said; and Nico knew her better than anybody.

Who was he trying to kid?

Nelly was dead.

Murderer!

Something nudged into Chas, making him jump like he'd been shot. But it was only another German sailor edging in, trying to block his view of Sven. All the sailors were edging in, trying to protect Sven. To them, he was their mate. A hero. Like Cousin Robert. . . .

Why did they hang spies anyway? Everybody used them. Was spying worse than sinking unarmed merchant ships? Yet these sailors would only be sent to a POW camp. Why weren't spies just sent to a POW camp? Then he would give Sven away without . . . remembering his face the morning they took him out and hanged him.

He couldn't take his eyes off Sven's face. A nervous twitch had developed on Sven's forehead, making his beret twitch up and down too. Sven kept swallowing, swallowing. And jerking his head sideways, then back, as if some fly was bothering him. But there was no fly.

He could even smell Sven now: sweaty skin and urine.

Sven was falling apart. Like the daddy-long-legs Chas had seen one evening, caught between an electric light bulb and its shade. It kept beating itself against the hot bulb, *ping, ping*. Then one of its legs broke off, then another, then there suddenly wasn't very much left of it. But it still kept pinging against the bulb till it died. . . .

Like Sven now.

And he was doing it to Sven.

He glanced round desperately. Lovely morning. Sun shining and little waves hitting the beach like kisses. Soldiers kicking their boots around in the sand, bored, wanting their breakfast. The bosses, still having a *lovely* time. The German sailors tense now, worried.

But Sven was in Hell.

He was alone with Sven in Hell.

A laugh came from the bows of the U-boat. A braying boss-laugh that owned the world and didn't give two buggers for anybody.

It wasn't Sven he hated.

But he had to know about Nelly.

"Sven?" he whispered harshly. *"Sven!"*

"Get that young lout out of there!"

Chas came to earth with a bump. The chief constable was pointing at him. A policeman rushed up and pushed Chas away from the Germans; so hard that Chas tripped and fell in a puddle.

A titter ran through the bosses. Smythson said something, then everyone was laughing openly.

Only the sailors didn't laugh; they watched Chas with solemn eyes.

"Get that young lout off the beach!" shouted the chief constable.

But now Cousin Robert was coming down the ladder from the conning tower, a spare sailor's beret in his hand.

The bosses froze. Robert walked across to Chas and handed him the beret, very ostentatiously. You could tell he was as mad as hell with the bosses.

Then came an order, shouted in German. The U-boat captain, with pale tattered dignity, was taking command of his crew for the last time. The German sailors jerked back to attention. They turned to the left, kicking their feet feebly in the sand, in half-forgotten parade-ground drill. Then they began to march away, toward the stairway in the cliff.

Sven went with them.

Chas watched, still unable to open his mouth.

What about his revenge? What about Billy Mason,

frozen dead? And Mrs. Mason, rocking, rocking? What about all the dead sailors?

But if he blabbed on Sven, that wouldn't bring them back. The bosses would just take Sven and make another garden party of him, with a know-it-all judge in a long wig and black cap. They wouldn't care if Sven cried and wet himself. Then Dolly would be rocking, rocking, like Mrs. Mason. And her unborn kid . . . fancy growing up with everybody knowing your dad had been hanged as a spy. . . .

Then Chas realized the chief constable hadn't finished with him; he was walking across, same old mad-lion eyes. "What did you say to that German sailor?"

Chas took a deep breath and said:

"I called him a filthy Nazi swine."

"Don't you know it's a legal offense to speak to Germans?"

Cousin Robert cleared his throat, gently. But somehow it was as cold as the Arctic.

The chief constable wavered; he could never stand up to a *real* boss. "Just watch it, lad, that's all!"

Chas did just watch it; it was all he had to do. Watched the German sailors break step to climb the cliff stair, and vanish forever. At least Sven was going where he couldn't do any more harm. And he would spend the rest of the war wondering if Chas would blab.

Punishment enough.

It was over. The bosses were driving away to their hearty off-the-ration breakfast.

"You look jolly smug all of a sudden," said Robert. His eyes were terribly sharp.

Chas looked down at the sailor's cap in his hand, and waved it cheerfully.

"Glad you're so easily pleased," said Robert. "Well, cheeroh. I'm off to Hexham Sanatorium in a couple of hours. Come up sometime and help me sail a bed!"

"I will."

They shook hands.

Chas trailed across the Sands, feeling so weary he doubted he could ride his bike home. But that wasn't the worst.

The world was upside down. Whores were heroines; heroes sick invalids; magistrates twisted the law to suit themselves; policemen were stupid bullies. Nothing was what it seemed. Least of all, himself. That dizzying poem again.

> *Full fathom five thy father lies;*
> *Of his bones are coral made;*
> *Those are pearls that were his eyes;*
> *Nothing of him that doth fade,*
> *But doth suffer a sea-change . . .*

You could trust nothing.

Then he saw the man on the cliff top; old black bike and greasy cap. Waiting for him.

He laughed, a little wildly. The poem was wrong. Everything had suffered a sea-change *except* his father.

Dad was the same, forever and always. . . .

"Aah often went fishin' when Aah was a lad," said Dad. "But Aah never caught owt as big as that." He nodded at the U-boat. "Pity you can't have it put in a glass case." He rummaged in his saddlebag. "Aah browt ye a bacon sandwich. Thowt ye might be peckish, and. . . ."

He handed Chas a pale-blue envelope. It was a moment before Chas recognized Sheila's writing.

"It came early, afore yer mam was up. Aah thowt ye might be needing it in a hurry, like." His eyes twinkled for a moment, in his whiskery face. Then he said, "Aah'll be off to work. This won't buy the bairn a new shirt."

Chas watched him pedal away. Then he dug open the envelope, with fingers still greasy from the bacon sandwich.

AUTHOR'S NOTE

The hyperefficient, supersexy master spy is largely a creation of postwar fiction. The vital attributes of spies in World War II were humbleness, ordinariness and the ability to remain unnoticed—and alive. German spies were highly effective in the conquests of Poland, Norway, Holland, Belgium and France. Only in Britain were they ineffective, because Hitler had never prepared fully to invade Britain; the Fall of France took him by surprise.

The ill-trained spies who were hurriedly dispatched to Britain after the Fall of France were usually caught within days. They made ludicrous blunders such as paying for a meal in pounds instead of shillings. By 1944, the entire German spy network in Britain had been rolled up. The spies were either executed or "turned round" by their new British masters in time to radio false intelligence to the German High Command about the location of the D-Day landings. Anyone interested in this incredible story should read J. C. Masterman's *The XX System* (Yale, 1972).

I have modeled the behavior of the River Gar in this book on that of the River Tyne. The Tyne harbormaster, Captain A. W. R. Smith, writes:

"The maximum flow is about two knots on the ebb tide. . . . It is difficult to say how far out to sea rubbish is carried, but about one mile off the mouth of the Tyne, the discolored water of the ebb can be clearly seen diverting to a southerly flow. I would suggest there is a similar pattern for rubbish. My staff have recovered such things as dead cattle, uprooted trees, drowned stags and floating islands of mossy soil."

The suction effect of a ship's propellers within the confines of a river is remarkable. Walter Lord, in *A Night to Remember*, records an incident which occurred while the *Titanic* was passing down Southampton Water on her maiden voyage: "As the *Titanic* started downstream, the suction of her propellers pulled the smaller American liner *New York* from her moorings. Hawsers snapped and the stern of the *New York* swung toward the *Titanic*. Just in time the great ship stopped her engines, allowing tugs to pull the *New York* to safety." In World War II, it was a foolish sailor who leaped into the water before the engines of his torpedoed ship stopped running.

Mr. McGill's statements about Winston Churchill in Chapter Twenty-three of this book are quite unfounded. They are based on a legend that grew out of Mr. Churchill's action in sending cavalry to cope with striking and rioting miners at Tonypandy in 1910, when he was the Liberal home secretary. Nevertheless, this legend was widely believed on Tyneside in 1943, so I have felt entitled to use it.

Much of this book is autobiographical. We did haunt the Low Street and torment the luckless Maltese. We did spend whole days scavenging Fish Quay Sands (still as excitingly smelly today). I even had a distant cousin, Commander Robert Atkinson, D.S.C., R.N., who sank a U-boat but whom I, alas, never met. And before I was born my parents did take a jaunt to Hartlepool on the tug *Hendon*. So in all fairness I must make it clear that my parents are not the parents of this book. My picture of parent-adolescent friction comes from twenty years' experience as a father and schoolmaster.

R.A.W.

ROBERT WESTALL, who lived in a town much like Garmouth during World War II, holds degrees from Durham and London universities. He has written several other critically acclaimed novels for young readers, including *The Watch House*, the Carnegie Medal-winning novel *The Machine Gunners* (which is the prequel to *Fathom Five*), and, most recently, *Ghost Abbey*.

When the world's at war,
there's no such thing as innocent fun. . . .
THE MACHINE GUNNERS
by Robert Westall

Chas McGill, who's already got a fair-size collection of scavenged World War II souvenirs, has just found the greatest prize of his young life. It's a machine gun, still attached to a Nazi fighter plane downed in the woods of northern England. Enlisting the help of his closest friends, Chas hides the gun from the prying eyes of safety-minded adults—who soon notice that it has disappeared—by building a secret bunker around it. As the local authorities mount a search for the lethal weapon, Chas and company have their own agenda to attend to. There are rumors of an imminent German invasion—and guess who plans to be prepared with a carefully orchestrated counterattack, and the perfect weapon?

"The best book so far written for children about the Second World War." —THE TIMES (London)

"A bloody good story!"

—SCHOOL LIBRARY JOURNAL

Winner of the Carnegie Medal
A *Boston Globe–Horn Book* Honor Book
A Child Study Association of America
Children's Book of the Year

BORZOI SPRINTERS PUBLISHED BY ALFRED A. KNOPF, INC.

They came from beyond the grave to . . .
THE WATCH HOUSE
by Robert Westall

Anne encounters spirits far more troubled than her own when she's sent off to a small seaside village away from her parents' disintegrating marriage. A dead man scrawls desperate messages to her in the dust. A demonic dog digs up the bones of drowned sailors in the graveyard. Terrified yet intrigued, Anne opens herself to other-worldly (and violent) forces. Before she knows it, she finds herself drawn into a century-old tale of shipwreck and murder that was never resolved—and is haunted by anguished phantoms in the old Watch House on the cliff and on the deadly rocks below. Unable to resist the pull of these supernatural forces, Anne finds herself stranded in a time and place from which it seems no one can save her. Desperate, she must fight for her sanity—and her life!

"A real bone-rattler."

—SCHOOL LIBRARY JOURNAL

"Well-paced with carefully built tension . . . an engrossing novel."

—BOOKLIST

BORZOI SPRINTERS PUBLISHED BY ALFRED A. KNOPF, INC.